RIOT ACT

RIOT ACT

ACT I

SARAH LARIVIERE

Alfred A. Knopf
New York

THIS IS A BORZOI BOOK PUBLISHED BY ALFRED A. KNOPF

Visit us on the Web! GetUnderlined.com

Educators and librarians, for a variety of teaching tools, visit us at RHTeachersLibrarians.com

Library of Congress Cataloging-in-Publication Data is available upon request.
ISBN 978-0-593-47995-7 (trade) — ISBN 978-0-593-47997-1 (ebook)

The text of this book is set in 11.25-point Adobe Garamond Pro.
Interior design by Jen Valero

Printed in the United States of America
10 9 8 7 6 5 4 3 2 1
First Edition

Dedicated to Susan Marie Levin,
my beautiful friend

HUNG BE THE HEAVENS WITH BLACK

Champaign, Illinois, 1991

Summer's over and I'm still fucking dead. They buried me in the cemetery south of town where everybody goes to have sex. Nobody in my family is buried out here. Nobody knows anybody who's buried out here. For miles around in every direction it's just a wasteland of shredded cornfields. If anybody had ever really known me, they would've cremated me and tossed my ashes in the dumpster behind Ye Olde Donut Shoppe. Instead I've spent my summer vacation buried under a gnarled apple tree that's just aching to crap wormy fruit all over me. A full moon shines on my stone:

MAXIMUS BOWL, 1972–1991

Born.
Dead.
No nickname.

No memorable quote.

Tonight, Giselle and Axl drove out to the boondocks to visit me. They're parked in Gigi's big brown turd, the 1979 Chevy Malibu Classic she bought for six hundred bucks from her dad's friend Mosquito.

They're not having sex. Never having sex, for reasons that have always been unclear to me. I'd kick it with either one of them, no hesitation.

Then again, I died horny.

Gigi is in the driver's seat, chain chewing Red Vines. Bright red lipstick. Joan of Arc buzz cut. She looks like some corn-fed pixie, the type that's a magnet for doom.

She's remembering the day we met.

We were Thespians. High school drama dorks. Actors, lighting geeks, sound nerds, scenery designers, stage managers, and other assorted freaks who rehearsed nights and weekends to stage twice-yearly productions under the guidance of our fearless leader, theater teacher Fiona Lee.

It was fall of '88, Gigi's first Saturday-morning set construction. Gigi was the Ghost Girl with the long black hair hiding in the wings of the Champaign High School theater while the Doors (illegally) blasted from the sound booth, and center stage this corpulent beast of a sophomore (me) drilled holes in flats, bellowing with Jim Morrison.

Gigi can hear me now, singing, *"This is the end . . . my only friend, the end. . . ."*

See me wearing that Little Bo Peep hat with the pink plastic flowers I used to rock to scare the kiddies away.

Ms. Lee was bitching me out about safety goggles.

I got so caught up in bitching back that I dropped my drill.

Ms. Lee kicked me in the butt.

Ghost Girl laughed.

I looked up.

"Giselle!" called Ms. Lee. *"Glad you made it. Will you teach this scene-stealer how to use a power tool?"*

Tiny Ms. Lee, hands on her hips, straight black hair in a high pony, inexplicable suit jacket, inexplicable sandals, was smiling the smile that Gigi would later learn the teacher reserves for new kids, the smile that's so defiant it's almost loud.

Gigi walked downstage, to the edge. She appeared to be walking on water. Looked out, into the house, the sea of empty seats where an audience would be.

Turned to me.

"Can I borrow your hat?"

"Certainly." I struggled to my feet, tipped my bonnet. With a flick of the wrist, I presented it to her. *"Fair warning, freshwoman. This hat renders its wearer preposterous."*

When she put on the bonnet, Gigi shape-shifted.

"Check out me lump of lead. Spittin' image of the baked bean!"

Translation: In this hat, I resemble the queen.

Her cockney accent was dead-on.

We had an actress on our hands.

"A light hussy, I'd say," I retorted.

"Up yer arse!"

From that moment, Gigi and I were inseparable.

Axl is sitting shotgun. Paint-spattered pants tucked into black Doc Martens, fists like boulders on his knees. Wild hair. Complexion pulsing with tawny health, like some feral lumberjack. Eyes the color of arctic waters crawling with Vikings. He's clutching a Zippo.

He flips it open.

Lights a flame.

Flips it shut.

Axl is remembering the night I died.

The first shot was shattered glass skidding across the Ping-Pong table, Axl and me turning our heads, seeing the hole in the wall.

Axl yelling, *"Fuck!"*

Dropping his soldering iron.

Running for the door.

And me, looking back at the broken window, at my fractured reflection, understanding that it had come to this.

On the armrest between Axl and Gigi, a boom box blasts the Raincoats. *"This! Is just! A fairy tale! Happening in the supermarket!"*

Thanks to Axl, you can still get outlawed music here in Champaign, Illinois, and all the baby farm towns that surround us. Films, too. In fact, Axl can get you pretty much any illegal hunk o' culture that your Midwestern heart desires.

Short on cash?

Still worth asking. He might hook you up on principle.

The Fischer brothers have an ethic about these things.

When the Raincoats song ends, the cassette keeps spinning. America's Favorite Dictator is in the middle of a sentence.

". . . the Market respects those who respect the Market. The SYXTEM respects the Market. Join the millions who have already discovered the SYXTEM's trademarked techniques to increase your personal value—"

But the party sales pitch is cut off by the xylophone stylings of the Violent Femmes.

"Why can't I get / Just one screw?"

Gigi tosses her Red Vines into the back seat. "I can't do senior year."

Axl drops the lighter into the chest pocket of his flannel. "Okay."

"Fuck it," she says. "I'll drop out."

"And hide where?" asks Axl. "Rolling Acres?"

Rolling Acres: a cluster of ranch houses, a half mile by a quarter mile, plopped smack in the middle of the cornfields south of Champaign.

Rolling Acres, the neighborhood where Gigi and Axl grew up.

Rolling Acres, the place where I died.

Gigi shrugs. "Maybe."

"I'm off at eight tomorrow," says Axl. "Come to my theater after. We'll find somewhere better to stash you than that."

Gigi clenches the steering wheel like she's revving up. "I mean—I'll be at school on Monday. Of course. Just saying. Anyway, can't tomorrow. Dinner shift."

"So, after work."

"After, I'm going to Orin's."

Axl smirks. Takes his ciggies out of his chest pocket, looks at them like he's going to shove his tongue down their throat.

Gigi eyes him.

Axl hasn't lit a butt since I died.

While we fled Rolling Acres, dodging bullets (mostly dodging), trying not to trip over the pack of poodles and pugs gone feral who had joined us, slipping in their ubiquitous shit, the way Axl was hacking, I thought his lungs were trying to escape his body. Like if we didn't get away, the lungs still might.

Axl opens the glove compartment. Six unopened packs are stuffed in there with a pair of rainbow-striped gloves, because Gigi and I once decided that something called a glove compartment should contain them.

He crams in the fresh pack, smacks the liquid-poop-colored

plastic door shut. Bangs his skull against the headrest to help the craving pass.

Quitting smoking is by far the easiest thing on Axl's to-do list. Still hard.

"Orin Ellis," he says. "Did that pretentious cyberfuck not graduate?"

"He lends me books to read," says Gigi. "For the Defiance."

Axl's dimple appears out of nowhere like he wants to laugh, but his eyes say he doesn't have the juice for it. "Orin has nothing to do with the Defiance. He just needs people to believe he does."

Gigi shrugs. "Guess he's trying to impress me."

"Probably," says Axl. "Because you're playing so hard to get."

Gigi punches Axl in the arm.

"You know Orin disdains human flesh," Axl goes on; he can't help it. "He thinks it would be better if we became cyborgs with electric jacks and plugged ourselves into each other to bone. Do not let that guy put his tongue in your mouth."

"Stop."

Axl presses eject on the boom box, removes the cassette tape labeled *SYXTEM: Side 3: Take What You Deserve.* He flips the tape, cranks the volume.

It's Prince, "Let's Go Crazy."

My song.

Gigi hits the fog lights. They roll down the squeaky windows of the Malibu, push open its heavy doors, jump out. Their boots sink into the soil I'll call home until my body disintegrates completely, fat cell by fat cell, and I become it. Gigi is wearing a bright green Irish whiskey T-shirt belted like a dress, her father's old Navy jacket with *DURANT* stenciled on the pocket, ankle boots the color of dried blood. Axl is a giant in his ripped Hüsker Dü T-shirt and beat-up leather jacket. They meet in the muddy gravel in front of the car.

"Oh no let's go! Go! Go crazy. . . ."

Axl throws his massive arms over his head and thrashes like he's in his own private mosh pit. Gigi dances in a carefree, aerobic way, like the high school heroine of one of the '80s movies she loves way more than it makes sense to, given how little they have to do with her life. Gigi's America looks nothing like the America in those films, but she refuses to let the fantasy go. Why *shouldn't* her problems be limited to living on the wrong side of the tracks, resolvable by a cool vintage prom dress? She clings to the wish like a life preserver as she and Axl dance on their best friend's grave in the headlights, kicking up mud to Prince and the chirping of the field crickets.

The living Max would've appreciated this twisted memorial.

As for the dead one?

I'd like to tell these kids to be more careful.

The party is watching.

Possession of Anti-American Thought can get you a one-way ticket to a reeducation camp in North Carolina.

Gigi and Axl shouldn't need me to remind them about the New American Way, but here they are, blasting their soundtrack, tempting fate.

Alas, I can't berate them. The only place I exist anymore is inside a living person's thoughts. It's the sole dead-guy revelation I've had, and I've got no idea what it means, so I'll repeat it.

The dead live in your thoughts.

We feel your feelings.

The dead are in you, and we have much to say.

All right—I'm just trying to sound ominous, using the royal *we;* I'm the only dead guy I've ever met. So far, being dead is exactly like living in the Midwest. Shit's a booniescape. Nothing supernatural has gone down since I shuffled off this mortal coil, except I can park on Gigi's psyche like some goober who loiters at Burger King trying to creep with underage girls. *There's* a super-power.

The thing is, I died with a secret.

Insert "Ooh" from live studio audience here.

Really though, I have a hunch it's why I'm stranded between Heaven and Hell.

To be released from purgatory, I must confess my sins.

Tell Gigi what I did and why I did it to absolve myself, and warn her, so she doesn't end up buried in a sex graveyard, like me.

I guess?

There's no one to ask.

The afterlife is like a diner at three in the morning.

Seriously understaffed.

But even if I'm right about what I have to do to get out of here, the girl won't listen to me. She's never listened to me, and I sure as shit don't know how to make her start now.

Don't get me wrong. When I was alive, our dynamic worked for us. I talked too much; Gigi selectively ignored me. We cared about exactly nothing together, and it was perfect.

Not nothing.

Theater.

Just theater.

Still, I keep trying.

Original Pervy Bisexual paging Unoriginal Pervy Heterosexual— can you hear me? There's something we need to talk about, Gigi, and I daresay it's long overdue. . . .

My friends keep dancing. Electric guitars echo over the shrill stridulating of the crickets. Bats spiral in spiky darts, sucking up mosquitos, snatching one last piece of action before the summer is gone. I can almost smell the night air, sweet and fertile, like the moment before something starts to rot.

Yoo-hoo, freak girl, it's Maxy, the ghostest with the . . . Yeah, never mind.

I need to talk to you, Giselle. Seriously.

Ding-dong! Delivery for Dr. Dirtypants! I've got a very large *package for you. . . .*

Ugh.

Just—I've been trying to get your attention all summer. Can a girl take five seconds to tune in to the afterlife and check her messages?

Hello?

Can you hear me?

Are you listening?

2.

WOULD I WERE DEAD!
IF GOD'S GOOD WILL WERE SO;
FOR WHAT IS IN THIS WORLD
BUT GRIEF AND WOE?

The thing I can't get used to about being dead is my complete lack of ability to do shit.

Which is ironic. When I was alive, and the choice was (1) Do shit, or (2) Avoid doing said shit, numero dos was my numero uno every time. Except for numero three, self-pleasurization, which it should go without saying doesn't count as doing shit—or didn't, until now. In my current, Johnsonless state, I'm in horndog Hell.

The gods have a sick sense of humor.

When I was alive, I dug the gods. Not just the bossy, paternal, Catholic god I grew up with. All of them. The giggly pothead with the long earlobes. The blue Betty with ten arms and the necklace of severed heads. The one who's such a diva he won't even let you draw a picture of him. Not only are gods drama queens, they're comedy gold.

I believe in comedy; therefore, I believe in god.

Incidentally, this is what Ms. Lee called a Maxologue. If we were alive, she'd be giving me a verbal spanking about hogging the spotlight.

Alas, I'm not the only new corpse in town.

Last spring, our theater teacher ended play rehearsal early. The next day, we heard she'd sucked down a fifth of gin, sealed her garage, revved up her Ford Mustang, and drunk the fumes.

Ms. Lee is dead too.

We wanted to be angry at her.

We weren't.

Some of us actually blamed ourselves.

. . . But if we *were* alive, Ms. Lee would be all *You're monopolizing, Mr. Bowl,* and I'd be all *Chyeeuh, kinda what I do, beb,* and I'd bait her into a battle of wits until she booted me out of rehearsal.

Now that I think about it, maybe Ms. Lee had a point. If I go silent for a spell, the next time I try to get Gigi's attention, will she be so shocked that she hears me?

It's worth a try, no?

Ms. Lee, you win again. Apparently, even the dead can take direction.

It's Sunday night. Gigi is leaning on the hostess credenza at the Stand-Around Barn, forcing herself to read the book Orin lent her while her Creepy Dead Friend loiters in her thoughts not doing shit.

The Stand-Around Barn, aka the Round Barn Restaurant, is an actual barn that is actually round. Gigi's father used to swing on a rope tied to the hayloft back when he was a kid and the parking lot outside was a dairy farm. Now the hayloft is the second-floor smoking section. On Sundays there's a buffet piled with chicken limbs drying out under a hot lamp that makes them glow as red as Satan's ass cheeks, and a mountain of instant mashed potatoes that coat your tongue like paste and sink in your belly like paper-towel pulp. All you can eat, $7.95.

As usual, SYXTEM-sanctioned music blares on a six-CD changer programmed to random shuffle.

And random it is. We don't know how the party decides which music is Anti-American and which isn't.

We do know that in order for a song to be legal, it must suck.

That goes for pretty much all art, thanks to the Culture Initiative, which Bud Hill launched in '88 *to uphold American values.*

First thing he did after he canceled the elections.

That's his name, by the way. The Dictator's—Bud Hill.

Once, when he was a baby, someone named him that.

Buddy.

Customers seated in the wooden booths that line the barn's curved walls shovel in the meat and potatoes while Gigi twists Orin's paperback in her hands, keeping one eye out for her boss, Don Peluk. She's not supposed to be reading at work, and she's certainly not supposed to be reading a book about anarchy.

And she isn't reading it. Not really. Since I died, concentrating on anything has been a massive fucking chore.

Still, she keeps trying. She needs to say something intelligent about anarchy to Orin. Gigi lost me, and she lost Ms. Lee. Her virginity is one thing she's determined to lose by choice, and she's going to lose it tonight.

With Orin.

Because of her intelligence.

She flips to a random page. *You cannot buy the revolution. You cannot make the revolution. You can only be the revolution. It is in your spirit, or it is nowhere. —Ursula K. Le Guin.*

Gigi feels a painful longing in her heart.

She knows exactly what that means.

It was fall of Gigi's sophomore year when the Dictator hijacked the Thespians. A directive was issued: from now on, American high schools would only produce shows the party chose. Our first order was to do a stage adaptation of the 1984 box office smash hit film *Red Dawn*.

The plot of *Red Dawn* is straightforward: hot high school students shoot up evil Soviets who are occupying the USA. When it was originally released, it was hailed by the *Guinness Book of World Records* as the most violent movie ever made.

When the Thespians heard the news, we were overjoyed. I howled my barbaric yawp in approval. Our scenery designer, Spatz Ammons, jumped on a stack of flats and pantomimed mowing down the whole Thespian troupe with her imaginary Uzi submachine gun. Even Axl couldn't act like he wasn't a little bit amped.

For despite our all-black outfits and our memorized Monty Python skits, we had not yet grasped theater's power.

If you tell the story right, people will buy anything.

Theater is the Dictator's most dangerous weapon.

Ms. Lee's response to the Thespians' juvenile enthusiasm about *Red Dawn* was simple.

She decided we would do something else.

Namely, the 1963 pinnacle of modern theater, *The Brig,* written by former US Marine Kenneth H. Brown. The play is a gruesome depiction of a single day of abuse in a Marine prison. The original production was described by the *New York Times* critic as "a feverish fetish of realism" wherein "hardly anything happens except the bestial rituals of confinement." In summary, "a painful evening in the theater."

Two shows oozing brutality and bodily fluids.

With one difference.

The party wanted to teach us to dehumanize our enemies so we'd lust to fight in a patriotic bloodbath. Have fun with the guns, kids! Want more? Join the war!

Ms. Lee wanted us to feel the crushing humiliation of following orders so we'd lust to fight authoritarian control. Bow down, maggots! We're gonna destroy your humanity and eat your soul!

By the end of the first—and, thanks to Vice Principal Smith, only—performance of *The Brig*, not a single Thespian wasn't weeping.

VP Smith chewed us out big-time. Slapped Fiona with a warning, put her on the party's shit list. Shut down the theater department for the rest of the school year.

It was the greatest experience of our lives.

The night the Thespians became outlaws.

A cluster of cowbells jangles aggressively. Gigi slips the paperback into the top drawer of the hostess stand as the barn's front doors gape open and a cold wind blows inside.

More customers.

Gigi asks, "Four for dinner?" Scrawls with a grease pen on a glass-covered seating chart, leads the citizens to a booth for their meat. When she pushes open the swinging doors to the kitchen to grab a basket of rolls for her table, the music changes: hair metal. Illegal, but the odds of a SYXTEM soldier taking time to press pause on the tape deck and slap cuffs on the kitchen crew seem low to nil, the cooks a couple of ex-convicts too mentally deranged to be useful to the party.

She calls, "Four-top on nine."

Ironman is on the grill. "What's up, Grizzella," he says. Sleepy eyes, flattop fade, Christian cross dangling gold and lonely from his neck. "Got a boyfriend yet?"

"Thousands of them," says Gigi, pulling open the heated metal drawer where the dinner rolls live, soft and comforting.

"I miss your hair," says Droopy Sterling, who has a face like melting wax, one eye that doesn't open anymore, and is never cooking anything, only ever leaning on the salad bar, longing for something for whom any woman in his path is an equal-opportunity substitute. "You look like a dyke now."

Gigi gives him the finger without looking up. "Homophobe."

Buried in the rolls she notices the corner of a piece of paper. When she tugs it, she pulls out a booklet.

Damp, black-and-white photocopies, folded in half and stapled. On the cover, a fuzzy collage of a garden; the blooms are severed hands, flipping the bird. In the sky, letters in a jittery mix of fonts float ransom-note style:

RiotRite | Hot Deals | Savings

Gigi feels a thrilling jolt of panic.

This is it.

The Defiance zine.

She's heard about *RiotRite,* of course—but she's never actually *seen* a copy. They quit coming out a couple years ago. Rumor has it the kids behind it were sent to a reeducation camp.

The cooks are suddenly quiet, cooking or pretending to be. A spatula scraping, the sizzle of scorched meat.

Gigi checks over her shoulder. Her boss isn't lurking in the dark corner with the mops, so she flips through the zine.

It's a mix of drawings, collages, typewritten . . . articles? Poems? Sentences that make no sense. She lingers on a comic strip. Two truckers, pigs with eyeballs popping out of their heads, lean out the windows of their vehicles to talk. But instead of words, the dialogue balloons are filled with scribbles. There's an article with the headline "Listen to Your Friends":

> *Sweetheart, I hate to break it to you, but youth today meet where the worms eat. Don't miss tomorrow's party. Turn that frown upside down! We've got recipes, recipes, recipes. New! Improved! Carburetors! Don't miss our EXCLUSIVE interview with Harry Houdini. . . .*

There's an illustration of a girl wearing cat's-eye glasses holding a knife, using it to carve a treasure map in a pumpkin.

She heard it was like this.

Nonsense.

In Gigi's hands though, the zine feels charged—like more than nonsense. It feels like some absurd anonymous love note. Supposedly, it's coded. Meaning you used to be able to get real news from these pages, if you were in the know. It's still a crime to have one.

Gigi looks up. Which cook is this cool?

Neither of them.

She remembers a fellow employee she's never previously thought directly about. Skinny taxidermist from the trailer park, a couple years younger than her. What's his name?

"Where's the dishwasher?" Gigi asks.

"Stu quit last night," says Ironman.

"Why you wanna know?" asks Droopy, holding a squirt bottle of white salad dressing above his head and letting its jizzy contents drizzle on a pile of iceberg. "You doing him?"

"Douchebag," says Gigi, newly fascinated by the thought of the ex-dishwasher, Stu.

She slides *RiotRite* into the waistband of her skirt, fluffs her granny blouse to hide it. Grabs her basket of rolls.

When she leaves, nobody calls after her.

She pushes open the swinging doors and almost falls over.

The boss is at the hostess stand, reading about anarchy.

Don Peluk is the Round Barn's owner, its manager, its live-in troll. Built like a flagpole, no shoulders. Eyes the color of a loogie. He probably asks his babysitters to fold his underwear and watches them do it. He probably has a fuzzy brown cozy on his toilet seat.

Peluk holds up the book. "Anarchy, eh? Yeah, I used to be into philosophy."

Gigi drops the rolls on her table, stops as far from Peluk as she can get away with while still appearing to resume her hostess post.

He's leering with his pimento-olive eyeballs at her breasts.

She'd like to snatch her book and whack his stupid head with it.

But she controls herself. Reminds herself how much she likes her job, typically. All she has to do is stand around. Hence, the Stand-Around Barn. She earns enough cash to buy groceries when her dad is running low, which is always; keep gas in the Malibu; impulse-buy lipsticks at Walgreens. She just needs this horndog to leave her alone so she can do her dumb job without him breathing on her.

"Can't keep letting you get away with reading at work. Problem is, Gigi, girls who look like you bring in the cabbage. With a body like that, who needs long hair?"

Gigi bites her tongue. Wonders if she could tolerate the pain if she decided to bite it off. How much pain can she tolerate?

The cowbells jangle angrily.

A swarm of soldiers barrels into the restaurant, guns drawn.

Gigi stops breathing.

It's a raid.

She feels the zine pressing against her body.

Why did I take this? How stupid am I?!

Time to break my vow of silence.

GIGI! I scream. *YOU MUST CHILL! Do Not Panic! I repeat! Make yourself absolutely calm!*

Gigi's heartbeat is speeding up, not slowing down.

She doesn't hear me.

Or does she?

My tone isn't exactly soothing.

Can you blame me?

Last soldier I met put me to bed with a shovel.

The barn lights flash on and off. Soldiers in royal blue uniforms bark commands. Two flank Peluk.

Peluk raises his hands, still holding the book.

One of the soldiers snatches it, flips through the pages.

Gigi feels nauseous. That book belongs to her, not Peluk. He shouldn't be arrested; she should. But if he tells the soldiers it's hers, they won't ask questions. They'll arrest them both.

Why would they raid the Round Barn? Peluk is a SYXTEM fanatic. He's always listening to Bud Hill's wealth-building seminars in the basement office. . . .

The soldier locks the handcuffs, marches Peluk around the hostess stand. The cowbells ring a jagged exclamation as they exit, and the barn doors thump shut.

The other soldier stays behind. His eyes dart around the restaurant like he's looking for some specific thing.

Gigi's heart feels woozy.

Her skeevy boss just saved her.

From what?

When democracy was "temporarily suspended," the military replaced the cops. Since then, buttloads of people have been arrested. The ones they release rarely talk about it. The rest go to the reeducation camps that Bud Hill simultaneously brags about and won't admit exists. What happens there we *really* don't know. Nobody has come back to tell us.

And Gigi isn't out of danger yet.

She still has the zine.

The soldier is standing so close to Gigi that she smells the starch of his uniform mingling with the sharp scent of his sweat. His head has a noble shape, like a landmark. . . .

Wait: Does she *know* this person?

She does. They sang together in a regional chorus in elementary school. He was a soloist. She hears him—what was his name?—singing full-throated, like a brand-new bird, a song from the musical *Oliver! "Who will buy this wonderful morning? Such a sky you never did see. . . ."* Gigi lets her eyes spiral into the secret curl of his ear. She has whispered into it. *"Do you want a Starburst?"* The boy's name was . . . Benjamin?

The choirboy stands alert while his colleagues usher out customers at gunpoint.

Folks with feathered hair, ice-washed jeans, wristwatches, polo shirts, mock turtlenecks shuffle past Gigi and out the barn doors, accompanied by the peppy grooves of the electronic flute that's blaring from the Round Barn sound system. No handcuffs.

Everyone cooperates, their expressions blank. You can't tell who's terrified, who's happy to help, who's both.

As the customers leave, Gigi suppresses the urge to make sardonic comments, like *Hope y'all enjoyed your meal!* Or *Next time, cheesecake is on the house!*

The more disturbing the situation, the stronger Gigi's urge to make a joke.

"To feel your feelings in the moment they are happening can be terrifying. Like it will result in a catastrophic overload of your heart. Your brain develops ways to avoid feeling, some of them more destructive than others. . . ."

Ms. Lee told us that.

Ms. Lee, who gave up and is gone.

Wait: Why didn't the soldiers march Gigi out along with everybody else? They appear to be wrapping up—why is she still standing here?

A firm hand on Gigi's shoulder startles her.

The choirboy.

Her head is spinning. If he arrests her, she'll . . . what? Bust out her secret kickboxing skills? No! *She'll be arrested!* If they send her to North Carolina, what will her father do? Her poor father!

The zine is digging into her flesh; she's gonna ralph.

The soldier says, "Go home."

Gigi hears a small, sweet voice singing, *"So what am I to do? To keep a sky so blue? There must be someone who . . ."*

The soldier whispers through gnashed teeth. "Or do I have to take you in with everybody else, Gigi?"

It *is* him. Benji.

The flapping sound of the swinging kitchen doors. Ironman and Droopy stumble out with their hands behind their backs. A soldier appears behind them. Unlike the parade of customers, the cooks are handcuffed.

They cross the matted brown carpet in their grease-spattered aprons, pass Gigi without making eye contact. The soldier prods them as they descend the winding steps to the basement, where the bar is, and the bathrooms.

Handcuffs?

Now Gigi definitely feels something appropriate. She feels panicked for the cooks. Certainly, Ironman and Droopy will be questioned and let go.

She turns back to Benji. He's totally staring at her breasts.

Gigi grabs her purse from the bottom shelf of the hostess stand and rushes out the big barn doors.

3.

O PITEOUS SPECTACLE!
O BLOODY TIMES!

America's Favorite Dictator has a serious fan base.

In 1980, when Bud Hill ran for his first term as president, I was in elementary school. His stump speech was the same get-rich-quick sales pitch he hawked in the late-night television infomercials I used to fall asleep watching.

"Don't let them stop you from experiencing abundance beyond your wildest dreams!" said the man with the pockmarked face and the bulging jugular. *"Remember the SYXTEM Core Value: You deserve what you desire. . . ."*

The SYXTEM wasn't a political party then. It was a twelve-cassette set of wealth-building strategies that Bud warned us was a limited-time offer.

It wasn't.

He's still talking.

When he won the election, my father was one of the many Americans who celebrated.

"Now, by law, everyone in this country has the same opportunities, Max. Finally, the free market is free!"

"Free from what?" I asked. *"Jail?"*

"Not jail. Taxes! And regulation, which was murdering small businesses. No more government handouts. We're gonna strengthen national defense. It's time for America to grow up."

The First Lady never hurt for admirers either. Christie Hill is both unattainably physically attractive and barely relatable. Smoking-hot combo. Doesn't speak much in public, but when she does, it's usually about the power of positive thinking.

In 1984, Bud ran for a second term. The guy who ran against him presented a portfolio of innovative civic policies, which he explained, in great detail, again and again.

Guess what's not exciting?

Policies.

Guess what is exciting?

Getting rich!

Bud stayed.

Of course, the Dictator also has his critics. Even before he started a bunch of wars, plenty of people hated his guts.

First of all, how does a guy whose sole accomplishment in life is creating a self-help cult with an impossible-to-pronounce name—I mean, SYXTEM? As in, "system" with an "x," but in ALL CAPITAL LETTERS? What *is* that? How does this guy get elected president of the United States?

When I was in middle school, people could still make jokes about Bud Hill in public. On television, comedians made him feel like the star of a fart-joke comedy, like *Police Academy*. Or, at worst, the bad guy in an entertaining thriller, like *The Shining*.

There was straight-up reporting back then, too. On the nightly news television broadcasts, in the daily papers, on public radio. Commentators contextualized the party's philosophy, analyzing its massive appeal. The Bud Hill phenomenon was nothing new, they argued. Nothing surprising. Humanoid history loves its snake-oil salesmen. Its pull-yourself-up-by-your-bootstraps mythologies. Its tough guys. Its nationalists. Its despots.

The older I got, the more Dad and I argued.

"If eliminating taxes was so smart, how do you explain the empty storefronts downtown?" I'd ask. *"Skyrocketing poverty and drug addiction. Busted streetlights and sinkholes the party doesn't fix. Curable diseases killing people who can't afford medical care. Raging rivers of dog poop—people can't even afford to feed their pets!"*

"Have faith in the Market, Maximus. The Market will show you the way."

"Gee, Dad. I have a twelve-cassette set of trademarked wealth-building techniques you'd enjoy. Never mind; you memorized them."

"Son, if you weren't so busy being sarcastic, you might notice the millions of people the New American Way is helping. The government was paying people not to work. You want oppression? There's your oppression. Thanks to the SYXTEM, everyone can be wealthy."

"Everyone cannot! You think a country founded on genocide, built on slavery and womanhating and gay bashing and earth rape—"

"You're trapped in the past! Just like the universities—"

"So look at the present. Do you, Bernie Bowl, truly believe that this country has leveled the playing field, as you love to put it, because everything must be a manly sports analogy, by instituting mandatory raw-doggin', free-ballin', fuck-you, winner-take-all, psycho-killer capitalism with zero regard for the human consequences—"

Dad's voice would careen with sarcasm. *"Actions have consequences, Max! Gee whiz! Imagine that!"*

By the time Bud canceled the '88 elections (*"We must protect these great United States from those who would divide us"*), not only had Americans picked sides.

We were loyal to them.

There were—O, god, seems forever ago—humongous protest marches. For a few days that winter of '88, you could watch colorful clips of them on the news. Hundreds of thousands of Americans shouting through bullhorns, singing songs, waving signs, wearing hats.

Dad refused to let me watch downstairs, so I'd turn down the sound on the TV in my bedroom. It was so inspiring. Badass America was *on* this! The country that belonged to Harriet Tubman, Harvey Milk, and Susan B. Anthony was obviously gonna crush the wannabe dictator with its pinky finger.

Then, one day, the party took over the news, and you couldn't watch the marches anymore.

Or listen to public radio.

Local newspapers?

Gone.

And the buttloads of stories about the end of democracy became a buttload of celebrity home tours, froofy cocktail recipes, sitcom reruns, and profiles of citizens living their Best Lives under the New American Way.

Round about the time the rumors started flying about reeducation camps, Christie Hill did a prime-time television interview. When the reporter asked why the Hills were jailing opponents of the party, the entire country gasped.

The First Lady responded with her megawatt sympathetic smile. *"Americans are optimists. They want unity, not division. Bud and I refuse to let Anti-American Thought tear this country apart."*

And then, to make sure we all stayed optimistic, the raids started.

SYXTEM military cleaned out video stores. Record shops. Cafés.

And the party took over the universities as part of the

Education Initiative, *to "review the relevance of the curriculum in a wartime economy." Professors were fired; classes were "paused."*

Dad justified that, too. *"The University of Illinois was teaching the blame game. Massive waste of cabbage."*

Whenever Dad would look me squarely in the face with his beady brown eyes and multiple chins, I'd sigh audibly.

"What?" he'd ask, swirling his wine.

Sometimes, I'd say, *"Forget it."*

It's uncomfortable to completely disagree with someone you love.

You start to feel like your skin doesn't fit, or something.

We both hated it.

Feeling the distance between us winning, conquering more and more space in our house.

Pushing everyone in our family farther away from each other.

Smashing us up against the walls.

At some point we started hearing talk about an underground opposition called the Defiance. Which sounded tough, but nobody seemed to know what it was.

Even now, it isn't clear to me if the Defiance is a real thing or an expression we use to reassure ourselves that someone, somewhere, is doing something in secret to stop the country from becoming the thing we're becoming, even if nobody agrees on what that thing is.

Now that Madame Death has shat upon my dignity, it's safe to brood about my role in Our American Drama.

The things I said.

The things I didn't say.

The things I did and didn't do.

Or is it?

I shouldn't get cocky. Double-killing dudes may not be a thing yet, but I'd bet my decomposing left nut Bud Hill is working on it.

Meanwhile, the Dictator keeps ruling from the White House, and since the party took over the news, there is none. Champaign has always felt stranded, like an island plopped in an ocean of corn. Now it's even more isolated.

What I'm trying to say is that over the past few years, it's become impossible to get real information. Like, I want to explain how things got to be the way they are, but I can't say for sure that I *know* how they are.

I can't speak for other places. Cool places like Chicago, or New York.

But these days?

Nobody where I'm from knows what the flying fuck is going on.

Gigi and Axl are standing outside Champaign High School, staring down its dilapidated façade.

Pardon me; did I just use two SAT words?

Staring down the festering bunghole oozing perverts with gonads for brains. The beige exterior is permanently stained with drippy streaks, like it had diarrhea and didn't wipe. A third of the windows are nailed over with plywood boards. The undergloom, suspended in a state of condemnitude. Abandon All Hope, Ye Who Enter Here! That's Dante, bitches, and the King of the Purgatorio I be.

Yes, Ms. Lee; I get it now. Drama isn't a superfluous invention crafted to entertain the masses. It is dictated by the Dead to dignify the fate of the Living.

Gigi and Axl approach the school, Styrofoam cups of coffee and a bag of bliss from Ye Olde Donut Shoppe in hand. Dandelions sprout through cracks in the sidewalk. A squirrel nibbles on a syringe. Gigi kicks a foil Arby's wrapper with her ruby Chuck Taylors. There's no place like home.

Together, they pull open the front doors of CHS and hike the grand stairwell.

Over the stairs hangs a portrait of Bud Hill on a red-and-blue banner ten feet tall. Most people's faces look better as a drawing, and the Dictator's is no exception. In the picture, he's ageless, a comic-book character with a swoop of black hair, clean-shaven with a dimpled chin. His skin lacks the acne scars that were so evident in his infomercials, back in the day.

Fifteen minutes till the bell rings and the main doors open; meanwhile, kids are perched on the stairs in clusters, smoking whatever they've got.

Axl licks a streak of chocolate glaze off the back of his He-Man hand as he takes a seat near the top of the stairs. Gigi sits below him, leans her head against his knee while she eats her powdered sugar.

Today, I force Gigi to hear my confession. Then I drop the microphone and exit stage Death. For once, I have a legit excuse to skip school. Yet here I am, trapped in this filthy stairwell, watching my friends eat doughnuts.

The comedy gods just took this joke too far.

Gigi? My love, it's Maxy.

Before I died, I committed a terrible sin—

Axl nudges Gigi with his knee. "You've been vibing weird all morning. Wanna tell me what's up?"

"Theater was the only thing that made this shithole bearable," says Gigi.

"Let's motor," says Axl. "I'm only here because you are."

"Right. Let's drop out of school and get jobs in the party," says Gigi. "Or enlist. Or we could go into hiding, get found, and get shipped to North Carolina."

"So, we're here," says Axl. "Tune it out."

Gigi remembers Ms. Lee lecturing us last spring during rehearsal for the Thespians' final, never-seen, underground production, Shakespeare's *Henry VI*.

"You're being bombarded with painful stuff, guys. You feel so much, you want to stop feeling. Our job is to do the opposite. Express ourselves with precision. Let our feelings animate us, and wake the audience from its deathbed. This is a skill," Ms. Lee told us, *"and you can develop it."*

"Don't you wonder what it would've been like to go to college after graduation, and study theater openly?" Gigi asks.

Axl says, "No."

She looks up at him. Axl's face reads like an ancient Greek mask, a tragic hero permafrown they dug up and preserved in the British Museum.

"No?" she asks. "Just, no?"

Axl shoves the rest of his doughnut in his mouth.

Gigi! I'm telling you key shit, here! Stop thinking about your own problems for, like, two minutes, so we can talk about mine!

"Now that we're here, though, I'm glad," says Gigi.

"Because?" asks Axl.

"Because I feel Ms. Lee here. I *feel* her."

Guess who else is here?

Me!

My tale is not for children. It pulses with violence and lust. Like Henry VI, *the play with which we Thespians struggled until my untimely end—*

Axl exhales audibly, pulls a napkin out of the doughnut bag. Cleans icing from his fingers carefully, like he's giving a manicure.

"Heard the Round Barn got jacked last night," he says. "You ever gonna tell me?"

Gigi sips her coffee. Last night after the Round Barn was raided, she didn't feel like losing her virginity. Instead, as soon as she was safe inside the Malibu, she shoved *RiotRite* into her glove compartment like it was radioactive. Then she drove home, ate half a pan of microwave brownies, and watched her pirate VHS tape of *Pretty in Pink* for the ten billionth time.

"You okay?" asks Axl.

"I mean—are *you*?" she asks.

"Why wouldn't I be?"

"Because the maggots will probably raid CHS today and make a spectacle of dragging you out on your ass!"

"You know they won't do that."

"No I do not. Why wouldn't they?"

"Because the party needs me."

"To what?"

"Placate people. Gigi, we've talked about this."

According to Axl's big bro, Frank, the party ignores the illegal buying and selling of bootleg culture so people are less motivated to fight censorship.

"They'll never stop harassing us," said Frank. *"We're the hottest piece of ass in town. But as long as we don't make them look like fools, they need us around."*

Nobody ever called Frank Fischer modest.

Modesty isn't a trait typically associated with smugglers.

"Then why did they come for you the night they killed Max?" Gigi asks.

"You know why," says Axl. "We've been over this, like, many times."

"Reassure me."

"So, you're *not* okay."

Gigi throws her hands into the air, her face exasperated, with the froggy eyes. "Of course I'm not fucking okay!"

The stairwell is filling with kids and noise and the dealing of illicit substances palm to palm. There's a thick scent of stale sweat and hair spray.

Axl lowers his voice. "It was a fluke, Gigi. Rogue maggot, trying to impress his party superior by putting an Anti-American in a body bag his first week on the job. My sources are absolutely clear on that; nobody was supposed to be in Rolling Acres that night. Guy who killed Max is in North Carolina now, wishing he'd opened a shoe store or some shit instead of enlisting, accidentally murdering Commissioner Bowl's kid. They're really not supposed to be out there hunting down citizens in the streets. It's not, like, legal for them to do that."

"Yet."

"Yet."

"They can ship you to North Carolina, though."

"They can, Gigi. But they won't. Frank said—"

"Frank was always convincing, Axl. But he was often wrong."

Axl's nostrils flare, but he doesn't respond. Gigi is the only person who can criticize Axl's big bro without getting shouted down.

Axl crumples the empty doughnut bag. "The real question is what the fuck is wrong with me? Why didn't I think about the fact that when I ran, Max would take the hit? That's the shit that keeps me up at night. Reliving it. Did I truly just not give a fuck?"

Axl is obsessing over my death?

I mean, it doesn't crush me.

"Come on, Axl. You loved Max. Anyone would've—"

"I'm not anyone. And Max and me had a different relationship than you two," says Axl. "And your obnoxious—"

Axl seems to think better of finishing his sentence. He scratches his stubbly chin.

Gigi and I cross our arms. *Obnoxious?*

Axl looks directly at us. Sometimes his eyes have this dazzling sheen, like some faraway body of water. "I loved Max like a brother. I treated him like shit. I owe us both an explanation."

The stairwell resonates with the murmurs of the crowd, the off-key hum of the horndog chorus, managing the messes of their own lives, their own sloppy first days of school.

"I'm sorry, *what's* obnoxious about us?" asks Gigi.

Aw, Gigi, don't change the subject—Axl was about to elaborate on how much he loves me! And you already know why he hated us. He was jealous, because he wanted to get in your pants, but he isn't gay enough to have the privilege of rolling around in bed with you eating Sour Patch Kids and smoking cloves.

"I could've saved Max and I didn't. Just like I could've saved my brother."

"That's not true, about Frank. And you know it."

"I don't. Can we stop talking about this?"

Gigi frowns, stretches her legs in front of her. She's wearing the leopard-print miniskirt we found on clearance at JCPenney, black fishnets, her Navy jacket over a T-shirt she artfully ripped herself. The costume she chose to help her face another grueling day without theater and me.

Gigi, please.

Listen to me.

"You know what scares me the most?" Gigi asks.

Axl says, "Tell me."

She lifts her heels and drops them on the ground, repeatedly, like she can't sit still with the thought. "Without a play to focus on, the whole year is gonna be like this."

"I know," says Axl. "Relentless."

The color scheme of the CHS interior is pus gold with accents of bacterial-infection green. As Gigi carves a wriggling path through her peers toward homeroom, I can almost smell the rancid bodies of the mice who spent their summer vacations rotting inside the walls.

Gigi?

GIGI?

Giselle, my belle, it's me, in Hell—

Well, Hell's waiting room—which has NO snacks—

"Giselle Durant," calls a voice, garbled and wheezy, like it's being amplified through a bad sound system.

Gigi looks up.

She hears *Vice Principal Smith* but not me?!

Thanks, Gigi. Way to make me feel more dead than I actually am.

VP Smith is the tallest person at Champaign High, thanks in part to the four and a half extra inches provided by her decades-old, "I'm still standing" bouffant of white-blond hair. She has a pancake-powdered face and painted-on eyebrows, each one shaped exactly like the Saint Louis arch. Last year, when Ms. Lee led us in the exercise about how to empathize with your worst enemy, Gigi chose VP Smith, which is why the elaborate makeup endears her to us now, if fleetingly. Because VP Smith puts on a face each morning, as Gigi does, and that's something.

Gigi says nothing, just follows.

Smith unlocks the door to the windowless closet that used to belong to the janitor, flips on a blinding fluorescent light.

Gigi looks at the posters on the wall and resists the urge to salute. It's been a whole summer since she's laid eyes on the multicultural menagerie of muscular boys and white-toothed babes encouraging her to join the SYXTEM military before graduation.

Smith takes a seat in a plastic chair shaped like a shoehorn, crosses her legs. Her varicose veins make it look like she's flowing with blue-green antifreeze, the kind the Malibu guzzles.

"Well then, Miss Durant. Here we are." Smith tilts her bouffant toward the other chair.

Gigi sits. She resents the enemy intimacy Smith tries to bait her into. If Gigi is a delinquent, VP Smith created that delinquent. Gigi is here, but nobody can make her play.

"May I see your ID card?"

"You've called me by my name, like, five times in the past three minutes."

"ID card?" Smith repeats, unblinking. One of Smith's painted-on eyebrows is raised, the other is lowered. One the good cop, the other the bad. She's someone in a play who's trying too hard to reveal her character's stature.

We consider telling Smith to *stop indicating; it's bad acting.* Don't show someone you're doing a thing; just do the thing!

Gigi opens her backpack, hands over the card with her name, her ID number, and her freshman-year photograph—the old Gigi with the long black hair.

No party stamp. By now, most people have them. They make life easier. Even I caved, eventually. I needed to join the party to buy my Range Rover.

VP Smith makes a production of inspecting Gigi's card, handing it back.

"Axl Fischer has quite the little business going. What can you tell us about it?"

Gigi resists the urge to snort. *This* again?

In a surreally direct continuation of Gigi's last conversation with Smith three months ago, Gigi says, "I told you. I know nothing about Axl's job at the 7-Eleven."

"It's not the 7-Eleven that interests us," says Smith. "I ran into Didi at the IGA this weekend. In the freezer aisle. She's looking well. But she was very concerned about you."

Gigi's hand rises to rub her neck, and a harsh noise works its way out of her throat.

"Groan away, Miss Durant. Your mother is rightly concerned that you're affiliating with a known Anti-American."

Gigi snarls. It's the only appropriate response to the word "concerned." Gigi hasn't seen or heard from her mother in fully a year.

How do Didi and Smith even know each other?

Not that they wouldn't, thinks Gigi. *Everyone in Champaign over the age of seven knows each other.*

Gigi inspects the Vice Principal's cockeyed face. No justification is needed to snap up Axl. Nor Gigi, for that matter. Every time Smith drags her in here, there's an ulterior motive. Invoking Gigi's mother is a new one. . . .

Of course.

This is coming from Didi.

Gigi's mother wants information to help her husband, Marty Eckhorn, advance in the party.

Gigi's stepfather, Farty Marty, Champaign County Culture Commissioner, outburst-prone self-proclaimed self-made man.

Marty, the little gnat man.

Who will, in turn, pull strings for Smith next time she needs it.

Didi and Gigi.

Gigi and Didi.

It's astonishing, no? That way back when, Gigi's mother had thought it would be cute to have rhyming nicknames?

"Axl Fischer believes himself to be beyond my reach," says VP Smith. "He is not."

"Great. May I please be excused?"

"*No.* And the sarcasm in your voice is unattractive. Fiona Lee convinced you children that it is your birthright to question authority. Her suicide unmasked her as a fraud. The Thespian Society will continue under the leadership of Mrs. Knoxville. My greatest wish for you, Giselle, is that you will distance yourself from Fischer and use your considerable talents as an actress to support the party's vision and the New American Way. In doing so, you may inspire students who were tragically misled by Fiona Lee's Anti-American propaganda."

Knoxville, the *marketing* teacher? Whose entire curriculum is Bud Hill's SYXTEM seminars?

Gigi suppresses a very strong urge to snort.

VP Smith stands. "I've been a school administrator for thirty years. I know a bad egg when I encounter one. If you affiliate with Axl Fischer further, it's your bad. You don't want to share his fate."

Gigi nods as if in agreement, while we contemplate which phrase is more disturbing: "it's your bad," or "share his fate."

Anyway, she does want to share it.

She shares her friends' fates already.

All of ours.

* * *

Gigi exits the janitor's closet absently reading the back of her ID card, the part below the 1-800 number.

Anti-American Thought in word, deed, or intention destroys lives and puts your freedom at risk. Citizens whose tips lead to arrest may receive a cash reward of up to $2500.
IT'S OUR AMERICA. LET'S KEEP IT THAT WAY.

—BUD AND CHRISTIE HILL

She peeks in the window to Axl's homeroom.

Kids are tongue wrestling, scribbling in notebooks, sucking down nourishment from flasks. Axl is kicked back in his chair, boots on a desk; he appears to be fully asleep. A sign that says *Self-Directed Study Leads to Self-Sufficiency Is a SYXTEM Core Value* hangs above a chalkboard. Below it, someone wrote, *Fuck your face.*

After *The Brig,* VP Smith locked the Thespians out of the CHS theater for the rest of the year.

The next year, Ms. Lee had an idea.

The Thespians would do the shows the party ordered. Public performances would be Friday and Saturday nights in the CHS theater. Sunday, we'd strike sets.

Immediately after, we'd hold a secret, invitation-only performance of an underground show we'd been rehearsing, simultaneously.

Yup.

Under Ms. Lee's direction, the Thespians memorized lines, built sets, and designed tech for two entirely different productions—the party show and the underground show—and performed them on the same weekend.

It's called commitment, motherfuckers.

Last spring, the party's show was *Seven Brides for Seven Brothers,* a heartwarming musical about horny woodsmen who kidnap a village of women to be their unwilling brides.

Don't worry!

The women fall in love with them.

Secretly, Ms. Lee was directing us in the aforementioned rarely produced Shakespeare, *Henry VI,* Parts I, II, and III. A tale of a divided England, Joan of Arc, teenage warriors, and a king with a pacifist's heart.

She died before we could perform it.

So did I.

Honestly?

Can't say I miss it. The best thing about being dead is being done with *Henry VI*. Shit is slow, you know? *Slow.* And for some reason, half the characters have the same name, which never stops being confusing.

As she walks toward homeroom, Gigi remembers one particularly miserable *Henry VI* rehearsal.

I was sitting in the audience, blue high-top Chucks propped on the seat in front of me, unlit ciggie stuck to my bottom lip, flapping as I griped.

"Why should I keep risking my life and wasting my time with the most boring play Shakespeare ever wrote? Henry VI *didn't save the world, and neither will we. Who's with me?"*

Nobody exactly laughed, but you could feel it in the air, that the Maximus was speaking for the masses.

Ms. Lee was standing center stage, her suit jacket tossed on the battlefield. *"How am I supposed to know why you do things?"*

I shifted my large ass uncomfortably in my seat. *"Because . . . you're kind of obsessed with me?"*

I had a piquant premonition that I was about to be verbally spanked.

"Why you kids do or do not do things—theater, or anything else? This is not my problem."

A wise man in my shoes would've held his tongue.

The splooge bucket who was actually in my shoes did not.

"So why are you doing this play?"

"Me?" said Ms. Lee. *"I'm doing it because they told me I can't."*

4.

BUT IN THIS TROUBLOUS TIME
WHAT'S TO BE DONE?

A chain jostles as the door to Orin's apartment opens a crack, then all the way.

"Hey, Gigi," he says in his voice that is always so surprisingly quiet.

Orin Ellis. Tall, short black hair, slender without being slight. His thoughts flicker across his dark eyes like reflections of a film the rest of us can't quite see. Often, Gigi feels like Orin is looking at her from another dimension. One where she so wants to join him.

Gigi feels a shiver of warmth. Why do they call it *losing* your virginity? she wonders. "Lose" makes the whole experience sound accidental, not to mention unfortunate. In fact, Gigi has precisely envisioned every detail of what this experience will be like, down to the underwear she'll be wearing, until she isn't. Losing her virginity to the smartest boy in town?

That will be a *very* big win.

Gigi follows Orin inside.

I'd like to interfere with this entire situation. Tell Gigi that

Orin plays a role in my story. Without him, shit wouldn't have gone down like it did.

But I'll never get Gigi's attention with those biceps in the room. He's a hacker; why is he so toned? I always found it a bit much.

The warlock has thwarted me, again.

"I'm just finishing something. There's coffee."

Gigi gets herself a mug while Orin proceeds to the living room with the standard-issue curdled-cream semigloss walls, metal window blinds, drop ceiling that feels a tad too low. In the corner, an L-shaped assemblage of fiberboard resting on filing cabinets is a makeshift desk. On it, three computer screens connect via nests of wires to a clutter of electronic boxes. A telephone cord shooting from one of the boxes plugs into a wall jack. Orin sits in the fractured office chair he and I lifted from a defunct cubicle at the University of Illinois late last year, rolls it toward the screens.

Orin was never in our scene; not really. Isn't into theater at all. Our connection is *The Anarchist Cookbook.* He got it from Axl, who, under Frank's tutelage, by fall of his junior year was already dominating the smuggling racket from Carbondale to Kankakee (even the Fischers weren't cocky enough to cross the underworld professionals of Chicago).

Frank was still alive then; his band, Pater Cida, had just released their big album and was touring the underground club circuit in the Pacific Northwest.

The Fischers had lost the house in Rolling Acres, though. Not because their business wasn't profitable. The problem was Frank's love affair with smack, which loved him back like a jealous husband. It took away his world, and then it killed him.

Anyway, the Fischers didn't typically deal with books—too

much competition; not their interest—but sometimes got a few and had to shake them.

The night Orin stopped by to pick up *The Anarchist Cookbook* from the boarded-up community theater where Axl was squatting, we weren't sure what to do with him. We Thespians were onstage battling in a nerdilicious fashion, props like lampposts and picket fences conscripted as swords and shields, when this unnervingly handsome ghoul slid into the house—the very same phantasm who used to glide through the hallways of CHS in silence, emanating superiority. The bitch had been intimidating since middle school. None of us had ever even considered opening a conversation with him.

Axl gave him the book, and Gigi—who was probably, now that I'm thinking about it, having an insta-crush experience, the world caving in and reconstructing itself in a whole new geography—told him if he didn't have anywhere he needed to be, he should hang out.

We were shocked when he did.

Orin started showing up at Axl's on the regular. Sitting in the audience reading a book, looking like a profound vampire, while we Thespians carried on with our fuckwaddery, donning wigs and building medieval catapults.

Of *course* Gigi fell for him.

"Sorry about that," says Orin as he rolls back his chair, stands. "Your haircut is so flattering. It shows off your eyes. Sorry. I keep saying that."

Gigi smiles shyly at her Chucks as she crosses the matted carpet, sets her mug on his desk. Orin's body has fueled so many of her fantasies that sometimes she's embarrassed to look at him.

"I brought you something genius tonight," she says, tone of voice most flirtatious.

"Ooh, goodies," says Orin, rubbing his bicep, just in case she hadn't noticed.

Gigi reaches into her bag, pulls out the zine she found at the Round Barn.

"Ahh," says Orin. *"RiotRite."*

He sounds unimpressed.

"You . . . already have one?" Gigi asks.

"No, no. I mean, yes—of course. The zine was important, at the time."

We assume he isn't *trying* to insult her, but ouch. The cyberfuck does have a knack for popping one's bubble of self-satisfaction.

Gigi's face must look like she feels; Orin blinks like he just woke up.

"I'm sorry; I don't know how to talk. Thank you, Giselle. This is a really interesting historical document. You know what I meant."

Sometimes dude is about as emotionally perceptive as a vending machine.

Gigi does that thing she does when she's uncomfortable, twisting the piercings in her ears: faux sapphire, her birthstone; faux pearl, like someone's grandmother; gold stud, smaller gold stud, cubic zirconia . . .

"I've been wanting to show *you* something too." Orin goes back to the computer cockpit, gestures for Gigi to take a seat facing the screens. "This is what I've been working on."

Gigi feels off-balance as she slides the zine back into her bag, goes over to Orin's busted office chair.

What is she even doing here? Trying to get laid? The thing that never, ever happens, no matter how hard she tries?

The screens are crammed with bright green letters and numbers.

"The SYXTEM is developing an electronic net. Within a decade, the entire world will be using it to communicate. They're going to know everything you're thinking, Gigi. Everything you want. Everything you need. What you've said, what you're going to say. They'll know everything you've done and everything you're going to do. The internet will expose your hopes, your fears, your dreams. It's a magnificent tool of control."

A *net*? Like a *fishing* net?

Orin is looking at Gigi like he's expecting a reaction.

Now it's her turn to be brutally honest.

"No offense, but conspiracy theories annoy me. I don't need to make up shit to worry about."

"I get it, Gigi. But this is different. In the hands of people like Bud Hill? The internet will make Neighborhood Reports and ID cards seem like child's play. Its revolutionary potential has always been obvious too, but it's been difficult for people who aren't programmers to access. Before the Education Initiative, I would sneak through the steam tunnels to break into the supercomputing lab at the U of I. That's when I started designing a tool to make it easier."

Either Gigi isn't good at flirting or Orin isn't good at getting flirted with. Whichever it is, they're apparently going to talk about the internet.

Gigi sighs. "Why would you want to make it easier to access something the party will use to control us?"

"Because the internet will also allow us to exchange information," says Orin. "Get actual news. Connect with each other, all over the world. And we're going to use it to destroy them."

Gigi loves the passion in Orin's haunted eyes. It's what she wants to see when he undresses her.

But that's not what this is. Orin is telling her the new plan to take down Bud Hill, and she doesn't care. Not because she doesn't think it's a fine plan; she has no reason not to.

There's too much happening to care about all of it.

Or even a fraction of it.

She needs to redirect this conversation to someplace more satisfying.

Sex.

"Wait. Who is going to use the net to destroy who?" Gigi does that thing she does with her eyelashes. "Or is that a 'whom' sentence?"

"The *people* are going to use the net. And we won't only destroy the party. We'll destroy authority in all its forms. Let me show you. . . ."

Gigi stands and Orin sits, starts typing again.

She crosses her arms. "Is this like the movie *War Games*? Where the kid launches nuclear weapons from his bedroom?"

Orin sniffs a laugh. "Well, it's not unlike that."

Ugh. *War Games* bored the crap out of her.

As Orin types, Gigi's eyes trace the curve of his shoulders.

For one night, she thinks, *I want to distract myself from how much everything sucks. I want Orin. And I want Orin to want me. It's so simple. Shouldn't it be simple? Max would understand . . .*

Do I ever! I shout. *And I'm here, my love! Your twin in horniness. Though our tastes diverge—the opalescent anarchist never did it for me—*

Gigi inhales—

Sees me—

Facedown, bleeding out in Rolling Acres—the scene she didn't witness personally, but imagined in sickening detail, to try to understand what happened—

Alive and laughing, holding a paintbrush—

Dead and immobile, eating asphalt—

Shotgun in the Malibu, cranking the Styx—

Alive and crying, about that boy from Tolono—

Tottering around her bedroom, my bigfoot paws crammed into her stilettos, crowing, *"Could I come near your beauty with my nails, I'd set my ten commandments in your face!"* My drag queen interpretation of Eleanor in *Henry VI*—

Gigi imagines that she's holding me, dead and leaking—

Dead. Silent. The sky above my broken body spangled with disinterested stars, the evil queen, cruel and glamorous—

The cowbells jangle; the doors open; soldiers raid the Round Barn—

Gigi drops her palm on Orin's makeshift desk, knocks over a joystick.

Gigi! I shout. *I'm here!*

Orin's hands pause above his keyboard like a pianist.

Gigi says, "I can't breathe."

Orin jumps up, helps her to the La-Z-Boy. "Gigi, what's—?"

"The Round Barn got jacked."

"*What?* When?"

"Last night. That's why I didn't come over. I was too . . ."

"Fuck! How—?"

"I knew one of the soldiers," says Gigi, seeing Benji the choirboy's familiar ear, the strange new adult in his eyes. "They arrested my boss. A couple of cooks."

"Anyone else?"

Gigi shakes her head. "But I had the zine in my skirt. And they took your anarchy book."

Orin crouches beside the chair, lets his head drop. Grasps her hands. "*Fuck.* I'm so relieved you're okay."

The warmth of Orin's touch releases something in Gigi.

Is she okay?

"It's not like things weren't bad before," she says. "But when

Ms. Lee was alive, I had a focus. A way to express my feelings about the horrible things that are happening all around us. Now, without Ms. Lee? Without Maxy? It's brutal."

"Max," says Orin. In lieu of forming a sentence, he frowns.

Hey, man. I know you're probably full of regrets about me and shit. Please; let it go. Whatever happened between us was probably, like, 87 percent my fault.

It always is.

"And I know that Fiona Lee was your favorite teacher. . . ."

Gigi looks at Orin like he changed the subject to basketball.

"Ms. Lee wasn't *my favorite teacher*," she practically spits. "She was the only person in this backward-ass town who cared if we *lived or died*!"

Orin squints like he's confused. "Oh. So, I'm guessing . . . you still see her?"

Gigi spots a tissue box on Orin's desk, gets up to grab one. Orin, who *never* kisses her, and *continuously makes no sense*. Nothing is ever what she wants it to be. Things seem like they might not suck, and then they do suck, and then they're gone.

"Do you visit Fiona Lee in hiding?" asks Orin.

Gigi feels a surge of genuine annoyance. "Stop."

Orin's flickering eyes search Gigi's face. "You know she's alive."

Oh, *dude,* you are *so* buggin' right now. I kid you not. Screwing with Gigi about Ms. Lee? What's the premise here?

Gigi doesn't blink. "What could you possibly be saying, Orin?"

Orin's lips part, but he looks away from her, like the words he needs have floated across the room.

A shiver crawls up the back of Gigi's neck, spreads over her scalp; I feel it rattle my brittle bones.

And I realize: Orin isn't lying.

Ms. Lee is alive.

Or he thinks she is.

Goddamn, dead dudes know a frustratingly limited amount of shit!

"You didn't know," says Orin. "I assumed Axl told you."

Oh, *No He Didn't.*

Obviously, Axl would've told us that Ms. Lee is alive—*if it were true.* Gigi is stalking toward the door.

Orin follows. "Gigi, hang on. This isn't what—I wanted us to watch a film tonight—"

You wanna seduce her *now*?

Read the room!

"I'll call you," says Orin as Gigi pulls out her car keys, already mentally halfway to Axl's theater.

5.

MY THOUGHTS ARE WHIRLED LIKE A POTTER'S WHEEL

If Ms. Lee is alive, why didn't Axl tell me?! I, Maximus, who needed to know? If he'd told me—

Axl might be dead, instead of me.

I mean, no.

I don't want *that*.

But if I don't have to confess to Gigi that my sin led to Ms. Lee's death—

What do I have to do to get the fuck out of here?

I used to assume that Death would be the end of the questions. That the end meant THE END, not the beginning.

My afterlife is going seriously off script!

The night sky is a hot shade of magenta, thick with ash-black clouds. Gigi is pounding on the heavy wooden front door of Axl's theater. It's the first raw cold of fall, and Gigi is shivering like mad.

Axl squats in an abandoned theater on the edge of town. It's a railroad station that was refurbished as a community playhouse in the '30s, left to fester in the '80s, and boarded up. A couple of winters ago, Axl and I broke in together, and were shocked to discover how well the place was preserved. The Art Deco lobby with its painted geometric ceiling. The heavy velvet curtains, caked with dust. The chalkboard-black walls of the house. The door hardware is solid brass, and the arched mirrors behind the glossy walnut ticket counter are perpetually foggy, with cracks that look like veins. Once Axl reconfigured the water and electricity, employing wells of deep nerdery I lack the expertise to describe, we were golden.

Gigi stops pounding on the door, fumbles with her keys, unlocks it. If he's in the middle of something embarrassing? Serves him right.

She bolts the door behind her, crosses the lobby. Parts the velvet curtains that lead to the theater proper. Spots Axl onstage, hammering in the dim glow of the footlights.

Music streams down from the elaborate sound system Axl and I patched together over the past year and a half, the pained voice of Morrissey singing: *"And now I know how Joan of Arc felt! . . . La-da-da, da-da . . ."*

Two Thespians, Leticia and Butt, are lounging in the second row of the house, talking quietly, high-top Chuck Taylors propped on the seats in front of them.

"'Sup, Gigi," calls Leticia.

"What's up," Gigi calls back absently as she crosses the house.

"Just being really fucking sad in a dark theater," says Butt. "Telling stories about Max and Ms. Lee."

Aw. Go on. . . .

"Same shit different day," says Leticia. "Care to join?"

Axl marches offstage with purpose.

"Axl!" calls Gigi, skipping up the steps to follow him into the wings.

Off stage left, she glimpses Axl's black fisherman's sweater as he slips through the steel door that leads to the brick vestibule and the emergency exit.

Gigi runs to catch up, grabs the door before it slams.

"Dude!"

Axl spins around. "Oh, hey. What's up?" Red light from the EXIT sign splashes on his kinky hair. His green cargo pants are tucked into his boots. He looks like a commando styled by a dark-wave Goth band.

Gigi crosses the vestibule and looks up into her friend's face, his eyes so hard that when you stare at them long enough, they become soft again, like polished stone. Touches his sweater sleeve, stiff from washing his clothes by hand.

"Orin says Ms. Lee is alive."

Axl is silent.

Gigi searches his face.

I search his face.

Wow.

Wow.

"Oh god." Gigi takes a step back.

Axl puts his hands on her shoulders, as if to steady her. "Giselle. If you knew how many rumors. How many urban fucking legends—"

"Why didn't you tell me?"

"*Unsubstantiated* rumors, designed specifically to keep people unclear about what the truth is. You know that, right? That they want to keep everyone off-balance?"

"I don't understand why you didn't—"

"Why would I tell you, Gigi? To upset you even more?" Axl

is raising his voice now, that thing he does when he shouts you down for your own good. "To get your hopes up, that she's gonna be okay?"

Gigi can't believe he didn't tell her.

And I'm horrified that he didn't tell me.

"You should've told me"—she speaks slowly, simmering—"because you knew I'd want to know. The party wants to drive us apart. Make us stop trusting each other. Congratulations, Axl. You're helping them."

Ditto!

And also, you shithead, it might've saved my life!

Gigi pushes past Axl, cuts through backstage. Passes tables piled with wood scraps, a pyramid of cans, the paint we use to make new things look old and old things look new.

Storms onto the stage, weaves between random set pieces the Thespians rolled out for our amusement. The spiral staircase that leads to the balcony with two folding chairs and a faux geranium. The boat, nose down, an oddly angled shipwreck from some play nobody can name. The country porch swing, spotlit, Axl's leather jacket tossed on it like he's gonna be right back.

The house seats are empty; the Thespians are gone.

Morrissey is singing "How Soon Is Now?" as Gigi jumps off the stage and heads to the lobby.

When she pushes through the velvet curtains, she barely avoids a head-on collision with Piper Aurora.

"Hey, Gigi!" says Piper, her voice as sunny as orange Kool-Aid.

Peachy white skin, farm-girl freckles, green skater dress, black Chucks. Long red waves that shimmer in the lobby's golden light, like she's some landlocked mermaid.

Piper is the nicest Thespian in the world.

Gigi's oldest friend.

And Party Royalty.

Piper's mom, Melinda, is First Lady Christie Hill's cousin. They grew up neighbors in Kenilworth, Illinois, and have been White-Anglo-Saxon-Protestant-ing out together ever since.

Technically, this makes Piper the First Lady's first cousin once removed, but nobody understands how cousin shit works, so "First Niece" became the shorthand.

Gigi and Piper bonded in kindergarten, when Bud Hill was still a joke. Gigi's father was almost always working at the tavern; her mother was . . . her mother. The Auroras treated Gigi like another daughter, fussing over her, asking her thoughtful questions, feeding her hot, delicious meals.

The Auroras were the stable, loving family Gigi longed for.

Gigi was Piper's fiercest defender when the rumors started that the Auroras tortured people in their farmhouse outside of town. That Piper spied on kids, informing on their Anti-American activities to her parents. Gigi knew for a *fact* that Piper was trustworthy. When Gigi joined the Thespians in high school, she insisted Piper join too.

Ms. Lee put a hard stop to the whispering at rehearsals.

"Who here volunteers to be judged by the behavior of their most abhorrent relative?"

The Thespians gave Piper a chance because of Ms. Lee.

She won their trust by being herself.

Piper works harder than anybody. She's organized, dedicated, sharp. And *kind*. Piper could smell the sweetness in an old sock.

Now all the Thespians stand up for Piper.

Except one.

This spring, Gigi had a change of heart.

The Royal Family is responsible for my death.

Piper is one of them.

Their friendship is a childhood relic.

And like Gigi's childhood, it needs to be over.

Piper hasn't gotten the memo.

"Axl is such a flirt," says Piper conspiratorially. "How are you two not a thing? And I mean, if you're not gonna be . . ."

Piper's glossy lips are downturned, her cinnamon eyes blatant with hope.

"Wait," says Piper. "Gigi, are you okay?"

Gigi is on the verge of saying something sarcastic and jetting when she's hit with an urge that gives her whiplash.

She wants to tell Piper the rumor about Ms. Lee. Gigi imagines Piper saying, *We've got to find her!* Like something out of Nancy Drew.

Or Scooby-Doo . . .

Gigi keeps walking.

Piper follows. "Giselle? What's *up* with you lately? Can we talk?"

When Gigi opens the door to exit, a bracing night wind blows into the theater.

Gigi turns around.

"Axl's ideal woman is a porn star who is also a rock star. But also, somehow, a monk. In other words," says Gigi, "he's a dick. Good luck with that."

Piper nods in that slow, awful way that means she's looking through Gigi, through whatever Gigi thought she'd effectively said or done, and seeing what she actually felt and meant. This familiar realization pisses Gigi off just enough to make her leave the theater without bothering to shut the door behind her, a move I find melodramatic, but we Thespians have our moments, I suppose.

Gigi crunches through the gravel to the Malibu.

Slides into the driver's seat, punches the gas several times as she turns the key.

The Malibu coughs, clearing its throat, then growls, awakening.

The first deep chill is always difficult for the beast. We wonder how many winters it has left. Gigi watches the fuel needle go from wild gesticulating to slumping near the E zone.

She leans her head on the headrest and looks toward shotgun. Pretends I'm sitting beside her, wearing a houndstooth newsboy cap, lighting a clove.

Imagines me saying, *Let me get this straight, beb. Ms. Lee might be alive, and Axl didn't tell you. I've been extinguished, Piper is unforgivable, and Orin doesn't want to have sex with you; he only wants to talk conspiracy theories about robots.*

You've got no play to rehearse. No job. And you're almost out of gas.

Hate to break it to you, honey.

You've got nothing.

Gigi takes comfort in what she interprets as permission from me to feel sorry for herself as she throws the car into reverse, backs onto the gravel road.

But she was talking to imaginary Max.

The real me went through a thing since the last time he rode shotgun in the beast on a despairing autumn night, and today's Max would never tell Gigi she has nothing.

You're alive, my love is what I'd tell her.

There is nothing else to have.

6.

FLY THOU HOW THOU CANST, THEY'LL TANGLE THEE

The Durants' ranch house in Rolling Acres is tiny but tidy. What they can't afford to fix they keep clean. Gigi hands her father, Dick Durant, a mug of coffee, joins him at the dining room table.

Other than the occasional breakfast, Gigi and her father rarely see each other. His shifts tending bar at the tavern begin when her school day ends.

This morning, a thunderstorm pounds on the small skylight above their heads. Dick keeps looking up at it, as if he can hairy-eyeball it into not springing a leak.

I've recovered from the shock that Ms. Lee may be alive. Yes, it's infuriating that Axl didn't tell me; if he had, who knows how things would've turned out?

But in the end, it doesn't matter.

Whether she's dead or alive doesn't change what I did.

The fact remains that I committed a terrible sin. And as all religiously promiscuous cultural Catholics know, every sin requires a tearful confession.

Time to make like a tree and get out of purgatory.

Top o' the mornin', Gigi! Max again, here to grovel and wail and pound my chest and show you this miserable world in a new and still more miserable light, like the scary stepbrother of some toothless ghost in the great Charles Dickens tale A Christmas Carol.

Which ghost is the most ominous?

Future, right?

Did I ever tell you I was an extra in that show, in Catholic school? I played "a great fat man with a monstrous chin." Harsh casting for a nine-year-old, no?

Gigi?

Are you getting all this?

Gigi stirs her coffee. "Do you remember my theater teacher, Fiona Lee?"

Her father pulls a neon-orange lighter out of his T-shirt pocket, fires up a cigarette.

"Course."

"Have you heard the rumor about her?" she asks.

Dick blows smoke over his shoulder so Gigi doesn't have to breathe it in. "Which one?"

"What's that supposed to mean?"

"It means when your theater teacher came into my tavern, she ordered a gin martini, and when I say a martini, I mean several. And the hillbillies who live at the bar, because they can no longer stand their wives, their lives, or themselves, never bothered to restrain themselves from speculating on the comings and goings of a Chinese woman who likes to sit alone drinking hard liquor. The fact that she could hand it back to them with a threat she appeared to be capable of making good on? Let's just say it didn't allure them any less."

"Ms. Lee is *American*, Dad. By the way."

"People say she lived. People say she died. People say she's working for the Chinese government. What I can tell you is Fiona Lee tipped well, and she didn't love to chitchat, which is a far more flattering description than I can give you about most of my customers."

Gigi recoils at the thought of Ms. Lee rolling into Rollo's Tavern to get lit after rehearsal. Or after school. Or before school, or whenever she went.

She watches her father open a box of doughnut holes from the IGA. "Do you think Ms. Lee is dead?"

"I don't think shit about shit, Gigi," says Dick. "And I try to keep it that way."

Gigi takes a bite of a cinnamon sugar. It's the preservatives that make boxed doughnuts extra sludgy when they slide down your esophagus. If you eat too many, your stomach turns into a sack of wet cement. Naturally, Gigi would prefer to stop in for a proper cruller from Ye Olde Donut Shoppe on her way to school this morning, but beggars can't be choosers, and a beggar Gigi be, now that she's unemployed.

"How hard is it to leave town?" Gigi asks.

Dick shrugs. "It's been done, but the checkpoints are a bitch. Bribe the wrong soldier, you've bought yourself a problem. Why? Somebody want you to fly away with him?"

Gigi sips her coffee. What a strange idea.

Since the travel ban, you can't leave your town of official residence for any reason without special permission, which is nearly impossible to get. Except you can go to our twin city, Urbana; we bleed into each other enough that it doesn't count. And people sneak around, locally, too—you can get to a baby farm town like Homer, or Booty, without too much hassle, if you're not on the party's radar, and have cash for the bribe, and are just dying to go. Only Commissioners and their families, like mine, can move freely, though—and the Auroras, of course.

Even if people were allowed to flee, Gigi can't imagine where she'd go. Not that she wants to be in Champaign. But where else is there? What would you do when you got there?

"Are you?" asks Dick.

Gigi looks confused. "Am I what?"

"Flying away."

"*Me?* Come on."

Dick shrugs.

It's true that Gigi has never considered leaving Champaign—but Ms. Lee might. She used to live in New York City. That's far, though; it'd be hard to get to. Maybe she'd try to sneak up to Chicago. It's the biggest city in Illinois, and less than half a day's drive. Chicago wouldn't intimidate Ms. Lee at all.

"If your theater teacher wants to disappear, she's better off staying put till she's not such a hot topic for speculation. I'm guessing she knows that." Dick raises his mug. "Refill?"

Gigi shakes her head, stands. Goes to the screened-in sun porch to watch the storm.

On the other hand, Axl might be right—that it's a rumor. It's the simplest explanation. Ms. Lee probably got drunk and decided to call it. It's a less romantic story than that she snapped her fingers and disappeared in plain sight to start a revolution, but the theater teacher never claimed to be the Good Witch of the Midwest.

Dick appears on the porch. "Before you and Fischer run away together, you'd better stockpile some cash."

"I told you, I was asking about Ms. Lee, not me. And you know Axl and I are just friends."

Her father's face looks like it does when he's humoring a

door-to-door salesman. "Okay. Regardless, without the hostess gig, you better find something new."

I wish Dick would ask his daughter *how she's doing,* not where she's going to get another job. But Gigi is used to their dynamic. Dick isn't so much her parent as he is her fan. He wants her to do well, but there's only so much he can do for her, and they both know it.

"True," says Gigi. "The Malibu is almost out of gas. I'm about to be desperate for cabbage."

"Cabbage," says Dick, pursing his lips like the SYXTEM slang for dollar bills tastes bad. "You and me both. Anyway, when you run away with him, don't do it on an empty wallet."

"For the millionth time—"

"Fortunately, you've got a new job."

"What does that mean?"

"You'll be waiting tables. Better cash than hostessing. Serving's where the money's at."

"Where?"

Dick extinguishes his cancer stick in a chipped red ashtray, twisting it slowly, like he's sorry to see it go. "The Market abhors a vacuum. So I've been informed. I'm replacing Don Peluk at the Round Barn. Supposed to keep the place problem-free for them. Call it a promotion."

Gigi feels the anger sting her throat. "Who is *them?*"

Dick doesn't respond.

Wind blows the rain horizontally, beating on the porch screen.

"You said you'd never work for the party," says Gigi. "You said the SYXTEM is all pissants with penis envy."

"Don't let's hop on the merry-go-round, Giselle. We're finally gonna have a little stability. I might even bring home a steak once in a while."

If the party has finally realized that they need Dick Durant, a widely disliked but wholly trusted figure in Champaign taverns for the past two decades, Dick Durant may have just realized that he needs the party, too—if he wants to feed his daughter, or heat the house this winter. Last winter, Gigi wore two pairs of long underwear and a stocking cap to bed, and she still has scars on her knuckles from the frost burn she got during that freak ice storm.

"I'm gonna screw around with the bike for the next few days before I put on the monkey suit and go play manager on Monday. Call it a vacation. So."

"They're reopening the Round Barn *next week*? The body isn't even cold!"

Dick pulls a wad of cash out of his pocket, peels off a twenty, hands it to Gigi. "Fill your tank this morning."

She squints at the money like it's covered in snot. "Is this from *them*?"

Dick seems to be waiting for Gigi to say anything else she needs to before he leaves the porch for the garage, where his motorcycle lives—Dick's less-unhappy place.

Looking at him standing there, Gigi feels more sad than angry. Her father shouldn't have to worry about her opinion of him, along with everything else.

"Sorry," she says. "I'm not trying to be an asshole."

Have fun with the hog, Dick. I'll put in a word with the angels of Harley for you if you use your new income to buy your stubborn daughter a Ouija board, or a crystal ball, or some other freaky head-shop shit I can use to contact her from the other side.

Dick Durant definitely doesn't hear me. He's mastered the art of tuning out long-winded monologuists. Most bartenders have.

"It is what it is," says Dick. "We'll get you training next week."

* * *

In the CHS parking lot, vehicles speed toward the single exit in a lawless mayhem. Lunch period only lasts thirty-four minutes, and everyone wants to be first in line at the Arby's drive-through.

Gigi is hopping across the lot like she's in the video game *Frogger* when she sees Axl leaning on his Toyota, playing with his Zippo.

"Gigi!" he yells.

She pretends not to hear him, stalks to the Malibu. Her lunch plans are to sit in her car rereading *RiotRite* and eating her bologna sandwich, alone.

Axl jogs up behind her. "I owe you an apology."

Gigi spins around, both hands giving him the middle finger. She's wearing black leggings, black combat boots, heavy black eye makeup, violet lipstick, and a white tank top that lets her red bra straps show—the outfit she chose for her date tonight, with Orin. I advised Gigi strongly against this overtly come-and-get-my-virginity look this morning, when I was trying to force her to listen to my tale of woe, but as usual, she ignored me—and ended up looking kinda badass.

"That's the spirit," says Axl. "Can I buy you lunch?"

A flock of skaters coasts noisily past, a spectacle of colorful hair, chained wallets, and Vans.

"Is it for real Friday?" yells one.

"Indubitably," yells Axl.

"Is what for real?" asks Gigi.

"My back-to-school party," says Axl.

Gigi leans back. "No way."

"Yes way."

She follows Axl to his Toyota. "Come *on*."

"What, you don't like parties?" asks Axl as he slides into the driver's seat.

Gigi takes shotgun. "I like my life more."

"This is how tragedy works, Gigi. When you're cursed, you're cursed. You gotta sit back, enjoy the ride down."

Axl starts the car, stereo at top volume—Jim Morrison, howling, "L.A. Woman."

He does a doughnut spinout, jumps a median crammed with ferns, barely dodges a red Saab.

I shudder. Dude drives like he's mad at the road.

Giselle sucks in air like she's drinking through a straw, turns the music down. "So. My apology?"

"You're right, Gigi. About everything. They know what I do," says Axl. "They know where I live. They'll come for me. Someday. But they haven't yet. Today, I'm a free man, and I intend to act like it."

"I hate it when you're like this," says Gigi. "You've decided something, and it's inarguable; yet you need to argue about it."

"Come on, then. Argue with me."

"No matter how many favors you call in, a party is an enormous risk, and you know it. Not just for you. For everyone. Isn't broadcasting outlawed tuneage for half the county at your theater exactly what Frank meant by making a fool of them? What's the point?"

"The point is I'm not hiding from Bud Hill. Now or ever. I will not let them win. People come? They want to risk it? Their choice. Bring the cyberfuck!"

"Axl."

"Come on! Bring robot man. What, are you afraid he can't dance? He can't, by the way. I bet your ass he cannot."

Axl accelerates through a yellow light.

Giselle examines Axl's profile, the determination in those hard angles.

He wouldn't be taking such a huge risk out of the blue if he wasn't fighting his fear of them. Trying to prove to himself that they can't win.

Which means he's afraid that they can.

Axl has always been moody. But since my death, he's been flat-out unpredictable.

They're getting to him.

Mariachi music blares in the windowless, soundproof back room of Enchiladaville, the room that doesn't exist unless you're with Axl, or someone like him. Candles flicker in a handful of booths.

Axl points his fork at Gigi. "Rumors make people horny. That's why people talk about Ms. Lee. Think of the sewage people spew about the Auroras. Last week, somebody told me Piper has a sexual relationship with her horse."

"Maybe she does."

Axl leans back. "Jesus, Gigi."

"Piper is such a little girl, you know? She's so Strawberry Shortcake, with her red braids, like she's in third grade. She acts like she's got no responsibility for what her family does. It's fucked up. She's—"

"Hey!" Axl snaps. "You have no idea what you're talking about."

"I'm just tired of defending Piper when she does literally nothing—"

"You're wrong, Giselle."

"Am I?" she asks.

Axl sinks his fork into his vegetarian chimichanga. "Check yourself. New topic."

Gigi slices off a curl of custard flan. It feels gross, talking shit about Piper. She just wanted to try it, see if it helped.

It didn't.

Gigi pushes the flan aside.

"Listen," says Axl. "When I knew for sure Ms. Lee was safe, I was gonna tell you. I thought it'd mess you up, this maybe—maybe not shit."

"It does, obviously. Can't you ask around?"

"Nobody wants their supplier asking them questions about stuff like this. Frank drilled that into me. Keep the business clean. Don't probe each other's butts. Too messy."

"Probe each other's butts. That visual was definitely necessary."

Spatz slides into the booth beside Axl, takes a long sip of his coffee.

Axl looks at her. "Care to join us?"

Spatz is a preternaturally sophisticated Thespian with a lanky skinny-boy physique and a serious talent for scenery design. One of the handful of die-hard Thespians who is Black; the only female at CHS who is out. Her private life takes place entirely off campus, but as far as I ever deciphered, it involves velvet vests, hard-core music, and a universe of somewhat older, crushingly attractive individuals to whom we theater dorks have zero access.

It's not remotely surprising to find Spatz in Enchiladaville's back room.

Spatz sets her motorcycle helmet on the seat beside her, takes off her messenger bag, and pounds the table. "Who else is depressed as fuck?"

Axl almost smiles. "That question was weirdly enthusiastic."

"Life is hell and Ms. Lee and Max Bowl are dead. Without

Thespians, what's the point of senior year? And who am I supposed to take out my anger on, if not Max Bowl?"

Miss you too, honey.

The waiter offers Spatz a menu.

"Tacos to go," says Spatz, "no meat, no sour cream, no rice. Beans, lettuce, and salsa. Please and thank you."

Spatz digs a tortilla chip into the guts of Axl's chimichanga.

"You're pretty touchy-feely for someone who went missing all summer and showed up just the fuck now," he says.

"Dude, I had this girl in Farmer City making me crazy. I took a serious mental dip. As in, *Gilligan's Island* reruns and instant oatmeal all day long. I didn't need to weep in the back row with my fellow grieving theater dorks to remember how shitty everything is. That incident with those kids in Urbana didn't help."

Gigi is afraid to ask what Spatz means by that.

She sees the look on Gigi's face. "You didn't hear? Kids broke into Urbana High School, desecrated the party banner. Drew a dick on Bud Hill's nose. Soldiers who arrested them would've been seniors this year if they hadn't enlisted. The good guys and the bad guys *literally* went to kindergarten together."

Gigi thinks about *RiotRite*. Wonders how those kids got caught.

"Do you guys know the Defiance zine?" asks Gigi.

"Course I know *RiotRite*," says Spatz. "DIY word vomit. Riot grrrl shit."

"Hard to get," says Axl. "Butt ugly, but it has legs."

Gigi won't ask Axl if the Round Barn's ex-dishwasher got the zine from him. He wouldn't say, and she can't be sure the zine is Stu's. But she's curious—

"What do you know about Stu Perloff?" Gigi asks.

"Stu? Not much," says Axl. "He hunts. Last year he brought

a stuffed squirrel to shop class. He'd posed the sucker so it was, like, midleap. Shit was bonkers."

"That's Stu. Kid digs scary nonsense," says Spatz. "Like that zine. But I guess you knew that. What's going on, Gigi?"

"You two knockin' boots?" Axl asks.

"You and li'l Stu." Spatz nods. "I could see it."

Gigi brings to mind an image of Stu: slim Black kid with a long face, thick eyebrows, serious expression. Not a chatter. Wears short-sleeved button-down shirts in plain colors, blue jeans, oxfords. Thoughtful profile.

Oh shit, we think, simultaneously. *Stu is hot.*

The quiet ones always sneak up on you.

Axl piles guacamole onto a chip. "What, the hacker hasn't kissed you yet?"

"As a matter of fact, we have a date tonight," says Gigi.

"Do you?" Axl eats the chip, talks with his mouth full. "I'm telling you, the cyberhunk has no mojo."

"We'll see about that."

"Will we?"

"We will."

"Ominous."

Spatz is shaking her head. "It's so fucked up."

"What is?" Gigi asks.

"How much you two flirt. Listen, the goons went after Stu," says Spatz. "Confiscated his trailer. Thankfully, nobody was home."

Gigi closes her eyes. By now, she should know better than to ask a question about anyone without bracing herself for an answer like that.

"When was this?" Axl sounds surprised.

"Sunday night."

O, shit, we think.

Stu might be who they came for when they raided the Round Barn.

"Why did they want Stu?" asks Axl.

"Kid was into some computer hacker stuff," says Spatz. "Told me once that all the computers would be talking to each other in a couple years. I was like, spare me if you're about to quote *Tron*."

Stu is a hacker?

Gigi will ask Orin about him, tonight.

The waiter returns with more coffee for Axl, hands a paper bag to Spatz, who gives him cash.

Spatz gathers her things and slides out of the booth, motorcycle helmet tucked under one arm. "I'm bringing actual cool people to the hoedown at your theater on Friday, so you better not get raided."

"Won't," says Axl. "Called in multiple favors."

"You were here for like two seconds," says Gigi.

"Can't be late to class," says Spatz. "I'm not trying to get drafted into the military because I was wasting away with some tragic heterosexuals in Enchiladaville. I don't do uniforms. Unless I'm onstage. God, I miss theater. Holy fucking fuck."

Spatz flashes a peace sign, disappears through the back door. A sliver of blinding daylight slips into the restaurant.

Festive music fills Enchiladaville. Men crooning in glorious harmony; jubilant horns.

Gigi leans over the table and speaks quietly, despite the fact that the music is so loud that nobody could possibly hear her.

"Stu Perloff brought *RiotRite* to the Round Barn. That could be why they raided the restaurant. The zine is in my car right now."

Axl leans back as if his confusion about these statements had a physical impact. "The who to the what?"

"Stu!" says Gigi.

"Giselle. You cannot drive around town with that zine in your car."

"Says the man who was yelling about his house party outside the high school."

"Don't fuck around."

"Back at ya!"

"You're gonna give me a heart attack."

"*You're* gonna give *me* a heart attack."

"Jinx."

"That's not how that works."

"I know you are but what am I?"

"Dork."

Orin's bedroom is as empty as the rest of his apartment. Just a mattress on the floor, several sets of weights, and on the carpet, a ceramic lamp that casts a warm glow on his gray blankets.

That evening, Orin and Gigi are sitting cross-legged on the mattress, facing one another.

"Sorry I ran out last night," says Gigi. "When you said Ms. Lee is alive, I just . . ."

Her eyes wander to Orin's arms, lean and defined. She looks at the weights; briefly imagines him using them.

Orin's eyes trace Gigi's bare shoulder. "I'm glad you're here now."

Gigi feels the blood rush to her neck, tries not to smile.

Sexual tension heals all wounds.

"On that subject," says Orin, "can I tell you something about Fiona Lee?"

"Of course."

"I do know that she meant a lot to you personally. But she's a diversion. I wouldn't waste too much time worrying about her."

Aaand there goes the sexual tension.

The man will stone-cold *execute* a mood.

Gigi leans away from him. "Are you *joking?*"

"I'm not. Fighting the party has become my entire life. I've thought about this a lot. One missing person means nothing in the big picture. If we want to win, we have to focus."

"Yeah. And the party wants Ms. Lee because that's *exactly* what she was teaching us. How to focus on what matters. How to use our most overwhelming feelings to make art."

"Art doesn't matter, Gigi. At least, art doesn't matter now."

Gigi looks at Orin like he just told her he's a werewolf.

Words race to exit her mouth. "Of course art matters now!"

"Why?"

"Because—" Gigi has never articulated this. Why art matters. "If art *didn't* matter, it wouldn't be threatening to every single dictator since, like, the dawn of time!"

Orin looks at Gigi with tenderness. As if she's his sister, or his cat.

"Stop making that face! The reason they're afraid of art is because it connects us. The party tells us we're all exactly the same. If we're rich, it's because we try harder. If we're poor, it's because we don't try hard enough. There's no such thing as race anymore; we're color-blind. But we're not the same. Our differences matter. Learning about each other, listening to each other, instead of dehumanizing each other, that's how we stand up to power. The party tells us freedom of expression is too dangerous for us. That we're too easily manipulated, too fragile, too whatever to handle it. The truth is, it's too dangerous for *them.* When we care about each other, they can't convince us that we're enemies. The Hills say they want to unite us, but it's a fucking lie. They silence us to keep us apart. When we hate each other, they win."

"I agree, Gigi. We're interdependent. I'm not saying art doesn't matter at all. But art won't remove the party from power. It's been proven, again and again, in social science experiments, that with *anyone* in power, over *anyone*? Humanity is fucked. Anarchy is the only way we can be truly free from oppression. Anarchy is the only ethical power structure, because the structure is obliterated. The structure is—" Orin waves his thin hands in the air. "Gone. The internet can help make anarchy possible. That's why I work all the time. Not to attract attention to myself and make people admire me, like an artist. When an autocratic government is methodically dismantling basic human rights, you have to do more than make an amusing zine. You have to think strategically and fight."

"You have to start with empathy, though," says Gigi. "And—warmth. Humanity. Without that, you have nothing. And fighting can be nonviolent."

"Gigi, the party is slaughtering innocent people."

"You think I don't know that?" Gigi snaps.

"No, I— Of course you do." Orin rubs his eyes.

Gigi sits up. "I'm sorry. It's late."

"Don't. Please." Orin puts his hand on Gigi's knee.

The surprise of his touch stills her.

"I miss Max too," says Orin.

Does he?

Hmph.

"That's why it's so important to stay focused," he says. "On what makes a difference and what doesn't."

Gigi sighs. "It *all* makes a difference, Orin. Have you ever read the Jean-Paul Sartre play *The Flies*?"

Orin shakes his head.

Spring of '90, when we were locked out of the CHS theater to punish us for our underground performance of *The Brig*, the Thespians staged a reading of *The Flies* in Ms. Lee's backyard. We sat in a circle on folding chairs and read the play aloud. When the sun set, Ms. Lee turned on strings of lights. It felt as magical as any theater. The story cast a spell.

"*The Flies* is about a town full of people who are miserable because they don't know that they're free," says Gigi. "They're cursed with this plague of flies, which is driving them nuts. They think they need the gods to free them from the curse. But they don't need gods. They can free themselves. They just need to act. He based the play on a Greek myth. All I'm saying is that if you do what they tell you not to, you take away their power. Even if it's just, like, playing music, or telling a joke. Resistance inspires more resistance. Every act counts."

Orin opens his mouth like he's going to say something else.

Instead, he blinks. Smiles softly at Gigi, as if he's seeing something he's never seen before.

Gigi says, "What?"

"You're . . . so."

He leans toward her. Takes her chin in his hand.

If this moment could last for the rest of 1991, it might salvage this miserable year.

It's a hard kiss, with soft edges, and Gigi wants more of it—

Okay, this is messed up. I'm inside my best friend's head while *Blade Runner* feels her up, and I can't even enjoy it!

Being a peterless peeping Tom is pointless.

Maybe this *is* the Inferno.

Plus all this talk about doing the right thing is giving me flashbacks. My rotting flesh is breaking out in hives.

The dead are supposed to haunt the living.

So why is my life still haunting me?

My attempts to reach Gigi are obviously futile. She talks to me like a child talks to a stuffed animal. Pretending I'm real.

Yet I *am* real, if she'd only choose to know it!

Or—fuck. Maybe I'm the crazy one, imagining I can still talk to her.

I'm as useless now as I was when I was alive. The dumb goof with the bit part in the play I don't even understand.

In Death as in Life, the fool.

7

AH, WHAT A LIFE WERE THIS! HOW SWEET! HOW LOVELY!

For Axl's party, Gigi threw on a vintage Madonna concert T-shirt and ripped jeans, scruffed her hair with a dab of lemony pomade, and painted her lips stoplight red. Tonight's the night she loses her virginity, and she knows it.

She really, really wants to talk to me about this but refuses to acknowledge my ghastly presence, even now that I have resorted to tabloid headlines like:

I OVERTLY BETRAYED YOU AND IT LED TO MY GRIZZLY DEATH!

Which makes me wonder.

Are the gods torturing me for their own amusement?

Is purgatory payback for changing words in hymns to crack myself up during Catholic Mass?

At the time, I thought singing about "the holy toast" was hilarious.

Look who's laughing now!

As she drives, Gigi remembers a slumber party we had in Rolling Acres last winter.

I was stretched out on her peach bedroom carpet, eating gummy bears, wearing the pink satin robe we found at that killer garage sale in my neighborhood, the Cliffs of Capri.

How I loved that frock. It was rare to find such rad finery in my size. Worth every penny of that one dollar and seventy-two cents.

Gigi was lying on the floor beside me, dapper in her men's flannel pajamas.

"Do you think we could get sent to North Carolina for doing Henry VI?*"* she asked.

North Carolina. Home of Bud Hill's reeducation camps.

"I'd go right now if it would get me out of doing Henry VI.*"*

"Max."

*"*Henry VI *is too hard for us, Gigi. I don't see why Ms. Lee can't admit it."*

"Shakespeare isn't supposed to be easy. It's supposed to be big. Speaking of big . . ." Gigi rubs my lush black chest hair. *"The problem with you naked is the fur. You know they make a wax for that."*

"Some men dig my fur."

"Do not tell me there's a grown-ass man in your life."

"(A) Don't judge me. (B) I'm eighteen. (C) There's not. Unless you count the porn. Axl knows my taste. Anyway, you know I got mine last weekend. Age-appropriately. Three condoms, Gigi. The boy was divine. A little imp. Very Midsummer Night's Dream.*"*

"And he appeared out of the mist at a rave in Carbondale. And somehow, although Axl was with you the entire time, he never met him. I totally believe you."

"Shut up, you jealous bitch. I told you about those condoms because I was proud I figured out how to use them. I'm totally willing to teach you, by the way, so that you and Axl don't make a baby before you're ready."

Gigi parks in a cornfield a half-mile hike to the party.

Well, Max, she thinks, *at least you didn't die a virgin. And neither will I! Tonight, I reach the only goal I have left in my fucking life.*

I suppose I can't not give it up for that.

I sing wholeheartedly, as if I were in the cathedral:

Glory be to the tongue wrestling! And to the sex and to the holy toast!

I know.

I'm never getting out of here.

In the lobby of Axl's theater, brass wall sconces cast a warm glow over the crowd of thirty or so kids shouting to be heard over the music. Gigi scoots around people she knows and used to know, parts the velvet curtains, and enters the theater proper.

Gigi used to ridicule Axl's and my endless soundproofing, stuffing the theater's walls with blankets and foam. *"Are you gonna kidnap people and lock them up where no one can hear them scream?"*

Tonight, we've been vindicated.

The bass is bumping and the guitars are crying out in pain while a hundred bodies dance between the seats and the stage. The *Romeo and Juliet* balcony is spotlit, decorated with kids, climbing and dangling; more are draped on the sinking boat, drenched in sea-blue light. Spatz and her friends are crammed onto the porch swing pumping away together, ready to leap off and fly away.

Nobody's in the catwalks, which means Axl locked the stairs, and we're sure he locked up backstage, too.

When Gigi sees Axl bobbing in the booth, lit by a string of blinking holiday lights, she feels tender. For the first time in forever, he looks like he's enjoying himself.

And judging from the size of the crowd, Axl wasn't the only

one who was willing to take a risk tonight, to get the fuck out of their head.

How 'bout a round of applause for the Teenage Brain?

Stupendous at having ideas.

Terrible at anticipating consequences.

Or . . . are we?

Just because teenagers don't dwell on worst-case scenarios doesn't mean we're destined to be wronger than adults.

It's adults who voted democracy out of existence.

Not us.

Axl lands in front of Gigi.

"Yo!" he says, face flushed, Clash T-shirt drenched with sweat.

Gigi has a sudden urge to bite his neck.

An urge she immediately overrides.

She's not trying to make out with *Axl.*

BITE HIM! I yell. *Do you know how happy it would make me to see you kids smooching? Do you even know?!*

"So, what's what?" asks Axl. "You good?"

Gigi watches a new group of kids stream through the velvet curtains and join the dancing. The theater should always be packed.

"I am weirdly better than I've been all week."

"Sweet," says Axl. "What do you wanna hear next? I was thinking . . ." He trails off.

Gigi looks where Axl is looking, toward the lobby.

Orin is leaning against the ticket counter. A girl with dyed pink hair is standing on her tiptoes, kissing him.

Aw . . . dude. Come *on.*

Axl grabs Gigi's wrist. "Fuck that guy. I need you in the booth. You're picking the next tune. . . ."

Orin and Gigi have locked eyes. Orin raises his hand as if to say hello. The girl doesn't notice Gigi. She's resting her head on Orin's chest, facing the door.

Gigi pulls away from Axl. To leave, she'd have to pass Orin, so she makes a beeline for the corridor off stage right that hides the stairway to the costume attic. The door to the attic isn't locked, but it's invisible; if you didn't know it was there, you'd have to work to find it.

She runs up the wooden stairs, drops her purse on one of the makeup stations.

Her whole body is trembling. Since everything turned to shit, the point of her whole stupid life was to sleep with Orin. One single goal she was sure she could still achieve!

And now—what the hell? Does he have a girlfriend, or something?

Gigi refuses to get caught up in some cheesy boy battle. Screw that. She's a riot grrrl, dammit. Whoever was kissing Orin can have him.

Gigi sits on a stool, blinks back the tears she will not allow to fall. Stupid stupid *stupid* life.

"Gigi."

In the mirror's reflection, she sees Orin holding up his hands, like he wants to prevent something invisible from moving forward. "That wasn't— I don't want you to think . . ."

Gigi forces herself to sound casual. "What's up?"

"I—" Orin shakes his head.

Gigi closes her eyes. She's fighting it. The tide, rising within her. Her belly is hot, and her cheeks. She will not allow Orin to affect her like this. It was one night of kissing plus one year of fantasies that have blown up in her face.

"Hey," says the soft voice that she feels like she used to live to hear, but that means absolutely nothing to her now. "I got here, like, five minutes ago. I barely know that woman. She just grabbed me, and—people are in a weird state of mind tonight—"

"Don't worry about it," says Gigi. "You and I are better as friends. I was thinking that, before."

That's not true. Come on. What's she saying? She doesn't know what she'll say next. She's talking to avoid the silence that would allow her true feelings to intrude into the room. Her feelings, which fill her with shame. That she'd believed she could love and be loved by a boy so thoughtful and rare.

Orin crouches on one knee beside the stool. "Giselle, I'm trying to tell you—I don't want that. Let me speak."

Gigi scrunches her eyes shut. It hurts so much. So embarrassing! How is she supposed to deal with this?

"Move toward the pain, not away from it," she remembers Ms. Lee telling us. *"To experience your full range of feelings is the most important thing I'll ever ask you to do."*

Gigi takes a deep breath, lets her eyes open.

"What do you want from me, Orin?"

"Nothing, Gigi. I just want *you.* I tried to keep my distance. Half tried. But you're so— And I'm—incredibly lonely." He looks at the ground. "I don't"—his voice breaks—"know when that started. You're the last person in the world I want to hurt."

Gigi frowns. Looks down at Orin's head, the muss of thick black hair.

Well . . . Orin isn't the kind of guy who goes around, obviously full of shit.

It just stung.

She touches his shoulder, his scratchy wool sweater. ". . . Okay."

Orin stands.

"Okay?" he says.

Gigi nods.

He takes her hands, pulls her to standing.

Wraps her in his arms.

Holds her with strength.

She can feel, in her body, that Orin is for real.

He wants her.

And of course. *Of course* she wants him, too.

When Orin kisses Gigi, it's like he's been starving. Gigi doesn't think about it; she's just kissing him back.

You're kissing, and then you're really kissing, and then you're taking off his shirt. . . .

And then you turn the lights off, because you're not interested in seeing yourselves in a thousand different mirrors while you undress each other.

And then you're finished peeling off, and stepping out of, and you're on the wood floor, shivering, and warm, and kissing, and slowly, you find that it's happening.

And then it's painful. And odd, and out of nowhere, the rules change.

And then you're kind of there, just, being there, thinking about the fact that he's enjoying this. He is . . . in a state, anyway, and you focus on making him happy. How to do that you aren't sure. By sighing when he sighs and moaning kind of around the same time as he moans.

And then you are physically hot, as in way too warm, and your head somehow keeps knocking into the legs of this stool. Can you move the stool? Not with his arms pinning yours, and you don't want to ruin the moment.

Gigi feels herself detaching from her body.

What the fuck? she thinks. *I want to be here for this!*

She concentrates on staying inside herself, to feel this.

But it doesn't feel . . .

You know, it doesn't feel great.

I, Maximus, feel terrible.

This isn't how she hoped it would be.

And I may have exacerbated her disappointment by exaggerating about my own Big Day.

I didn't lie to Gigi about the imp I had sex with, and the three condoms.

But it didn't happen exactly like I told her.

I did consent. It was consensual.

But it wasn't heaven on earth.

Not sure why it's so difficult to talk about how things really go down, when it comes to the big shit. Not sure why we have to act like we know everything, like somehow we're some secret sex expert, even when we're talking to our very own very best friend.

I wish I'd told Gigi the whole truth about losing my virginity. How confused I felt when we were doing it, and the imp cracked up laughing and wouldn't tell me why. How alone I felt when he said, *"Don't worry about it. You're fine,"* and started laughing again, enjoying his private joke.

I wish I'd told her that I cried that night, wishing I could undo it; wishing I'd waited until I met a boy I loved.

It would've given us something scary to discuss. Something that we couldn't smooth over with a joke.

Which would've been a very healthy habit.

When Orin is finished—is he finished?

It's over, anyway; things stop.

Gigi is drenched with sweat. His sweat, beneath his heavy body.

Was that it? she wonders. *Did it happen?*

She's squinting at the chandelier above them, feeling her lungs compressed, with this ten-ton boy draped over her. Wondering what all the fuss is about, about sex.

She'd like to roll him off her and dive into a cold swimming pool.

Or drive out to the country and take a very long walk under the familiar indifference of the stars.

Then it clicks.

It happened.

She lost her virginity.

And she can never get it back.

Maxy! I lost my virginity, and it didn't take three condoms. I win!

Well . . . not exactly how the game is played.

But who knows how the game is played?

Rule one, try not to die. That's all I ever figured out.

In that respect, Gigi did win.

Nice work, I tell her.

She did work for this moment, you know?

And here it is.

Ya really can do anything, if ya try.

Orin and Gigi are dressed again, fixing themselves in the mirrors.

Gigi is ready to go. To leave the costume attic, the party—get out.

But she's not sure if that's okay. To leave, now. After they just did it. Are there rules for this moment? What happens next?

She glances at Orin in the mirror.

"You're very beautiful," he says.

Gigi looks at her face more closely. Her lipstick is gone; she forgot to bring it, to refresh. The tears she refused to let go of nevertheless managed to evaporate her eyeliner, and now her eyes look like someone else's eyes, a saddish blue, like a puddle. Her short black hair looks kind of like she'd hoped it would, before she cut it—messy, from rolling around on the floor. She wouldn't use the word "beautiful" to describe herself.

You look like a stranger, she thinks. *I wonder who you are.*

In the mirror, Orin is smiling at her, a smile that shows his small teeth.

Orin has small teeth.

When Gigi smiles back, she covers her teeth with her lips. What's she revealing about herself that Orin didn't know before?

She really has to go. "See you. . . ."

"Tomorrow," says Orin.

Gigi smiles, though she doesn't feel like smiling; she just feels like she should smile, to show Orin that she's happy, although happy isn't exactly what she is. She doesn't know what she is. And in the Midwest, when we don't know what to do, we smile. It's a revolting habit that I for one am still trying to break even now that I have lost my face.

Gigi leaves Orin in the attic. She'll say goodbye to Axl, run to the Malibu.

She needs to drive somewhere, anywhere less depressing.

In the lobby, Gigi realizes how much time has passed. The mood in the theater has changed, or rather, intensified.

The bodies have multiplied exponentially, and every single one of them is dancing—if not by choice, then because they're pressed together, forced to sway along with everyone else. Strangers are vamping, sexy-eye flirting, trying to make each other laugh. Rich kids, poor kids, kids from the baby farm towns, kids from the 'Paign, and our twin city, Urbana, a place with which we maintain an active rivalry for reasons nobody understands, that manifests itself in no particular way, including tonight.

Gigi wedges her way through the writhing mass of bodies. The Prince song that's been blaring winds down, but before it can end, there's the abrupt, truncated air-horn intro to a goofy party song born in the mystical 1980s we've all been trying to get back to, the pre-Dictator Paradiso of proms and nerds and keggers and boobs and jocks and punks and all the teenage shit we were long ago promised and are therefore entitled to experience.

A song so dumb and goofy—

A song so *fun* we can't believe Axl is actually playing it.

But soon enough, the reason Axl chose the Beastie Boys song "Brass Monkey" is evident.

Everybody knows the words.

The entire crowd is putting their left leg down, their right leg up, tilting their head back to finish the cup. The party is one leaning, pulsing mass of funky monkeys.

An exuberant confidence pervades the crowd. The kids are in unanimous, unspoken agreement that if the soldiers show up, they'll have no choice but to drop their weapons and dance.

Delusional?

Maybe not.

Soldiers are teenagers too.

Gigi makes her way through the theater, grooving with every body she encounters, until she reaches the stairwell to the tech booth, the door to which she has a key.

Gigi stands in the booth beside Axl, looking down at the crowd.

A few minutes ago, she was ready to get in her car and drive until she ran out of gas. Now she wants to hug Axl for doing this insane thing. For somehow knowing that tonight was what everyone needed. That it'd be worth the risk to show up.

Axl pulls an album from the crates, waves it at Gigi.

"Next song's for you, beb."

"What do I get?"

"You'll see."

Gigi spots Piper dancing downstage center, looking up at the booth. Piper is wearing a bright red tank dress and has curled her hair. Gigi assumes that Piper is dancing specifically for Axl. And that Axl has been up here, enjoying it. She wonders how long it will be until that happens. Piper and Axl. They're not an obvious couple—she's so light and cheerful; he's such a hunk of rye bread.

But in another way, it feels inevitable. However conflicted Gigi has been feeling about her friendship with Piper, she can see it clearly, why she and Axl would be into each other. Piper never pretends to be anything. Axl can't tolerate falseness. Piper is alone; Axl is a loner. Yes, the whole world is inside his theater tonight, but Axl is locked in the booth, not down there, mingling.

He's by himself, above it all.

Gigi has been a jerk to Piper all summer, avoiding her without saying why. *Of course* it's not the girl's fault who her relatives happen to be. Gigi has just been so fucking angry. She owes Piper an honest conversation. She's reaching for the doorknob when Axl grabs her wrist.

"This is it!"

Axl flips a level on the sound board; a warped bass line kicks in.

For the first time in my Death, I'd trade the ability to pleasure myself for one last waggle of my ass. For the King of the Obscure is spinning the only song I know that is goofier than "Brass Monkey."

Moreover, Axl is dancing.

To the sound of Shock G, rapping, *"Stop what you're doin' / 'Cause I'm about to ruin / The image and the style that you're used to. . . ."*

The song is "The Humpty Dance," by Digital Underground. Axl scoops his neck to the left, then to the right. He sticks out his tongue and scrunches his nose. He squats, and thrashes, and kicks like the Russian dancers in the *Nutcracker* ballet. He jumps on a chair, thrusts his pelvis. His rhythm is precise. His moves are loose, yet tight.

We've never seen Axl get down like this.

We didn't know it was possible.

Axl jumps off the chair, hooks his elbows under Gigi's armpits to lift her. She squeals, laughing hysterically, as he spins her around. He sets her down, leans, one hand stretching to the ceiling, the other to the floor, like he's about to do a cartwheel.

Gigi understands that the only appropriate response is to do the exact same move, but in the opposite direction.

And so Axl and Gigi become the funkiest human butterfly in East-Central Illinois. For the rest of the song, they improvise gymnastic dance moves with the uninhibited freedom of siblings.

It is, in terms of a physical experience, exactly the opposite of the sex Gigi just had with Orin.

"The humpty dance is your chance to do the hump!"

The crowd below is charged up, escalating toward the moment of degeneration. In another song or two they'll start peeling off. Bickering. French-kissing strangers. Telling each other to *Shutthefuckup!* as they leave, so they don't make noise and ruin everything.

Then they'll scurry back into the night, trying to remember in exactly which cornfield they parked their cars.

But right now?

It's all love.

When the song starts to wind down, Axl goes back to the crates.

Gigi, smiling and out of breath, looks out the windows. Below her, all the bodies move like one. The lights blink red, blue, green. The theater throbs with life. It feels *right*.

People are supposed to fill the theater. It's what it's built for. And Gigi is meant to be here. To create a world with the Thespians and share it with whoever shows up. To shine a light in this dark world.

She thinks about her conversation with VP Smith. *"Fiona Lee convinced you children that it is your birthright to question authority."*

She looks at Axl hunched over the turntables. Head nodding, T-shirt clinging to his torso.

When he turns around, Gigi says, "We're doing the play."

"We're—what?"

What?

"We're doing *Henry VI*. You and me and the Thespians. If we can get away with this?" Gigi waves her hand toward the crowd. "We can do Shakespeare."

"Here?" he asks.

"Here."

NO!

News flash: dead dudes can hyperventilate.

Axl stands beside Gigi. Folds his arms.

"Durant, you scare me," he says.

Gigi squints at him. *"You* scare *me."*

YOU BOTH SCARE ME! Guys, tune in to the afterlife, please! Feel my menacing vibes!

Axl says, "Good scary, though, right?"

Gigi's eyes shine like a coyote who just spotted dinner. "Yup."

O MALIGNANT AND
ILL-BODING STARS!

Mostly, Orin collects books that were hard to find even before the Culture Initiative.

Guerrilla Arsenals for Freedom Fighters
Surviving Torture
How to Disappear and Never Be Found

And, of course, *The Anarchist Cookbook,* which I admit is not my personal fave. The bible of mayhem mainly wants to teach you how to build bombs out of random shit. Bleach and a mailbox. Fertilizer and a floppy disk. A light bulb and a fart.

That's the obvious problem with a future led by anarchists, as I see it.

So many *bombs.*

"Say you're way too high. So high you can no longer feel your face."

It was February of '91, a couple months before I died. I was reclining in Orin's La-Z-Boy, holding that mug we stole from Weedman's Diner, drinking coffee dosed with the hazelnut syrup I kept stashed in Orin's rathole.

Orin was in his computer cockpit, typing, pausing, looking from one screen to the other.

His window was open, and the air smelled electrocharged, like raindrops and flowers. It was one of those preview-of-spring afternoons.

"You know what I'm talking about, Orin," I continued. *"You know you know what I'm saying, dog."*

Orin looked at me with the *Remind me what you're doing here?* eyes.

Since Dad was a Commissioner, I could get away with skipping school pretty much whenever, as you know. So I'd bagged it to chill with the Phantom of the Opera.

Had Orin given me reason to believe he needed our friendship to blossom?

No.

I was imposing, and I knew it.

But I truly believed it was for his own good. Orin hadn't stopped by Axl's theater in weeks. I was worried he was bugging out.

"Where's Gigi today?" asked Orin.

"Fuck if I know. School? So when you're high and you can't feel your lips, yet you still taste the Tabasco sauce? That's Szechuan peppercorns. Better than an orgasm. Almost. You know. Almost."

Orin looked at me like he was *almost* interested in what I was saying. *"Um—how do you know about this?"*

"My dad is a gourmet cook. Like, he used to subscribe to Gourmet *magazine. Our garden is nuts. He got into Chinese food when he and my mom toured the country on their honeymoon, like, forever ago."*

"They went to China?"

"They go all the time. I know, it's unfair—he's a Commissioner. What can I say, the SYXTEM worked for Dad. Bernie Bowl digs Bud Hill. But he also digs food, man. Travel. That's where I get it. We get fucking crazy in Italy. Gigi, by the way? No idea what food should taste like. Green leaves scare the diarrhea out of her."

"I really like Gigi," said Orin. *"She's unique."*

Yes, Gigi: he said that.

I said, *"If by that you mean stubborn and ferocious. I blame her twisted childhood."*

Yes: that was my response.

"Kidding, man," I said. *"She'll be flattered to know she has a secret admirer."*

"Well, don't—!" Orin sniffed. *"Don't tell her."*

You two horndogs were jonesing for each other hard-core. *That's* why I was slagging you, Gigi. If you became his girlfriend, I'd lose you.

I know.

I sucked.

I mean, I *sucked.*

I got up to leave. *"Sorry, man, for perpetually boring the shit out of you. Later days . . ."*

"No. I'm sorry, Max. I'm overwhelmed. Your father sounds worldly. It seems like you admire him."

"In some ways. In other ways—he's, shall we say, misguided. Hates the intellectuals, can't admit he is one. All about the party. Kind of a lost dude. But he's a decent human being. I love the asshole. You know?"

"That's heartening." Orin looked at his computer screens again, and I noticed how tired he seemed.

"Do you ever take breaks from all this Usenet hacker shit you're into?"

"Um—not really."

"Fighting the power is worthy and all. But once in a while, you must take a license to chill. Pop some corn and call your dogs and watch a flick. You know what's a tonic? Eraserhead."

"I'm working alone these days. They call themselves the Defiance. It doesn't matter. Who uses it. The name. We're not children anymore."

Had I missed something?

"Orin, I'm mentally deficient. What's the premise, here?"

"The Defiance makes art. I work for liberation."

"Huh. And there's . . . what's the distinction?"

"There's no overlap."

He lost me. But also, I honestly didn't give a toot.

So I said, "You should let me help you out. I know squat about hacking. But if you need renegade shit? Spy shit? I'm your man."

He was peering at me.

"What, dude? Your penetrating gaze makes me antsy."

"It's just funny you should offer. I've been approved for a project."

"My first mission? O shit! I'm listening."

"At the high school."

"I literally attend the high school."

"I'm going to be collecting information."

"As in?"

"Infractions against the party. Small things that could indicate bigger things."

I leaned back, trying to see the angle. "You're gonna narc on CHS?"

"I share leads with my party superior; she lets me direct the inquiry. I'll know everything that's going on."

I looked over my shoulder, like there was someone behind me with whom I could check in, facial-expressionally, to confirm I'd heard Orin correctly.

All I could find was that cat calendar, hanging on the wall beside his phone. The cat was staring at me with even less expression than Orin.

Until that moment, I'd understood that Orin was some anarchist hacker with leading-man pecs, or whatever.

I did *not* know Orin *worked for the party*. Like my dad *worked for the party*.

"Who's your party superior?" I asked.

"You know I can't tell you that."

I did. Nobody is supposed to know who anybody reports to. The party loves itself some secret shoppers.

"You wouldn't be an actual informer, Max. I'm feeding the party plausible garbage. So the real secrets at the high school stay secret."

I nodded knowingly. Felt a desperate need to pee.

"It's not what you were imagining," said Orin.

"I mean, shit, Orin," I said. *"Are you sure you want to be wading knee-deep in the piss pond, here?"*

"If it isn't me watching the high school, it's someone else."

I pondered this. Dad was always saying it's what you don't know that will bite you in the ass. Maybe Orin was onto something. We know what's happening at the high school, we keep all asses intact.

"And this is, you know. Safe?"

"Doing nothing is what's unsafe."

I nodded like I agreed with Orin, although I totally didn't. Everybody knows that nothing is safer than doing nothing.

"Do you feel safe now?" Orin asked.

Yes. Yes I did.

But Dad was a Commissioner.

Axl was right about me.

I was a rich bitch.

Spoiled rotten.

It was time the Maximus stepped up.

I bowed deeply. *"Your grace, I am ripe for this role.* More than I seem, and less than I was born to: A man at least, for less I should not be. . . . "

Don't get me wrong; you know I hated *Henry VI.*

Doesn't mean I didn't memorize everybody's lines. . . .

Gigi is sleeping deep, post-party. Dreaming of the sun, breaking through the night. A hot light that feels like an invitation and a warning.

When the phone rings, she opens her eyes.

Her curtains glow a vigorous shade of pink.

I can't tell if my story made it into her dreams.

Of course, I don't want the Thespians to revive *Henry VI.* Because it's an inconceivably dull and miserable slog of a play, and also because it might get them all killed. Which was just as true when I was alive and among them, but if dying taught me anything, it's that being dead blows. Not worth it.

The thing is, I know I can't stop them. I can't even get Gigi to laugh at a joke from the beyond. I'll never prevent her from directing Shakespeare.

All I can do is tell Gigi everything, whether she's listening or not. Hope my words land somewhere inside her. Help her somehow, in some way I can't foresee.

And I mean tell her *everything*—not just the part Axl already knows, the part where I look like an asshole.

The rotary phone is still ringing on Gigi's nightstand.

It's probably Orin. As soon as they talk, the next chapter

begins, the one where they had sex. She tells herself she wants to make this in-between moment last, when anything is possible.

I suspect she also wants to avoid dealing with her own mixed feelings about last night.

The phone stops ringing, but the answering machine doesn't kick in. Orin isn't leaving a message.

Gigi lets her head sink into her pillow.

Her father sticks his head in her bedroom doorway. "It's for you."

Gigi sighs. *Whatever,* she thinks. *It's fine.* Reaches for the receiver, wrangles the coiled cord so she doesn't have to get out from under her covers.

"Hey," she says quietly.

"Giselle?"

"—*Mom?*"

"Yes, this is your mother, Dierdre Eckhorn. Marty and I have a box of your things that is taking up space in Marty's office. He'd like you to come and get them, preferably tonight."

Gigi hasn't been to the Diamante Villas in, like, two years. What things could she possibly have there?

"What's in the box?" asks Gigi.

Her mother doesn't answer. "You remember how to get here?"

"I know where you live, Mom."

"And you're fine?"

Gigi blinks. She doesn't feel entirely awake. "I'm—what?"

"I spoke to your Vice Principal at the IGA. She says you're doing fine. So we'll see you at the house."

VP Smith says that Gigi is *doing fine*?

We both snort.

Her mother hangs up.

The last time Gigi spoke to her mother was . . . *Streetcar.*

* * *

When the lights went down, the applause was like a hailstorm. It was fall 1990, and Gigi had made her final exit as Blanche Du-Bois, one of the leads of the Thespians' underground production of *A Streetcar Named Desire*. She was off stage right in the CHS theater, perched on a crate, the shiny white gown we found in the dumpster behind the bridal outlet at Market Place Mall pooling at her feet.

It was our one and only Sunday-night performance, and we'd pulled it off without a surprise appearance from VP Smith.

To get me off her back, Ms. Lee had given me a nonspeaking role as an extra poker player. The applause wasn't getting any quieter as I exited stage right, feeling spicy in my jaunty New Orleans cap, ready to throw down at our cast Mardi Gras, the late-late show at Axl's theater.

I spotted Gigi, glossy eyed and tiny in the darkness, like a mouse.

"Curtain call!" I grabbed her hand. *"You're a beast!"*

We ran onstage, took our ensemble bows. When Gigi took her solo bow, she got a standing ovation.

If you've never been onstage, there are things to understand about lighting. You want to find people during the applause, but the cans glare. Sometimes, though, you can pick out some-one in the smear of faces, particularly if you're desperate to find them.

Orin wasn't on our radar yet; we wouldn't officially meet him for another couple weeks, so Gigi wasn't looking for him. Dick Durant was in the last row—he'd come less to see his daughter perform, more to intervene with creative bribes and blackmail if shit went down. Gigi spotted him right away and waved.

Axl and Spatz were in the booth, working sound and light. They'd stay there through the bows.

Piper, assistant stage manager, cheered from the wings.

Yolanda, who played Stella, also got a standing O. Her parents weren't sold on Ms. Lee's risk-taking, so they'd never let Yolanda join Thespians.

Yet her parents were in the audience. I saw them out there, one of a handful of Black families.

Gigi was still looking for someone. Her head was pulsing from the bright lights. Her mouth tasted tinny. She was pretty sure she'd just performed in this play. And that it was over now, and that she was herself again, but not precisely the same.

Everyone kept clapping as the cast left the stage for the last time. But Gigi didn't move, and her face looked weird. When I noticed her catatonic freak-out, I clutched her elbow, and in an eerie parallel to her last scene in *Streetcar*, when Blanche DuBois lets the doctor escort her to the insane asylum, she let me lead her offstage. I figured she was exhausted from acting her tits off. If she lost her shit a bit, she'd earned it.

Backstage, kids were fizzing and crackling and getting raucous. I was eager to join the revelry before we struck the sets and reconvened at Axl's.

But as soon as I let go of Gigi's elbow, she stopped walking, stood motionless in the darkened wing.

I turned around. *"Diva, come on!"*

Gigi says, *"Did you see her?"*

"Who?"

"Didi."

I was thrown for a loop by this question.

"Didi? As in who?"

Gigi stepped into the light. Her face was blank.

"Your mother?" I asked.

Gigi was silent.

I held up both hands. *"In the audience?"*

A look of shame was seeping into Gigi's eyes. Like the dog who ate the slipper.

"Dude. You did not invite your mother to the show. Your stepdad . . . ?"

I folded my arms and bit my top lip with my bottom teeth.

Gigi's stepfather isn't some generic ring-kissing party peon.

Marty Eckhorn is the Champaign County Culture Commissioner.

As in: he enforces censorship.

Gigi's stepfather was literally our problem.

He's also a legendary penis. Even my dad hates him. *"Marty enjoys his job too much. Limit your contact with men like that, who have nothing else going on."*

I hadn't even told *my* mom about the show. Lucy Bowl would've cried for weeks if she knew she'd missed seeing her big baby boy take a bow.

Gigi's saucer eyes were begging for something. Mercy, I guess, or sympathy.

I wanted to feel sorry for her.

I didn't.

"Stop. You're not actually Blanche DuBois. Did you tell the Eckhorns about the show? Just— I won't— Just tell me, did you fuck up?" I took her shoulders and shook her. *"Did you fuck up? Did you, Gigi? Did you fuck up? Goddammit!"*

A single tear rolled down Gigi's cheek. *"Mom wasn't out there. But she might be waiting backstage."*

Gigi ran into the scenery shop.

I covered my face with my hands. Just when you think your friend has overcome a massive emotional obstacle—having a mother who doesn't care to know her—you realize that this is a wound that doesn't want to heal. You can stanch the bleeding for a while, but then, like the stigmata, it gushes forth again, soaking everything in a desperate torrent of hot blood.

I kept the very major leak to myself as Ms. Lee quickly rounded us up for the after-show circle, Thespians laced with audience members, our trusted family and friends.

"Where's Gigi?" someone asked.

I shrugged.

Axl appeared beside me. For no discernible reason, he was sweaty.

"You smell manly," I said.

"As men do," said Axl, looking over his shoulder. *"She's probably hiding in the scenery loft. She doesn't like to be around people right after a performance."*

He sounded almost reverential.

Ms. Lee clapped. *"Let's gather."*

After every show, we circled up for thank-yous before she sent the audience back into the night. Time was of the essence. Nobody was parked in the lot, and we'd kept the school dark; people brought flashlights to navigate the halls.

Technically, the Thespians were allowed to be in the theater late to strike the sets for the party-ordered production. Still, at any moment, some hyperattuned neighbor might sense the extra creatures stirring within the high school—our audience—get suspicious, and call the 1-800 number on the back of their ID card to report Anti-American Thought, looking for the cash reward. We'd been lucky so far, but it could happen yet, as I was bitterly aware. To disperse with a quickness, we must proceed with the thanks.

"Art has power," said Ms. Lee. *"We've just witnessed that. Your children are brilliant and brave. Thank you for coming, and please get home safely. I'll ask . . . you to use the east exit"*—Ms. Lee circled her hand to indicate roughly half the group—*"and you"*—indicating the other half—*"the one by the football field. Stagger it, please, but don't draw it out."*

A handful of Thespians ran back onstage to disassemble the minimal *Streetcar* sets; everybody else vacated.

Ms. Lee, forehead crinkled in concern, turned to Axl and me. *"Where's Gigi?"*

Spatz was jogging our way. *"She's not upstairs. Fuck is wrong with your face, Bowl?"*

I was pressing my lips together, cheeks a-dimple. Not talking was wow. A feat of acting I hoped someone would appreciate.

Axl and Spatz and Ms. Lee were now all staring at me, as if I had, you know. Slob on my chin.

"What's happening right now?" asked Axl.

Ms. Lee said, *"Maximus, where's Gigi?"*

I widened my eyes. *"Who can say?"*

"You just made it obvious that you can." Axl flicked my ear.

"Ow. Cockmunch. I genuinely do not know. Dressing room?"

Ms. Lee and Spatz took off. It was out of character for Gigi to miss the postshow circle, and we needed to leave. I wasn't worried about her—I was sure she realized her fuckup, telling her mother about the show, and was crying tears of shame, as she damn well should've been.

Piper turned off the makeup lights one by one. Each made a smacking noise, a sound of finality.

I scratched my neck. My shirt was a sweat lodge. Fucking polyester. *"Let's motor. Before I start to smell like you."*

"You go," said Axl. *"I'm riding with Gigi."*

"Nice job tonight," called Piper as she opened the door to the dark hallway.

"Coming to my after-party?" asked Axl.

"Wouldn't miss it, Axl Fischer." Piper slipped out the door.

"Well, that was dirty-flirty," I said. *"You have a fan."*

"She's the sweetest," said Axl.

Axl and I were the only people left backstage. I fucking loved Gigi, don't get me wrong. But it could be taxing to be best friends with someone so traumatized. She put everyone at risk tonight, because she wasn't thinking. She was acting from her wounds.

I clapped Axl on his meaty shoulder. *"Brother, I must needs depart."*

The sound of sobbing. Ms. Lee emerged from the backstage corridor, arm tight around Gigi's shoulders. Gigi was weeping like a small child. Spatz followed, hands in her pockets.

Axl ran to them.

Ms. Lee looked weary. *"We have a problem."*

"I just thought she would come," said Gigi in a squeaky voice, an animal with its paw caught in a trap.

Spatz raised her eyebrows at me, like *Can you believe this diva?*

I shook my head, like *Believe this diva I cannot.*

Ultimately, nothing happened. VP Smith never came after us. Either Didi Eckhorn didn't report the Thespians' underground show, to protect her daughter—

Or she wasn't listening when Gigi invited her to come.

* * *

Gigi kicks off her covers, stands. Gets a head rush. Hangs up the phone feeling a mix of hopefulness and dread.

She wanted to say no. *No, I will* not *come pick up some random box at your house, Mom. What the fuck are you even talking about?*

But she couldn't. Because part of her wishes, every time the phone rings, that it will be her mother.

Not that Gigi wants to talk to her. It never goes well.

She just wants her mother to call. To be curious about her. To ask her questions. To listen to the answers.

The phone rings again.

Don't hang up on someone and immediately call back to apologize, she thinks. *Be polite the first time. . . .*

"What's up, Mom?"

"Gigi?"

This time it's Orin.

"Hey," says Gigi, remembering the strange dream she had this morning—the sun, shining in her eyes.

"Want to do something?" Orin asks.

To do something. Gigi flops on her bed again, stretches the springy pink cord between her fingers. *I used to want to do something. Now that we've done it, I don't.*

Orin suggests Weedman's Diner for breakfast, but Gigi doesn't hear him.

"Gigi?" asks Orin. "Are you there?"

The theater is probably trashed; Axl must be having a conniption right about now. He used to follow Frank around the Rolling Acres house like he worked there, picking up bottles and needles, emptying overflowing ashtrays.

She'll go over, help Axl scrub. And together they can call

the Thespians. See who's down to revive guerrilla theater in the
'Paign.

"Orin, can I call you back?"

"Of course."

"Thanks."

She doesn't know what else to say, so she hangs up.

Instantly, she feels like a hypocrite.

Gigi's mother hangs up on people—not Gigi!

She should call Orin back and apologize . . . but then she'd be
calling him back after hanging up on him, which she just decided
people shouldn't do. Plus she'd have to talk to him. . . .

She'll call him later.

A two-by-four props open the door to the theater. Axl must be
desperate to air the place out.

Inside, the lobby is gleaming. The red carpet runner is lush,
with fresh vacuum marks. The walnut ticket counter is polished
to a high sheen. The arched mirrors above it shine like water. Axl
must've spent all night cleaning.

Gigi pushes open the velvet curtains.

Piper, wearing last night's red dress, is sitting in the front row
of the audience.

On Axl's lap.

Maybe he *didn't* clean all night.

Piper turns to look. "Hey! Gigi . . ." She hunches her shoulders like she suddenly needs a jacket. Her smile is shy but un-
mistakable.

This is happening.

Axl leans forward to look around Piper. " 'Sup."

Gigi tries not to smirk as she plops into a seat a few away

from them. She wants to reply "'Sup" in the same fake-casual tone Axl just used, but she can't muster the cynicism.

Anyway, she won't tease Axl about Piper while Piper is here.

And she's glad Piper is here.

She needs to talk to her.

"Piper . . . I owe you an apology. For being such a bitch, lately."

Piper shrugs. "Everybody gets busy."

"I haven't been busy. I've been bitchy."

Axl looks at Gigi approvingly. Which would be annoying if he wasn't correct.

"And then, you're also grieving," says Piper.

"That's no excuse."

For a moment, nobody says anything. It's the type of silence that lets the truth take a breath.

"My parents miss you," says Piper. "My mother was just asking when you'll come over for dinner."

Gigi flashes through memories of her childhood self at the Auroras' farmhouse.

Lying in their garden in the summer, watching clouds make shapes in the sky.

Drinking hot cider on Christmas Eve by the fire, when her father had to work at the tavern.

Sitting at the Auroras' heavy wooden table, hungry and tasting real food. Hot stews, thick pickles, homemade vanilla ice cream. Plus sassafras candy—Gigi doesn't even know what that is, except it's delicious, and you get it with coffee when you're sitting by the fire, like it's the year 1905.

The Auroras' generosity was as endless as their love was genuine.

And Gigi's desperation for that love now feels terribly embarrassing.

These people are basically criminals.

Right?

"Wanna come over next week? Sunday?" asks Piper. "I'd suggest sooner, but Mom is in DC visiting Christie. And she wouldn't want to miss seeing you."

Visiting Christie. That's the type of phrase Gigi took for granted when she and Piper were kids. Now it's astonishing. That someone could *visit* the Hills. That the Dictator and his wife have human bodies that are visitable.

For the first time, Gigi wants to ask, *What's Christie like?* But she doesn't want Piper to think she's rekindling their friendship to dig for information. Piper has a hard enough time dealing with people who see her only as part of the Royal Family.

Gigi says, "Sure. Sunday."

Maybe seeing Mr. and Mrs. Aurora again will help Gigi figure out if she was wrong to love them then, wrong to hate them now, or what.

"Talked to Spatz about *Henry VI* after you left last night," says Axl. "She's in, but she has questions."

"What questions?" asks Gigi.

Axl says, "I mean . . ."

"She wants to know why *Henry VI,*" says Piper. "She won't be the only one."

Gigi finds this irritating. She never understood why the Thespians complained about the play.

"On *principle,*" says Gigi. "We finish what we started. To prove they can't make us quit. Plus the play is about civil war. Power. Violence. Why *wouldn't* we do it?"

"Let's have a Thespian meeting tonight," says Axl. "Hash it out."

"I'm in. Should I call people?" says Piper.

The Auroras have a secure phone line.

Axl says, "Beats pay phones and codes."

"Can't tonight," says Gigi.

"Why not?" asks Axl. "You going to tear the cyberfuck a new porthole?"

Piper makes sympathetic eyes at Gigi. "Axl told me about Orin and that girl. Asshole."

Fantastic. Not only are Axl and Piper going to be a couple. They're going to be one of those annoying couples who tell each other everything.

"That's not it," says Gigi. "Tonight I need to stop by my mother's house."

Axl and Piper both look at Gigi like they're not sure what she just said.

Yes: meeting with the Thespians is Gigi's top priority. But until she gets this thing with her mother out of the way, it's all Gigi will be able to think about. There's only so long she can contain the dread.

Of course, Gigi doesn't *have* to go at all. She could let this stupid box of whatever it is rot in Marty's office, taking up space.

But she wants to go.

She doesn't know why.

"Tomorrow, for the Thespian meeting?" Gigi asks.

They agree.

Gigi says, "Wish me luck."

"Good luck," say Axl and Piper simultaneously.

Luck. It strikes Gigi as sad that she asked for this, and that they wished it for her. As if there were so much of it, and wishing for it spread it all around.

9.

WHAT MADNESS RULES IN BRAINSICK MEN

Ancient Greek audiences expected theater to blow their heads off. To them, drama wasn't some jocks-versus-nerds rivalry that gets resolved in a dance-off at the high school prom. Drama was: you murder your father, have hot screaming sex with your mother, and stab your goddamn eyes out.

The acting was also different. Delicate fluctuations of feeling rippling across a damp and unreasonably attractive brow may be what Americans think of as an Oscar-worthy performance, but it interested ancient Greek audiences zero percent. They sat too far above the stage to see the actors' faces anyway, so Greek actors wore masks. Stylized faces of mortals, gods, and beasts, molded from stiffened linen, designed to help performers express emotions with power.

There were masks for comedy and masks for tragedy.

That's it.

The essence of humanoid life.

When I died, more than a hundred masks hung on the purple wall facing my canopy bed.

The classic theater duo cast in cheap white porcelain, five bucks from a trinket stall called "Things Forever" in Market Place Mall.

The plastic Balinese face, cackling and bug-eyed, with the long teeth and the painted flames swirling around its head, that Gigi and I snagged from a garage sale.

The replica of the Japanese Noh that Dad scored in Tokyo and brought home as a gift. An elderly woman carved from wood, her vibe wise yet unhinged.

We found Gigi's favorite at the junk store next to Radio Shack. A ceramic girl with a widow's peak that turned her face into a heart. Her skin was creamy yellow, and her big eyes barely contained some specific worry. Her purple lips were blurred. Tears stained her cheeks.

Whenever I added a new mask to my collection, it felt less like I was indulging my gay-as-hell hobby, more like I was rekindling ancient bonds and rivalries to last to the end of time.

Early March 1991. I was looking at my masks when I heard Dad come home from party headquarters and went downstairs.

Dad peeled off his suit jacket. His jowls were extra droopy, and his face was swollen. He looked like he needed a hug.

I wrapped my arms around his neck.

He gave me some classic back whacks, the kind that made me cough.

"Thanks, Max. Something smells heavenly."

"This lasagna seems to be working out, despite me," called Mom from the kitchen.

Mom's sentences always had a melody. Even if you didn't know she loved to sing, you could guess.

At the kitchen island, my parents clinked wineglasses.

I leaned against the refrigerator, tore open a bag of corn nuts.

Dad frowned as he swirled his wine. *"Do you remember, Lucy, when they made me Community Commissioner, I thought it was a real estate appointment? Community building, they called it. I can't imagine a description more misleading."*

"You were reading Neighborhood Reports today?"

"Grown adults tattling on each other like squabbling siblings. Looking to the American government to dole out punishment. Utterly juvenile."

When Mom pressed her lips together, her dimples appeared. *"I suppose that's exactly what the party asked them to do, Bernie. Turn against one another."*

Zing!

I tossed a corn nut into the air, caught it in my mouth.

I felt like this convo was flowing, so I decided to ask a question I should've known the answer to but totally didn't.

"Dad, what's your job, exactly?"

Dad tilted his head, looking puzzled. *"Why, I've been buying and selling real estate in every major metropolitan city in the Midwest since I was nineteen years old."*

"No, I mean, in the party. Specifically. Like, what do you do with the Neighborhood Reports?"

Dad put his free hand into the pocket of his slacks. Rocked onto his toes. The fragrance of lasagna filled the house, making it feel safe. As safe as anywhere ever was, or could possibly be.

"These days . . . not much."

"What's that mean?"

Dad exhaled forcibly. Like there was something heavy inside him that he was trying to lift up and launch out.

"Maximus, you're a man now."

I nodded with actorly confidence. *"A man I be."*

"*Things seem to have . . . shifted. In the party. Slid, inch by inch. Over the past, say, two to three years.*"

"*As in?*"

"*The New Way was supposed to be about encouraging citizens to take charge of their destinies. Removing roadblocks. Letting people thrive. Take responsibility for themselves in a color-blind society. Setting them free and watching them run. This is how America was born.*"

I resisted the urge to make some clarifying statements about genocide, slavery, imperialism, and the delusions of the patriarchy. I wanted to hear what Dad was trying to tell me, not lock into the same old argument.

"*People working their fingers to the bone to make something out of nothing. I'll have you know, Max, that I believe in that, even still. The beauty of hard work and individual responsibility.*"

The pause was long. Getting longer. Feeling final.

I said, "*. . . But?*"

"*But some party members, here in Champaign County—and also, you know. Chicago. Wisconsin. Minnesota. Forget Indiana. Arkansas. Swaths of the South. The obscure north, the Dakotas. Florida. And the Northeast is no bastion of clear thought either. Even California wavers. . . .*"

Dad stopped talking again, looked at Mom.

Raised his glass.

Took a long gulp of wine.

I felt like he was a car, stalling. We needed to turn the key, start him back up.

I said, "*Some party members . . . are?*"

"*Son, I voiced my concerns. Feedbacked, made calls, wrote letters, knocked on doors. My complaints have gone largely ignored.*"

Now, as I see it, a large part of my role as Community Commissioner is simply to prevent problems."

"What kind of problems?" I asked.

"If I'm the adult in the room, people who haven't hurt a flea don't have to deal with the hassle."

". . . Of being investigated?" I asked.

"I told them, Max. That in my opinion, the party's crackdown on Anti-American Thought has become a distraction from our mission of economic empowerment. In fact, I believe it's borderline harassment. The party—inadvertently, mind you—encourages yucksters and thugs to slap American flags on their vehicles and go around threatening people. Bullies, Max. Nosy Nellies with scores to settle. Anointing themselves 'Party Protectors.'" Dad pointed at my chest with his glass. *"Now, this is between us men. And Mom."*

I nodded, willing him to keep talking about Nosy Nellies, like, forever.

"A person must develop a philosophy to succeed in life. That's not an original idea. It's a SYXTEM Core Value. But I had a philosophy before Bud Hill. And when a person sees wrongness, they must act. Don't gloat."

I shook my head.

I would not have dared interrupt my father at that moment to gloat.

"Unfortunately, when some people see an opportunity to get what they want most? They will do so with a surprising lack of ethical— what's the word. Ethics."

"What do people want most?"

"You know the answer to that."

I wasn't sure I did.

But he was just staring at me, so I said, *"What people want most is . . ."*

Mom said, *"Power."*

I had the sensation that the Bowls were standing together in the halls of justice. And my parents were sharing a truth so profound as to be self-evident.

That's when I had the vision. My father was an elderly man, reclining in his leather chaise lounge, reading an architectural magazine. Mom's hair was totally white, and she was tucking his blanket over his knees. My boyfriend and I were in the kitchen, cooking Sunday dinner.

I saw it, Gigi. So clearly.

My family loved each other more than anything in the world. The Bowls were going to be okay.

"You and I disagree about the fundamentals, Max. I do not believe government should distribute handouts at the taxpayers' expense. Free money is an insult. A disincentive to thrive."

He stalled. This time, Mom started him again. *"But . . ."*

"But goddammit, our forefathers died for the country called the United States of America. Not for some numbskulls who wouldn't know a human right if they ran into one in a dark alley."

That's where human rights hung out now, wasn't it?

Dark alleys.

"I'd like to believe we're heading toward a détente of sorts. The easing of relations between the party and the citizens is inevitable," said Dad. *"We're one country. Nobody wants civil war."*

"Civil war?" asked Mom. *"Who's talking about that?"*

"We keep our heads down, guys. Make no enemies. Wait it out. We'll all be absolutely fine."

The only other vehicles parked on Bella Vita Circle are a gold Lamborghini and a service truck here to commit microcosmic genocide on some lawns. It's a bright afternoon, but you can feel the days shortening. Gigi slams the door to the Malibu.

Geese fly in formation away from the Diamante Villas' artificial lake as she walks up the sidewalk, then the brick path that angles to and fro for no apparent reason through the Eckhorns' front yard.

The house is a beige two-story McMansion with a three-car garage. A concrete statue of a pug dog wearing a sailor's hat stands guard beside the door.

Gigi is reaching down to pet him when the lights flick on and the door flies open.

"Hiii." Didi's liquid arms drape clumsily around Gigi and contract, squeezing her body loosely, like a poorly fitting straitjacket.

Gigi doesn't know what she was expecting, but it wasn't a hug.

Gigi inhales her mother's powdery perfume and alcohol-infused sweat, and she stiffens. She feels exactly like she did when she was ten years old and her lubricated mother became affectionate. Like the ground and sky are sliding in opposite directions, and Gigi needs to brace herself to avoid slipping through some invisible crack.

"Marty?" yells Didi. "She's here for that box."

Gigi follows her mother inside and hits a wall of dry heat. First sign of fall, the Eckhorns crank it up to eighty-two.

"It's like a desert in here," says Gigi.

"Wanna beer?" asks Didi.

"I don't drink, Mom."

"Well, *I do*," says Didi, shaking her empty oversized wine-glass above her head.

"What's in the box?" asks Gigi, but her mother doesn't hear her. She's on her way to the kitchen for a refill, walking like her bones are wet.

Gigi takes the moment alone to look around the foyer. Not much has changed. Same cluster of framed Sears portraits by the door—her mother, Marty, and Marty's sons, Rick and Ryan, at different ages, looking awkward against a variety of splotchy backdrops. Gigi is kinda glad she was never included in them, now.

"Nice haircut. Joining the Marines?"

Gigi turns around.

Marty Eckhorn, Champaign County Culture Commissioner, has appeared in the foyer. With the dyed-blond hair and the anguished smile, her stepfather looks like an aging movie star with a rage problem. He's wearing a red Izod sweater, holding his signature martini in a highball glass etched with a golf club. Same glass Marty has always used, since Gigi first met him, when she was nine and asked, *Is golf fun?* His response was, *Does shit stink?* For a second, she wasn't sure of the answer.

Before Gigi can say *Stop looking at me, fucko,* Didi returns with her refreshed spritzer.

Marty looks Didi up and down. "You didn't get the box?"

"It's in the garage," says Didi.

"Then why are we standing here?"

Gigi trails behind her mother and stepfather, who are bickering. Same wallpaper in this hallway, a scene of empty baskets with green vines winding around them. They're always trying to be pretty, these baskets, but they never quite are. Gigi looks closer. *Leaves of three, let it be. . . . Dude. Is that poison ivy?*

The garage is big and empty. Marty sets his martini on a card table, slides a cardboard box out from a metal rack.

Funny. Didi told Gigi the box was taking up space in Marty's office.

Whatever.

"What's in it?" Gigi asks for the third time.

"Your old photographs," says Didi. "I should've given them to your dad years ago. Marty keeps reminding me."

When Gigi steps closer, she sees her father's handwriting on the outside of the box: *Giselle, baby & little kid.*

Didi must've taken them with her when she left almost a decade ago.

Jesus Christ, Maxy, thinks Gigi. *They're giving me back my* baby pictures?

I say, *The brainwashing is complete. Marty convinced her she doesn't have a daughter.*

There was a time when a moment like this would've cut Gigi to the core. Now she's less shocked by the Eckhorns' offhanded rejections. Not that they don't burn. But Gigi is learning how to cope. At least, how to cope well enough so that *rejected* isn't, like, *who she is.*

It's a little bit funny, no, Maxy? thinks Gigi. *How blatantly insensitive it is. Dragging me here to give me this fucking box.*

I say, *Your mom nails the cringe factor, every time.*

Gigi thinks, *Didi is like if the comedy mask and the tragedy mask had a baby.*

I wish Gigi could hear me laughing. These are the moments when you need your best friend the most. Jokes can make the darkest pain less unbearable.

Marty downs his drink and turns to Gigi, a look in his eyes she can't place.

"You know what?" says Marty. "Stick around for dinner, G'selle. Been too long. Am I right?"

Gigi looks at her mother.

Didi is looking at Marty, her eyes wide.

Didi looks surprised. And—hopeful?

Gigi wants to say, *No fucking way, cornball. See you next lifetime.*

But she's watching her mother. Didi's expression reminds Gigi of a little girl whose father just gave her permission to do something.

Does her mother want her to stay?

Does she miss Gigi, sometimes?

Gigi hears herself say, "I guess."

There isn't dinner to speak of. Ritz crackers, Velveeta cheese. Something Midwesterners call "summer sausage" that tastes like spiced rubber bands. Copious alcohol. Gigi is sitting at the glass table in the dining room, leaning on her elbows, cheeks smooshed into her hands. She's been listening to Didi and Marty describe their recent cruise to Jamaica. It was a SYXTEM retreat, an award for Commissioners who can claim a certain number of arrests for Anti-American Thought.

"You want food and beverage? They got food and beverage," says Marty.

Didi nods, a wistful look in her eyes. "Twenty-four hours a day."

The way the Eckhorns rave about endless buffets, you'd think something was preventing them from eating in Champaign.

Gigi watches her mother sloppily tear open another column of crackers while Marty hacks away at the summer sausage.

Perhaps they do need someone to cook for them.

Gigi yawns. The novelty of this dinner has worn off.

"Thanks, guys," says Gigi. "For the box, and the—crackers." She scoots out her chrome chair, stands. "See you. . . ."

"You aren't leaving yet," says Marty. "Relax."

Gigi closes her eyes. She'd forgotten this. You're prohibited from leaving the table without Marty's blessing.

Fuck that. She's not his child. As they continuously remind her.

She zips her Navy jacket, grabs her box.

"You know, G'selle, I got a lotta men out there, looking for that theater teacher of yours." Marty nods, frowning. Swirls the onion in his empty glass. "Lotta resources down the drain."

Gigi looks at her mother.

Didi is squinting like she's gonna pass out, face in the Velveeta.

"I was informed that Ms. Lee is dead," says Gigi flatly.

"Maybe she is." Marty shrugs. "But if she isn't, doesn't look good for me. Can't let people think a known Anti-American— a *woman,* no less—can hide from us. Fiona Lee wants to make me look like a fool."

Gigi doesn't have to listen to this. She heads for the door.

"Shame what happened to the Bowl boy," calls Marty. "You knew him, didn't you? Maximus? His father is a friend of mine. Fine man, Bernie Bowl. Good golfer. Now? Goddamn mess."

We turn around.

"You don't get to talk about Max," Gigi hisses. "You don't even get to say his *name.*"

"Teenagers see the world in black and white," says Marty. "Guess what, honey. I'm not *evil.* I said minors shouldn't be targeted. When that order was issued, I'm the one who tried to stop it."

Order?

What *order?*

"Unfortunately, the Bowl boy was eighteen. And there's a

thing called chain of command. Respect it, you might be the one calling the shots someday."

What?

The soldier who killed me wanted Axl. *A rogue maggot,* Axl said, *trying to score points—*

"This makes no sense," says Gigi, her voice pressured. *"Max? Why Max? I don't understand why—"*

"Theirs not to reason why, / Theirs but to do and die. Alfred, Lord Tennyson. My father taught me that. My hero. Fought on the front lines. When an order is issued, you follow it. But I'll tell you what, G'selle. You and that dealer, Fischer, help us find the theater teacher? I'll put a good word in your files. That I *can* do. *Behind every problem is a win-win solution.* Bud Hill."

We're staring at Gigi's stepfather without seeing him.

I'm shuffling everything I thought I knew. Putting the facts about my death in a new order.

Was *I* the party's target?!

Did I betray my friends for no reason?!

Have all my fits and tantrums, all my sound and fury, signified a fat nutsack of nothing?!

Gigi takes one last look at her mother. She appears to be asleep in her chair.

Jesus Christ, Mom, she thinks. *Wake up!*

AND ALL THAT POETS
FEIGN OF BLISS AND JOY

That night, I'm frantic. I try to continue my story in Gigi's dreams, but her own dreams overpower me. We're in ancient Greece, and Gigi is directing me in *Henry VI* in a circular outdoor amphitheater with bumping acoustics, like the theater at Epidaurus. The stage radiates white light. I'm wearing a tragedy mask. Mouth open, eyes forlorn, a chubby-faced boy, permanently startled, like he's foreseen the stroke of bad luck that will end his life.

Gigi paged Axl after she left the Eckhorns', but he didn't call back. And she refuses to show up at the theater unannounced now that he's doing whatever he's doing with Piper. So she's been stewing, and I've been spinning in her head, an untethered soul in a tornado.

Gigi can't fathom why the party would want to kill me.

I can barely fathom it myself.

Death is a roller-coaster ride, and I'm puking my guts out.

The next morning, she's microwaving a frozen breakfast biscuit that looks as appetizing as a hockey puck when Axl finally calls.

"I have to talk to you alone," says Gigi.

"Same," says Axl. "Tonight, after the Thespian meeting."

Gigi takes her hot-and-soggy biscuit to the dining room table, where she's been studying *Henry VI,* to give herself a focus.

Theater will get Gigi and me through this, like it's gotten us through every other horrible thing. As long as we're working on a play, everything else we can handle.

That night in Axl's theater, Gigi is standing under soft lighting downstage center, twisting her earrings with one hand, holding her copy of *Henry VI* with the other.

So far, my Death has been an even bigger shitshow than my Life.

But tonight, I'm taking comfort in the one thing that always made sense to me.

I was born a Thespian.

I died a Thespian.

With a hundred masks hanging on my bedroom wall, shouting the tale of humankind in a thousand languages.

And my people have arrived.

The foul-mouthed prima donnas. The swashbuckling tech geeks. The sensitive monologue-aholics. The boa-wearing star-fucking diva-loving charlatans. The acrobats, the improvisers, the ingenues. The cornballs. The geniuses. The hams.

The Anti-Americans are here to make some noise.

I've never loved them more.

Axl and Piper are sitting together in the front row.

A few rows back, Spatz, dapper in her white bucket hat, is leaning forward to whisper to Yolanda, the actress who played Stella in *A Streetcar Named Desire.* Yolanda has high cheekbones, warm brown skin, and a chiseled face you can't stop watching; she looks like a celebrity even in baggy sweaters and no makeup. We assume she's sneaking out on her parents, like she did to rehearse *Streetcar*.

A few seats away, aspiring playwright Skeletor is smoking his stupid corncob pipe. Skeletor went bald prematurely, so he has a white gumball head, and he goes around in a purple raincoat. We've been sworn enemies since preschool, when he decided to make a full-time profession of copying me. I'm sure he thinks that with me out of the way, he'll be everybody's favorite. What Skeletor won't tell you is that his real name is Thad.

Emma, in all her preppy glory, is snuggled in the second row beside Hal, a friendly football star who wears tortoiseshell glasses and has a tall flattop inspired by the band Kid 'n Play. They're an earnest couple who do everything—acting, costumes, tech. They'll be devoted stage parents, someday.

Way to the right of them is Reggie. He dresses like a goof, but he has a decent singing voice and can wail on set construction on a deadline.

Lounging a few rows behind him is Butt. Butt is the nickname we gave Mateo Green when he was a sophomore and he pierced his hairy cheek with a needle and stuck an earring and a rubber band in it, like Captain Lou Albano from the World Wrestling Federation. We all agreed it looked like butt, and a nickname was born. Butt likes to play with lights.

A few seats to the left of Butt we're looking at a crunchy nut cluster of actors: Puppy Dog, high priestess of Goth droll, sharing sarcastic commentary with Zorro, the six-foot-three skinny white boy who's obsessed with new-wave music, and the one and only Leticia. With her splashy print dresses and filthy sense of humor,

Leticia is the only girl I ever successfully convinced to get naked with me, late one night in Robeson Park. We were tripping, and we ended up talking for hours, bare-assed in the moonlight. That was the night Leticia and I realized science fiction is the only realistic genre, and that if you say the word "mellifluous" as slowly as possible, over and over again, you'll have an orgasm.

Can the dead weep?

I think we can; I think I'm weeping.

That's what I miss most, you know?

Doing nothing with my people.

Nothing isn't nothing till it's gone.

Gigi keeps clearing her throat. As if before she speaks, she needs to be positive her voice still works. Finally, she says, "Hey, guys."

The Thespians quiet down almost instantly, a habit ingrained by Ms. Lee.

The silence makes Gigi nervous. She flashes back to our last *Henry VI* rehearsal. There were thirty of us then, gathered in the CHS theater. It was the last time we saw Ms. Lee.

Zorro breaks the ice. "Thanks for having the balls to call a meeting, Gigi."

Gigi reaches for her hair to smooth, to comfort herself, but the hair is gone. Her arm drops. "I just feel like we need to do this."

"We need to do something," says Yolanda. "I just don't know how we do *this* without Ms. Lee."

"My sister saw Ms. Lee working at White Hen Pantry in Dwight," says Emma.

Butt snorts. "There's no White Hen Pantry in Dwight."

"Ms. Lee is in Chicago," says Reggie. "She's living with the Pater

Cida bassist in that Defiance art commune. You know they're doin' it."

"I'd do Ito," says Puppy Dog.

"Why is everything about sex with you?" asks Skeletor. "You always take it there."

Puppy Dog snarls. "You wish."

"Ms. Lee is dead," says Leticia. "Stop disrespecting."

"It doesn't matter where Ms. Lee is right now," says Gigi. "I mean, it matters. Just, wherever she is, she'd want us to do the play. And so would Max."

"Max Bowl," says Spatz. "Come back to us, you infuriating clown."

"Goddamn you, Maximus," says Zorro.

Hal and Emma clasp hands.

"Quit talking about him," says Puppy Dog, her voice catching. "I can't do this now."

I'm touched by the outpouring. Dabbing my eye sockets with a scrap of the suit my parents buried me in. If you haven't gathered, my peers rarely told me openly that they loved me. They did not hesitate to tell me openly to shut the hell up. It kinda felt like "shut up" meant "I love you," but I appreciate the confirmation.

Gigi crosses her arms, takes a deep breath. "I want to direct *Henry VI*."

"*There's* an opening statement." Yolanda pulls a pencil out of her hair and a notebook out of her bag—the sign she's about to start analyzing the shit out of something.

"Yes to doing a play," says Hal. "When Piper called me, I was like, hell yeah. Let's go. And you directing works for me. But why Shakespeare if we don't have to?"

"To finish what we started," says Gigi. "Plus, we know it

already, which will make it easier. Thespians who graduated, or didn't want to come tonight, we recast. Some of us will have multiple parts. But since a few of you felt ambivalent about *Henry VI*—"

"What does 'ambivalent' mean?" asks Reggie.

"It means we hated it," says Zorro.

"Let's discuss," says Gigi.

"Okay. We're *risking our lives* for this shit," says Spatz. "Why do we care what happened to some royal white assholes five hundred years ago?"

"You never said that to Ms. Lee," says Axl.

"Nor did anybody else, except Max," says Leticia. "Who, in this case, was right."

See? Why was it so difficult for people to say that to my face?

Butt says, "Let's do something relevant."

"*Henry VI* is for sure relevant," says Gigi. "England is on the brink of civil war. Everyone who has power is selfish and grandiose and gets off on gore except King Henry. Who goes insane, because he's a pacifist. Plus he's a teenager. And so is his warrior wife, Queen Margaret. And so is the other greatest warrior in the play, Joan of Arc. This is a story about powerful leaders with petty squabbles who force common people to bleed and suffer."

"Scratch my previous comment. It's *too* relevant," says Spatz. "Let's focus on escapism. I wanna make something oozing positivity. An adventure, or some kind of earth rejuvenation thing. Outer space fantasy. I don't know. Fairies? If it must be Shakespeare, which I guess I don't outright oppose, how about *A Midsummer Night's Dream*?"

"No forest sprites," says Puppy Dog.

"Counterpoint." Yolanda is holding up her pencil like a torch. "I agree with Gigi. Ms. Lee chose *Henry VI* for specific reasons.

It's a story about us. And I like that the king is a pacifist. We can own this."

"Agreed," says Hal. "Rich people start a war poor people have to fight. Story of our lives. I want relevance, not escapism."

"Hold on, Yolanda," says Spatz. "Is the king a pacifist, or is he *passive*? Queen Margaret takes on all the responsibility the king can't handle and runs the war herself."

"True," says Piper. "It's not like King Henry makes any remotely effective attempts to broker peace."

"And Joan of Arc leads an army of Frenchmen into battle— this play has some marvelous female characters," says Skeletor.

"But there's so many dudes with the same name, talking and talking," says Reggie.

"Maybe the issue is Ms. Lee's adaptation," says Axl. "Show feels too long to pay attention to, not long enough to make sense. Wish it were more punk rock."

Gigi thinks of *RiotRite*. The zine doesn't make sense, but the way it's put together, it doesn't matter. Reading it doesn't suck the life out of you. It energizes you. Makes you feel like being obnoxious, yourself.

"Couldn't it be?" she asks. "There's plenty of action. What if we cut the slow parts, style it differently. Give the play a rawer, more stripped-down feel."

"You think we should make our own adaptation?" asks Leticia.

"Exactly. Shorten the scenes," says Gigi. "Cut and paste."

Skeletor points his pipe at her. "Get in, get out."

"That's what your mom said last night," says Puppy Dog.

Skeletor snorts. "Piss off."

Thespians snicker.

"Do you guys know the Defiance zine?" Gigi asks.

"*RiotRite*? Heard of it," says Hal.

"What's it like?" asks Butt.

"Unpolished," says Yolanda. "Scatology, energetic juxtapositions. My older brother had some copies."

"But do you like it?" asks Reggie.

Yolanda shrugs. "There's something about it."

Gigi feels a flash of the thrill she used to get when she was an actress, doing a monologue. When she'd hit that vortex of energy, connecting her to a universal force.

This is a strong idea.

"Let's adapt *Henry VI* so it feels more like the zine. Pick key scenes, cut the rest," she says. "Focus on civil war, female badasses, abuse of power. Make it explosive."

"Okay, now I kinda don't hate this concept," says Spatz, sitting up straight. "Hit the emotions hard, highlight the women. I design epic sets; Axl makes the soundtrack. We leave the audience wanting more."

"You wanna turn Shakespeare into scary nonsense?" asks Axl.

"*Henry VI:* the remix," says Zorro. "Sounds like it'd be more fun to work on."

"And much shorter," says Gigi. "Like, no more than an hour."

"Punk rock Shakespeare." Leticia rolls her eyes back in her head the way she does when she's seriously considering something. "Not uninteresting."

Puppy Dog groans. Her heavy black makeup makes her eyes look like flashlights in a cave. "Sounds like a fuckload of work. When would we be putting this up?"

Gigi looks at Piper.

"Election Day?" Piper suggests.

Supportive howling from the horndog chorus.

"What used to be Election Day," adds Hal.

Yolanda raises her thick eyebrows. "In two months?"

"*Fuckload* of work," repeats Puppy Dog. "I don't even like punk rock."

"Call it whatever you want," says Axl. "The point is, there are no rules."

"But, Piper," says Leticia. "Won't your parents throw us all in a cattle van if they find out we're doing this?"

"Probably," says Piper dryly.

There's some nervous laughter.

"But if you don't trust me by now . . ." Piper throws her hands in the air, like *Fuck it.*

"Right. If anybody needs to quit? Same as always," says Gigi. "No judgment. If you're in? Our thing doesn't work without trust."

The Thespians agree to rehearse most weekdays, and use weekends to build sets. Piper gives assignments for the new phone tree—who calls who if shit goes down and they have to postpone.

Nobody seems nearly as nervous as they should be.

Axl's party made them overconfident, I suspect.

It'll all change the next time someone disappears.

Till then?

It's hard to begrudge these kids their hope.

I woulda been first to the theater tonight.

Last to go.

Without me, Skeletor is the lingerer. When he finally drags his purple-raincoat ass through the lobby and out the door, it's almost eleven p.m. The door closes itself heavily behind him.

Only Gigi and Axl stay behind.

Gigi sits on the lip of the stage.

Axl is in the booth. He dims the house lights, drops the needle.

Big Star.

Me and Axl wore this album out. It's sad and not sad, simultaneously. Big Star was an early discovery for us at that age when hearing new music feels like finding your own pulse.

Axl slides onto the stage beside Gigi. His hair is mussed, and his T-shirt is torn, but he looks healthier than he did a few days ago. Gigi assumes this has something to do with sex. Obviously, the "afterglow," or whatever, was lost on her—but whatever.

"About your boyfriend," says Axl.

"Who's that?" Gigi asks.

"I don't know. Val Kilmer?"

Axl's silver eyes are boring into Gigi in a way she doesn't love.

"You're referring to *Orin*?" she says. "What about him?"

"Orin was making out with some girl at my party. It was a dick move. You were crushed. Now you're together? I don't like it."

Gigi can't imagine how Axl would know what happened between her and Orin. Did he see him follow her into the costume attic? Can he tell just by looking at her?

Has Orin told people?

Who would he tell?

"Why do you care?"

"You don't know him," says Axl. "Nobody does. I was talking to people after you left the other night. There's a rumor he works for the party."

Gigi feels a surge of protectiveness. "I thought you didn't listen to rumors."

Axl says, "This one's different."

"How did everybody in this town get to be such an authority on everybody else?"

Axl holds up both hands. "I'm not an authority on anybody."

"I mean, don't we both finally have someone? Isn't that a good thing?" says Gigi. "Or is that the problem? You get to, but you don't want me to?"

"I'm not jealous, Giselle. Go be sexy. That's not what I'm concerned about."

"What are you concerned about?"

"Nobody knows Orin. We can't take risks."

"Friday night you had a party and invited the entire state of Illinois and half of Indiana. Now a dozen of us are going to break the law to perform Shakespeare in your theater. Your new girlfriend is *the First Lady's blood relative*. Yet *I'm* the risk-taker? For dating one of our friends?"

"I just know you. You're all mesmerized because he's smart and shit. But I give more than a fuck about you, Gigi, and I cannot get a single person to vouch for this cyberbitch."

Gigi leans away from him reactively, like she's afraid to catch fire. "This went dark fast. What's your damage? How do I take you seriously when you sit here and use the word 'bitch' in a derogatory way? Who are you, your brother?"

For a few minutes, they're silent. The lonely, reassuring music wraps around them like a blanket.

"My turn." Gigi takes a breath. "Last night at my mom's house, Marty told me—that Max was the party's target, the night he died. Not you."

Axl shakes his head. "Wrong. That's a hundred percent—"

Gigi lays her hand on Axl's chest, as if to stop him from barreling forward, into an argument. "I'm not giving you my personal theory. I'm repeating what Marty told me. I don't know why he'd lie. I mean, he'd lie because he's an asshole. But I don't know what he would, like, get out of lying to me about this."

Axl's face is contorted, like he's looking for a place where Gigi's words can land. "Why *Max*?"

"No idea. Then Marty said some shit about if you and I tell him where Ms. Lee is hiding, he'll put it in our files for, you know. Extra credit. Which means we have files, so."

Axl exhales like he needs to clear the deck. Reaches for the phantom cigarette, the one that no longer lives behind his ear.

Gigi grabs her purse, fishes out a Red Vine.

Axl shoves the candy into his mouth whole, which kind of negates the purpose of it being a long, floppy thing you can chew on for six minutes to get your oral fixation, but okay.

"Fuck do I do with this information?" Axl mutters, shaking his head, his mouth full of gelatinous corn syrup.

I know he can't hear me, but I try anyway.

Think about it, Axl. Just . . . think about it.

The record ends; the theater is silent. It feels vulnerable to suddenly be without a soundtrack.

Gigi lies on her back. Imagines me in the catwalks, looking down. I wish I could appear there, see-through and smoky, like a proper haunt. Not only is my Death packed with new and confounding developments, I don't even have the skills of a basic-ass ghost.

But I did figure out why they killed me.

It should've been obvious.

It wasn't—but I figured it out.

Axl rubs his face. "Listen, I was being a dick earlier. My last couple days have been extra fucked up."

Gigi peers at him, but she doesn't want to reveal how curious she is about that statement. In the last couple of days, Axl found a perfect girlfriend to watch horror flicks and, presumably, have lots of sex with. Or whatever. What's fucked up?

"You finally got laid by your crush," says Axl. "That's . . . the ticket. Sorry I'm being weird about it. I have too much information and not enough information at the same time. There was a condom wrapper in the costume attic."

Gigi bolts upright. "*Eeeew!* What are you, my father?"

"I know. Sorry. Super awkward. But I just realized, I didn't want you to think he, like, told people. I mean maybe he did. But that's not how I know."

It's not a secret, but . . . she's glad Orin isn't telling people.

Axl's tragedy mask is more relaxed now. He looks at Gigi with soft eyes. "You wanna tell me about seeing your mom?"

Gigi examines her lap. Like it might contain words to describe the experience.

"She gave me my baby pictures. In a box."

"Nooo."

Gigi sniffs a laugh. "It's actually kind of perfect. The perfect thing for her to do."

"Your mom is a mess, Gigi." Axl leans into her, shoulder to shoulder. "And she's fucking missing out."

Gigi looks around the silent theater. Her mother *is* missing out. She's missing Gigi's whole life.

Maybe Didi is missing her own life too.

Gigi remembers how smug Marty was when he told her about me.

"Maxy—" Gigi's voice breaks. "Why would they hurt you?"

Axl wraps his arms around her.

Axl might figure it out too, you know.

Right now, it's hard to call.

The truth is a messy bitch, Gigi.

The truth entangles us all.

* * *

The Malibu is parked in the lot outside the shut-down VHS rental place Axl and I used to love, the one that carried foreign films, dark and stylish, the kind that look at the ugly truth and keep looking.

Gigi walks down the avenue toward the lot, miserable about me, frustrated that nobody trusts Orin.

And with herself, that she hasn't called him back.

She's never doubted that Orin is sincere. That's the whole reason she developed such a huge crush on him. Orin thinks deeply about things and comes to his own conclusions. He doesn't try to fit in. He stands out. That's what makes him beautiful.

Even if sex was . . . anticlimactic.

Gigi slides into the Malibu, opens her glove compartment to reread *RiotRite* for inspiration for *Henry VI*. The remix idea is solid, by far the best thing that came out of this night. She pulls out mixtapes, rainbow-striped gloves. Pack after pack of Axl's un-opened cigarettes.

Looks on the floor.

In the back seat; in the box of childhood photos.

Jumps out of the car and frantically searches her trunk.

The zine is gone.

LET NOT SLOTH DIM
YOUR HORRORS NEW-BEGOT

Mid-March 1991. I was sprawled on my velvet duvet, watching the first *Friday the 13th* on VHS, when my private line rang. Remember my red phone, Gigi? The kissing lips we scored at Spencer Gifts in Market Place Mall?

"*Beb! Talk to me,*" I said, assuming it was you.

"*Max?*"

"*Orin?*"

You know Orin's phone voice. So quiet it tickles, deep in your ear.

"*Big O! What's shakin', tenderoni?*"

"*Um—I'm calling you from a secure line.*"

"*That's sexy, Orin. But straight men are not my jam.*"

"*I'm not sure how to tell you this, Max. But I've learned that your father . . .*"

"*Dad? What about him?*"

"*He's on a list.*"

"*What kind of list?*"

"*A list of people the party is looking into.*"

"Back up the truck. You're talking about my father? Commissioner Bernie Bowl? Whom the party fucking loves?"

"I thought you should know."

"What am I supposed to do with this information? Tell my father he's on some list, but we don't know what list, or why?"

"Um—don't tell him where you heard it."

"Who's your party superior?"

"Max, I can't."

"A list isn't good, Orin! Nobody wants to be on a list!"

"Stop yelling at me."

"I know who your party superior is. It's a woman, and she approved your CHS project. You report to VP Smith."

"I didn't say that."

"Smith needs a hot bowl of spaghetti."

"Okay."

"And a mesclun salad."

"Max."

"Up her butt."

"I have to go, Max. I'm sorry. You must be feeling . . . I don't know. Please don't tell anyone about our conversation."

"Who would I tell?!"

"You have to know that if he's being watched, you're being watched too."

"Who isn't being watched these days?"

"I don't know."

"My goldfish is being watched. He's swimming fishily."

I hung up.

Fifteen minutes later, I was standing in the doorway to Orin's rathole. It was pouring rain. I probably looked like a drenched yeti.

I said, "Now is the part when you tell me precisely what in the holy turd division is going on."

Orin peered into his coffee mug, like it might help him figure out how he got into this situation.

"You told me about some list. For this you have my gratitude. Now tell me who your party superior is, so I can get Dad off it. Slip me her digits forsooth. If it's Smith, I'll be discreet."

"I can't—"

I pointed in Orin's face. *"I'm helping with your CHS project. Why? Because I'm an outstanding fucking friend. You owe me."*

I hadn't given Orin any leads yet. There was pretending to be a narc, and then there was narc-ing, and I was not clear on the location of that line, so I'd been stalling.

Still used it as leverage.

Something stirred behind me.

I turned around.

Frank Fischer was outside the doorway, swaying.

Limp, lanky limbs. Big, liquid eyes. White undershirt, tight black jeans. Something about Axl's big brother always made me think of a squid in a stocking cap. Only, hot. Frank was as unfairly blessed with edgy grunge hotness as Axl is with rugged lumberjack cool.

He'd gotten skinny, though. Like, see-through skinny.

Frank leaned toward me. *"Maxxxx. Sweet fatass little shit. I see you, baby."*

Frank's compliments and his insults intermingled seamlessly. It was an art form, the speed with which that guy could spin you into a state of uncertainty.

He pushed past us, staggered across the living room. Spilled into the La-Z-Boy like he was made of soup.

Orin glanced at me, obviously uncomfortable. Followed Frank into the living room.

I was on his heels.

"Oriiiin!" Frank crooned in his beautiful, mournful voice, that aching, longing voice that made your whole body hurt along with him. The man was absolutely born to be lead singer.

Frank's eyes locked on mine.

You remember Frank's eyes, Gigi. Like Axl's, that strange gray, but lighter. As if they'd been bleached by a long stare into the sun.

"My brother is tender like you, Maxy, but he don't have no balls."

I'd been around Frank often enough when he was like this to know I could speak as if he wasn't actually there, so I turned to Orin.

"Why is Frank at your apartment?"

"We're—old friends," said Orin.

"Why?"

Orin blinked. Like he didn't know how to answer that question.

"Axl is gentle like a flower, and I think this world could crush him, and he needs a friend like you by his side all the way, Maxy," said Frank. *"All the way home."*

"Max, you should go," said Orin.

"Dude, I'm out with a quickness," I said. *"As soon as you give me that number."*

Orin rubbed his eyes. Grabbed a notebook from the milk crate beside the La-Z-Boy. Ripped out a sheet.

I glanced down at Frank. He was murmuring quietly to himself now. Not awake, not asleep. I thought of a caterpillar. What was Frank Fischer morphing into? There was something on the other side. I feared, however, that it wasn't flight.

Orin scribbled something on the paper. When I reached for it, Frank intercepted my wrist.

135

Frank had a firm grip for a guy who looked like you'd have to scrape him off that chair with a spatula.

"Don't leave my brother alone, Max."

I looked at Frank's hand, wrapped around my wrist. He was wearing a bunch of bracelets made of leather and floss.

"I won't."

"You're our other brother. This shit is for life."

"I have to leave now, Frank."

I pulled away from him, shoved the number into my pocket, and left.

It was the last time I saw Frank before he died.

And the last time I ever saw Orin.

Despite my relentless pestering, the warlock never spoke to me again.

All day at school, Gigi worries about the stolen zine. Whoever took it didn't damage the car door. And they didn't take anything else. The boom box, the cassette tapes, even the unopened smokes, which someone could easily resell, no problem. She can't ask Axl what to do. He'll berate her for ignoring his warning, and she isn't ready to give him the satisfaction of being right.

By the time she gets to the Round Barn for her first-ever waitress shift, Gigi's nerves are fried. The last thing she's up for tonight is learning something new. Her father promised it'd be slow—nobody wants to be first to patronize a business the party raided and made their own.

Still.

Standing behind the hostess credenza is someone Gigi doesn't recognize. A petite girl with big blue eyeglasses and brown hair styled with hot rollers. Her lip gloss matches her violet vest, and she's wearing an achingly fresh silver secretary skirt.

Gigi looks down at the Round Barn decal stitched to her own shirt, atop her boob.

The server uniform is ice-washed jeans and a burgundy polo with the Round Barn decal stitched to the front, and the words *It's round-up time!* embroidered on the back.

We've never known what that's supposed to mean. Farmers in these parts do no wrasslin', no ridin', no lassoin', and no roundin' up, unless that's slang for detasselin' corn, or possibly bitch-slappin' soybeans.

Ms. Lee told me that the next time I used the expression "bitch-slap," she would bitch-slap me.

Which would be further proof she's not dead, if we still needed it. I'm all over this after-party, using the word "bitch" iffily, but her bitch-ass hasn't whooped me yet.

When she was a hostess, Gigi got to choose her own costume. Every shift was a solo performance of a one-woman show called *I Am Your Hostess.* Who is this beaten-down character she's playing tonight? Some off-brand Girl Scout? A champion of minigolf?

Gigi crosses her arms to cover her boob decal.

"Gigi Durant? I'm working with *you*? Dope. I'm Xia," says the new hostess. Then, more quietly, "*Streetcar* last year? Sick. My cousin took me. I heard about your teacher. And I'm sorry about your friend. The one who . . ."

Gigi wonders if Xia will finish her sentence.

I'm sorry about your friend who was murdered.

She wishes people would finish it. Dropping the end makes Gigi wonder if something worse happened to me. Something people can't say out loud.

Gigi says, "Thanks."

Xia nods, smiling in the empty way kids do now, like smiling is a leftover feature passed down genetically for reasons that no longer apply. Like a turkey's wattle, or an appendix.

"Anyway, you have a table," says Xia.

Gigi feels her stomach curl into a ball. Her dad made waiting tables sound easy, but he makes things sound easy because he doesn't see the point in talking about what's difficult.

Xia whispers, "I should tell you, though—"

Gigi doesn't hear her; she's already tromping into the server station, a cylindrical nook in the center of the barn.

She scoops ice from a bin into two glasses. Pours water, grabs a clean tray—people love it when their drinks come on a tray—and slowly, wobblingly, uses both hands to carry it into the dining room.

I should've practiced, thinks Gigi, her eyes locked on the too-full glasses threatening to jump to explosive deaths on the carpet. She looks up, scans the curving wall of booths to find her table. When she spots her customers, we gasp.

It's Mrs. Knoxville, the marketing teacher who took over the CHS Thespians. Her face is pinched, like she's about to shoot a spitball.

Sitting across from her is Mr. Derry, the PE teacher with the mustache he stole from Burt Reynolds in *The Cannonball Run*.

What if Knoxville sees it in Gigi's eyes—that she's stealing the most experienced Thespians to revive the underground theater program off campus? What if Knoxville pressures Gigi to join the CHS production?

Silently, Gigi turns away from the booth, hoping the teachers didn't notice her. She just has to make it back to the server station without these bitchy little glasses of ice water spilling.

Xia runs to Gigi. "Let me help." She takes the water glasses, holds them away from her body to drip on the floor.

The tray is suddenly light. Gigi has an urge to throw it like a Frisbee.

They go into the server station together.

Xia whispers conspiratorially. "Tried to warn you. Knoxville is unhinged. First Thespian meeting? She just yelled the entire time about how much trouble we'll be in if we break any rules. I don't blame you for not showing up. I wouldn't have either, except, I don't know. I just wanted to be in a play. I quit, though. Fuck that. I'd rather do monologues in my bathroom mirror than act out that punk-ass *Top Gun* military propaganda in public."

Gigi smiles at Xia. She likes the freshman.

From the dining room, Knoxville's voice floats into the server station. "If I knew where she was hiding, I'd report her so fast her head would spin."

"I'd arrest her myself," says Derry.

"With your handcuffs?" asks Knoxville, in a tone that strikes Gigi as creepy.

"Actually, yes. Did I tell you? I'm a Party Protector."

"Since when?"

"You know my neighbor Chad? We grill. Fellow T-bone man. Chad was like *'No reason not to join up, is there?'* I mean, I wasn't gonna argue that. Guy has a wall of shotguns. Chad says, *'Don't worry. We rarely have to give an actual beatdown. Stamp on your ID card gets you into rooms where mere mortals fear to tread.'* Better to be on Chad's team when the hammer falls, right? Gotta buy your own arsenal, though. You have no idea how many brands of handcuffs are out there, babe. I mean, *wow.*"

Gigi and Xia look at each other, eyes wide.

It's obvious the teachers think they're talking quietly. But the roundness of the dining room is strange, acoustically. People's words bounce off the curved walls and land in unexpected places.

"Can Party Protectors arrest people now?" asks Gigi.

"The party lets them get away with anything," says Xia.

"Lock her up," says Knoxville. "Fiona Lee deserves what she gets. Bitch thinks she's so much better than us. *Act from your conscience.* Like she's a fucking saint."

We gasp.

Will the drama ne'er cease in this 'Paign?!

"Where do you think she's holing up?" asks Derry.

"In the video, it looks like a basement full of spiders."

"Pick your Midwestern domicile."

Xia says, "They're *so* having an affair."

Gigi and I shudder. "What's this video?"

"Where the hell is our waitress?" snaps Knoxville.

That's us!

Xia shoves the water glasses into Gigi's hands.

Gigi composes herself, tries to look like she's been unaware of the teachers' presence and absolutely not listening to them. What's a good not-listening face?

Don't indicate that you're not listening, she imagines Ms. Lee directing. *Instead, be someone they can ignore.*

So they don't worry about me, thinks Gigi. *They just keep talking.* She rolls her shoulders, takes a breath. Tonight, she debuts her newest workplace improvisational theater piece: *I Am Your Waitress.*

Gigi approaches her teachers' booth, not overly surprised to see them, thinking nothing of the fact that they're together at a restaurant most people are going out of their way to avoid.

When they register Gigi, both teachers sit up straight.

"Miss Durant," says Mr. Derry, trying to sound like an adult.

"Hey, Mr. Derry," says Gigi.

"What a surprise to see you," says Mrs. Knoxville.

"Yeah," says Gigi, Your Appropriately Disinterested Waitress. "Got everything ya need?"

"We have nothing," says Derry.

"First day," says Gigi, apologetically. "Drinks are on the house."

Knoxville smooths some imaginary ripples in her sweater. "That's generous."

Make them comfortable, Gigi imagines Ms. Lee urging. *Let them relax.*

"Not really. I know the bartender," says Gigi.

The teachers laugh uneasily, and Gigi takes their orders.

"Anything else?" Gigi asks.

Derry's eyes move shiftily around the room. "To be clear, this isn't a social occasion. It's a meeting. Of a committee we're on."

Knoxville's lips twitch like her teeth itch.

Love affair confirmed.

Gigi takes an impulsive risk. "Come back anytime you need a quiet place to work. My father takes care of his regulars."

Derry laughs a knowing laugh. "Oh, we know Dick. We used to go to Leroy's up on University. . . ."

Knoxville grimaces.

Gigi tries to channel the innocent energy of someone like Piper. "My father says what happens in his tavern stays in his tavern. I work Sundays, too, which is all-you-can-eat fried chicken. Come on back, now."

Gigi scoots away, walking with more confidence than she feels.

Inside the server station, she collapses against the coffee machine.

"What happens in his tavern stays in his tavern?" Gigi moans. "What am I, auditioning for the mafia?"

"You were fine," says Xia. "I wonder what this video is about."

Gigi says, "Me too."

Me three.

I have no idea what's going on, ever. And I'm officially annoyed about it. My afterlife abilities are limited to pestering. After everything I've been through, I really feel like I should get omniscience!

For the rest of the shift, Gigi and Xia huddle in the server station, listening to the teachers' conversation, but it's not interesting. We're grateful we heard anything at all.

But what did we hear, exactly?

A video. A spidery basement.

What is Ms. Lee *doing*?

When her shift ends, Gigi runs downstairs to the bathroom, changes out of her waitress uniform into a white sweaterdress and a blue studded belt.

Then she digs in her purse for a quarter, goes outside to use the pay phone in the parking lot.

If she pages Axl now, she'll have to wait at the pay phone for him to call her back, which may not happen soon. She'll try him from home, tonight.

Meanwhile, she'll call Orin.

Orin is the one who told Gigi that Ms. Lee is alive.

If there's a video?

Orin will tell her about it.

She's been avoiding him because losing her virginity was so disappointing, compared to how she'd imagined it. But was that entirely his fault? It's not like she told him how she was feeling. She can't expect the boy to read her mind.

And last night, when Axl told her about the rumor that Orin

is working for the party, she felt protective. People love to talk shit about people they don't understand.

And she does understand Orin.

At least—she thinks she does.

"Gigi. Hey . . ."

"Just got off work," she says. "Can I pick you up?"

Orin agrees, and Gigi runs back inside to have a private chat with Xia.

It's unacceptable that the freshman might never know how it feels to do real theater. Gigi is dying to know what Ms. Lee is up to in that spidery basement. . . .

Meanwhile, Gigi is the director.

It's on her to make this right.

As she wheels the Malibu through downtown with Orin riding shotgun, Gigi is more anxious than she'd anticipated. She's having trouble starting a conversation.

They pass G. Harold's, the fancy department store, permanently shuttered. A mannequin's foot, bone white and featureless, has been stranded in the display window facing Main Street for two years.

Hello, foot, we think, passing it.

"Where should we go?" Orin asks.

"Kinda in the mood to drive around," says Gigi. "Go wherever the night, you know. Takes us."

"Okay."

Boo! Get off the stage, Durant! Worst acting you've ever done!

The truth is, Gigi is afraid to be in a specific place with Orin. Because it might lead to making out, which she'd probably like, but then she'd need to stop and talk about sex with him, which she one hundred thousand percent does not know how to do.

The Malibu rolls past a three-story yellow brick monster of a building with a row of arched windows with shattered glass panes, like blinded eyes. It used to be the local newspaper.

Gigi forces herself to focus. "I heard Ms. Lee made a video in hiding. Do you know anything about it?"

"Um—a bit," says Orin. "It just surfaced."

"Have you seen it?"

"No. But my sources say it's a teacher recruitment video. She's trying to convince others to protest the curriculum."

Ms. Lee *is* the Good Witch of the Midwest.

Hot damn!

But also—

Gigi glances at Orin.

Who are his "sources"?

They drive past the clock tower, which is missing the hour hand; the minute hand is stuck at 17. Me and Gigi want the number 17 to be symbolic of something.

It isn't.

Farther south, fluorescent lights make the big windows of a few cheap restaurants glow, including the second outpost of Ye Olde Donut Shoppe, which is open twenty-four hours and popping.

Too popping. The Americans spilling onto the sidewalk are hyperkinetic in that gimme-my-damn-drugs sort of way.

Maybe downtown at night isn't a great idea.

Gigi heads toward the old U of I campus and the Boneyard Creek.

At a stoplight, she looks at him. "You work for the party, don't you? Not the Defiance."

"I'm—not a fan of labels," says Orin. "Everyone needs to be able to access the internet without anyone looking over their shoulders. I'm going to make that possible. Which will, ultimately, destroy the party."

Of course Orin *doesn't care about labels.*

The problem is, other people do.

"To clarify. You're working for the party to destroy them from within?" Gigi asks.

"Of course, Gigi. Why else?"

Ugh.

Axl would call bullshit on that.

But Gigi knows Orin better than Axl does. She has no doubt he's telling the truth. . . .

Still. It doesn't make defending Orin any easier.

Gigi whacks the dashboard a few times to get the fan to stay on. Gives up, cranks open her window for some fresh air.

When the light turns green, she keeps driving.

"Incidentally. Last night, I read some chatter," says Orin, "Your teacher may be being held on the Auroras' farm."

Piper's family, locking up Ms. Lee?

This, at least, Gigi can deny with confidence. The Auroras may be related to the Dictator, but they aren't jailers.

"Anything you hear about the Auroras is bullshit. Besides, if Ms. Lee was on the farm, why would the party still be looking for her? They'd have her."

"It's one of those leads you can't prove or disprove. Local Commissioners would never authorize anyone to investigate. John and Melinda Aurora *are* the party. Listen, shall we go to the diner, or—?"

The Malibu's horn goes off, although Gigi isn't touching it.

She reaches under the steering wheel, yanks a wire.

The horn stops.

She does not want food.

She just wants to keep driving.

Her car is the most comforting place in the world.

How I miss riding shotgun while Gigi wrangles the quirky mechanics of her personal Millennium Falcon. My Range Rover was hotter, but it had way less personality.

We hate imagining someone breaking into the beast to steal the zine.

Besides that, *RiotRite* is inspiring her direction for the *Henry VI* remix—it would've been helpful to have it to refer to. Which reminds her. She's been meaning to ask Orin another question.

"Do you know Stu Perloff?"

"Um—" Orin looks out the beast's streaky window like he wonders if he'll ever leave this car. "Yes. Most local hackers know one another, at least vaguely."

"Do you know where he is now?"

"No. I mean, I did hear—that he's gone. Listen, Gigi. Can I ask *you* something?"

Gigi nods as she muscles the beast into a hard left, toward the creek. Who needs power steering?

Orin asks, "What did I do wrong?"

His dark eyes reflect an uneasy stillness.

Fuck.

"You didn't do anything wrong. I just," she stammers, "I don't know."

If they're really talking about this, she needs to park. She finds a spot under a tree.

"I think you do know, but you don't want to tell me," says Orin. "You didn't like being with me, the other night."

Gigi leans against the headrest, sighs. "It was . . . okay."

"Not—uh." Orin sniffs. "The word I was hoping to hear."

"Not horrible, Orin. For my first time, I expected rainbows, I think. A pot of gold."

Orin closes his eyes. "I should've asked how you were feeling."

"Well . . . you just did."

"I'm so sorry."

"I could've told you how I was feeling. Or asked you to slow down. But I was nervous. And I wasn't sure what I was feeling. Or if what I was feeling was, like, the right feeling. I think I was feeling, like, ten different feelings and none of them made sense together. And I wondered if I was doing everything wrong."

"Impossible, Giselle. I feel very stupid."

"Please don't feel stupid. I mean, I also feel stupid."

"Shit."

Gigi watches the dim light of the moon reflect in broken lines on the creek, the silhouettes of bare branches above.

"I did like being close to you," she says quietly. "And I love talking with you. I don't have these types of conversations with anybody, arguments about how to take down the party, and Bud Hill. Sometimes I have this feeling like between us, we can figure it out. I'm just not used to the other thing yet."

"Sex."

Gigi takes in Orin's mussed black hair, his lean body—his Ministry T-shirt, the shape of his arms, which has always made her feel warm.

"But you know," she says, "I want to be."

"Then let's slow down," says Orin. "I mean. If you still want—me."

"I do."

She thinks she does.

How would she know?

"Let's just talk, Gigi," says Orin.

"What about?"

"Anything. I love the sound of your voice."

Great. Now she wants to kiss him.

She cannot wait for the next *Henry VI* rehearsal. Theater is the only thing in her life that always makes sense.

She looks up, at the ceiling of thin brown fabric that sags above them, like the inside of a tent, then over at the zineless glove compartment. Remembers trying to share the zine with Orin, how he called it irrelevant.

"Why don't you like *RiotRite*?" Gigi asks.

"I do like it. I love how snarky and random it is," says Orin. "The problem is, it's apolitical."

"Apolitical? Are you kidding?"

"No."

Gigi rolls her eyes. For the smartest boy in town, Orin has a lot to learn.

"Guerrilla art is inherently political," she says. "Regardless of the content."

"No, Gigi. It isn't."

"Dude! You're wrong. Whenever we do something they tell us not to, it proves they can't control us. Like when we did *A Streetcar Named Desire* last fall with Ms. Lee. It's not necessarily a political play. It's the fact that we did it that matters."

"This is precisely the problem. People just want to be entertained. They're unwilling to join a movement that asks anything of them. That's why the internet will work so well as a tool of control. It will let us communicate without connecting. Look without paying attention. We'll be alone, stay alone, and the party will manipulate us. A lot of us won't care. People are willing to live very small lives if their basic needs are met. And they have, you know. Consumer garbage. Pizza delivery. Porn."

"But this is the same internet you want to use to start a *revolution,* right?" Gigi asks.

"Yes," says Orin. "People who *are* willing to act will be able to connect across distances to create a bigger, stronger alliance."

"Then what?"

"When the time is right, we take action."

"Action, meaning . . . ?"

"An effective revolution will have many components. Accumulating weapons, disseminating ammunition—this alone is a huge task. Many soldiers are ready to abandon the party as soon as the tides turn. When that happens, an armed citizenry will be more than happy to join us."

Gigi makes a crazy face at Orin.

"Everything you just said is insane! We need to have a *nonviolent* revolution. Like Gandhi, and Martin Luther King. If we use violence, we're as heinous as the party!"

"I strongly disagree. Nonviolence takes too long. The longer it takes to gather momentum, the more people Bud Hill murders. It's a numbers game, Gigi. Ethically, violence wins. We strike first, and with force. Our numbers grow quickly. Nonviolent revolutionary tactics squelched again and again by the military? We look ineffective. Nobody is inspired to join us and be slaughtered. A fast, violent revolution has a bigger impact, and *fewer* casualties."

"Decent people don't have the stomach for violence!"

"Not in normal times, when communities are healthy. But these aren't normal times."

"Do *you* have weapons? And . . . ammunition?"

Ammunition. There's a word she's never used in casual conversation.

"I mean, Giselle," says Orin. "Of course."

Gigi exhales in a big puff of air.

"So, you want straight-up civil war. Mass casualties."

"Yeah, Gigi. Just for fun."

"Sorry. I'm not trying to be a dick, I just—can't comprehend it. And in your scenario, once the Defiance wins, everyone in America is, what? An anarchist, all of a sudden?"

"Anarchy is a difficult concept. I get that. And no, of course not. But we could get there. You have to start with an ideal. Americans need to lose our toxic devotion to hierarchy and power. Men, in particular, and white supremacy. All Bud Hill's economic policies are a mask for that. But we *can* lose it. And live harmoniously, in communities that are mutually beneficial. We just have to behead the Royal Family first."

Behead the Royal Family.

He didn't say "kill the Auroras," but he might as well have.

"I agree with some of what you said, but I'm never doing any of that," says Gigi.

Orin sniffs. "Okay. What's your idea?"

"I'm directing a play."

". . . Hmm."

"Say what you want, Orin. Spit it out."

"Performing in public is extremely dangerous. It's willfully ignorant to think that art will save your life when someone is pointing a gun at your head. It's not worth the risk. It's a distraction from the big picture."

"It's my entire picture."

"Well, it's very small, Gigi. A play is a very small thing."

"All things are small things, Orin."

". . . Possibly."

"In my life, the play will be huge."

"I just wish you valued your safety."

"You wouldn't respect me if I valued my safety more than doing what I think is right. Anyway, it sounds like we agree."

Orin snickers. "Do we? On what?"

"That the revolution can't be just one thing."

For a few minutes, they sit in silence, watching the wind blow wispy clouds across the black sky, like it's painting with smoke.

"I'm glad this is happening," says Orin.

"What's happening?" asks Gigi.

Orin says, "Us."

12.

THE SANDS ARE NUMBER'D THAT MAKE UP MY LIFE

The next night Gigi arrives early to rehearsal. Axl is standing on a ladder in the lobby, fixing some loose molding near the ceiling.

When he hears the door swing open, he looks down. "Hey. Got the show photocopied for the new kid."

Gigi sees Xia's copy of the three parts of *Henry VI* on the ticket counter, held together by a fat binder clip. "Thanks."

She told him about Xia at school. For the video conversation, she wanted more privacy.

"What's what? You good?" Axl asks.

"So-so. I'm pretty sure Knoxville and Derry are fucking."

"*Yowza.* There's some amateur porn I can't unsee."

Right? And here I thought there was nothing in that category of which I wouldn't partake. O, Death, you and your futile revelations.

"They were in the Round Barn last night," says Gigi. "Talking about a video Ms. Lee made."

Axl takes a rag out of his back pocket, concentrates on wiping glue from the edge of the molding. "Wow."

Gigi folds her arms. *"Wow?"*

"I mean, yeah," says Axl. "Wow."

"Axl. You never say *wow.*"

"Sure I do."

"Dammit! You're not telling me something!"

Axl stuffs the rag back in his pocket.

"What is it?" asks Gigi. "Come *on!*"

Axl climbs down the ladder, scowling like a demigod exhausted by the part of himself that's mortal.

"Fuck it, Gigi. You're right. There are, like, three significant things I'm keeping from you right now, for your own good."

"Axl!"

"*Because,* Giselle, *I cannot let anything happen to you.* It's the only goal I have left in my life. You think I couldn't have saved Max. Or Frank. Prob'ly right about that, like you are about everything. But yes. I'm not telling you something. It makes me a happy camper. That I have the power to do this."

"This macho hero bullshit yet again . . ."

"Maybe! But also, *maybe not.* Some things everybody can't know. Any of them would make you vulnerable. You or someone else."

"This conversation is both boring and old. If you want to protect me, why the fuck are we doing a play?"

"Because we're all going to die someday. And if it's going to be me, next—and I swear to you, Gigi, *it is*—I want to live before they take me out. I don't want to go out waiting for the bad shit to happen. Bad shit will happen. I want to show up."

"For the sake of argument, how do you plan to protect me, in this scenario?"

"I don't know, Gigi! I won't pretend I'm, like, being super logical. Frank's death wrecked me. I lost him even before I lost him. Max's death broke me permanently. Now I'm rolling alone. With you. I mean—yeah, Piper, but that's different. I mean— no. I won't be able to protect you if we perform *Henry VI*. Obviously. Or anybody else. *If* we do it. Which, we'll see, you know? It's highly doubtful. Half the Thespians will drop out first time shit hits the fan. At *least* half, no matter what the show is. Anyway if I said *No, Gigi, we can't do Shakespeare, can't use my theater*, you'd be all over me until I gave in. Have I ever stopped you? From doing anything? Survey says—no!"

"Which is what you love about me."

"Exactly," says Axl, his eyes as serious as they've ever been.

Gigi lets her eyes linger on his for a moment.

Axl is a painfully sincere person.

Emotional.

Illogical.

Infuriating.

Like Gigi.

And me.

And pretty much everybody else.

Spatz pokes her head in the door. "Hey, kids. Shakespeare o'clock."

Spatz is wearing a torn black T-shirt and jeans. Her motorcycle helmet is tucked under one arm. She sets a paper cup from the Espresso Café on the ticket counter, beside the extra script.

Gigi turns to her, exhales. "How are Ginger and Mary Ann?"

"Their biggest issue is quicksand," says Spatz, "which I don't think exists. *Gilligan's Island* has nothing to do with my life, and I cannot stop watching. My dad wears earmuffs when I turn on the television. It's become an embarrassing problem. Almost worse than when I was drinking. Hopefully, it's easier to quit, now that I have sets to design. Please stop me if I start painting palm trees."

There's a faint knock on the door, although it's still partway open. Xia pokes her head into the theater, smiling nervously. She's wearing a white T-shirt over a black netted long-sleeved undershirt and a chunky resin necklace, plus her big blue eyeglasses.

"Hey, Xia!" says Gigi. "Xia and I work together at the Round Barn. This is Spatz and Axl."

Spatz says, "Welcome to the Thunderdome."

"'Sup," says Axl.

Xia steps into the lobby. "Nice to meet you guys," she says. It seems like she's unsure where to stand.

Gigi remembers how she felt at her first Thespian meeting. The peculiar alertness of knowing she was in exactly the right place, yet desperately hoping she'd fit in.

She hands Xia *Henry VI* Parts I, II, and III.

"Whoa," says Xia. "Long-ass play, huh?"

Gigi says, "We're only performing a few scenes."

"We're adapting it," says Spatz. "Turning it into music videos, sorta kinda."

"Eeeen-teresting," says Xia, her tone of voice curious but noncommittal.

Gigi feels a flash of self-doubt. There's more pressure, now that Xia is here. To make the underground play feel inevitable. As important as *The Brig* felt to Gigi. To create a home for Xia, the way Ms. Lee created a home for whoever needed one, whoever kept showing up.

Gigi is sitting on the edge of the stage, tapping her open notebook with one of the fountain pens we stole from Walgreens.

Fountain pens are sexy. The way the ink flows, all wet and drippy, like everything you write is a love letter, even your grocery list.

Stealing is also sexy. Secretly sliding valuable objects down your pants.

Ergo, stealing fountain pens?

Gigi and I agree that it's basically pornographic.

I know.

I'm undermining our impeccable credibility.

Thespians wearing every shade of black are scattered in the first few rows of the house.

Hal the linebacker is passing around a bowl filled with pumpkin cookies. "Did you guys see *America Tonight* last night?"

Emma takes two cookies. "That guy whose cat dances to the Bobby Brown song?"

"It's my prerogative," sings Butt nasally, shifting his shoulders back and forth in a decisive rhythm. *"The way that I wanna live. . . ."*

Puppy Dog is in the third row, munching a cookie. "I preferred Bud Hill's Mr. T impression," she says dryly. "If we'd known he could do impersonations, we could've given him a sitcom and kept the country."

Leticia is sitting in the front row, vibing like a kettle about to boil. She waves away the cookies.

"I'm entering the contest, though," says Reggie, digging into the cookie bowl with both hands. "A thousand bucks for the best Pro-America limerick? I'll write the *shit* out of that."

"Oh, me too, absolutely," says Skeletor, who is, for no obvious reason other than the need to draw attention to himself, sitting cross-legged on the dusty black floor in front of the seats, puffing on his corncob pipe.

Leticia stomps her feet and stands. Her tie-dye skirt swings around her ankles. "Did you all hear about the mob of Party Protector dipshits who flooded University Avenue last night? A bunch of grown-ass adults, with *torches,* chanting *Death to Anti-Americans! Death to Anti-American Thought!* For two hours, they caused a ruckus out there. I live on University. My grandmother was listening to her book on tape. And they're yelling about *Smoke 'em out!* We had to turn off her story."

The house goes silent.

"Do you think you are *safe* from them?" Leticia continues. "Do you think anyone is? Max Bowl and Fiona Lee are *dead.* What are you assholes gonna do about it?"

"I don't know, Leticia," says Reggie. "If I knew, I'd be doing it."

"Well, right now, all you're doing is wasting our precious rehearsal time sucking on the NutraSweet tittie the party feeds us to keep us drugged and passive," says Leticia. "I need some Thespians to find their fucking ovaries with me and make some goddamn theater, tonight."

Zorro purses his lips, kicks his Chucks up on the seat in front of him.

He says, "Button up, maggots."

Our favorite line from *The Brig.*

Leticia sits. "Thought so."

Gigi stands. "Leticia, thank you. I needed that. Anybody have anything to add?"

"I'm sorry about your grandmother," says Skeletor.

"Don't apologize to me," says Leticia. "Apologize to yourself for killing your brain cells watching *America Tonight.* Let's move on."

"Okay, maggots," says Gigi. "Tonight, let's wrap up casting. Who wants to take over the role of King Henry?"

Everyone is trading a look that says, *Not me.*

Spatz clasps Yolanda's shoulder. "I feel like it's Yolanda."

Yolanda shrugs. "I liked playing York, but I wouldn't mind a new part to shake it up. I'd much rather be Joan of Arc, though."

The senior who was playing Joan in Ms. Lee's production graduated.

"Yolanda is the new Joan la Pucelle. Anybody object?" asks Gigi. "We have a winner. Who wants to replace Yolanda as York?"

"Too many lines," says Zorro.

Nobody volunteers.

"Since Lizbeth graduated, can I play Gloucester?" asks Skeletor. Gloucester is the advisor who makes decisions for King Henry while he's an infant. "I've already got a velvet cape. And a puppet we can use for baby King Henry."

"There's no baby King Henry in the play," says Piper.

"Ah, but there could be," says Skeletor. "We could open with a coronation scene, to show that Henry was crowned as an infant. From the beginning, he was a puppet."

"And nobody gives a shit what he has to say. He's a literal puppet," says Hal. "I like that."

Puppy Dog says, "Of *course* Skeletor has his own cape."

Of *course* he does.

Attention whore.

"Any objections to Skeletor playing Gloucester? No? Great," says Gigi.

Emma takes out her ponytail, redoes her scrunchie. "Opening with Henry being crowned, it's pretty British. People might not get how it relates to us."

"We're turning the play into music videos, right? Let's add an American soundtrack," offers Xia, who's sitting alone near the entrance to the lobby. "American punk rock. Iggy Pop or something."

Axl points at Xia emphatically. "You and me are about to be best friends."

Tragicman is never not turned on by a solid cultural reference.

Gigi introduced Xia at the start of the meeting, but some of the Thespians seem to be noticing her for the first time.

"What's your name again?" asks Yolanda.

"Xia."

"Do you wanna play King Henry? Everybody else is chicken shit because they don't want to follow in Gigi's footsteps."

Xia looks at Gigi, as if asking permission.

"That would be fantastic," says Gigi. "If you're game."

Xia shrugs. "Why not?"

"Done," says Gigi. "Let's switch gears for a second and talk about the adaptation."

"The remix," says Zorro. "All we have to do is improve on Shakespeare."

"If *RiotRite* is our inspiration, shouldn't be that hard," says Axl. "It isn't super precious. In one issue they just stapled together a bunch of Xeroxes of somebody's tush."

"As long as we're changing the play, let's make it more political," says Butt.

Hal turns around. "It's about a civil war. How much more political can you get?"

"We could make the York crew talk like Bud Hill," says Reggie. "Insert speeches about the New American Way. And the Lancaster crew is the Defiance. That would be badass."

"Doesn't map well onto the story," says Yolanda. "Lancaster is King Henry's party. They're already in power. The play isn't a direct analogy for the New Way. That's not why Ms. Lee chose it."

"It's about the carnage," says Hal. "Ruling classes start wars in their pursuit of power, regular people suffer."

"Maybe in the background we could project horror films, with the sound off," says Piper.

Axl squints at her. "Like what flicks?"

"I dunno," says Piper. "*The Thing*? A big, scary force that makes everybody paranoid . . ."

"I don't even understand what we're doing," says Puppy Dog. "Like, at all."

"Yeah, and if we change a bunch of stuff, how will the story make sense?" asks Emma.

"Why should it make sense?" asks Skeletor. "My next-door neighbor went missing last week, and my nonna says it's because he was *in flagrante delicto* with some soldier's ex-wife. That makes no sense."

Your Latin is what makes no sense, *Thad*. Just say boinking!

"Yeah, but that's why the *play* should make sense," says Emma.

Thespians talk over each other.

"If we're gonna get arrested for this, it has to be sexy. I don't want to risk my life to bore the audience."

"So you're saying Shakespeare is boring. *You're* boring."

Axl leaps onto the stage, disappears.

The Thespians keep arguing.

"King Henry should stay the focus. He's a peaceful king. If we add stuff, it should be about the challenges of keeping peace in a country where people hold opposite points of view on how to run it."

"It's wartime, not peacetime. We should focus on the overwhelming violence. Make it as grotesque as possible, to show how devastating it is to normal people when leaders start these ego-driven wars."

"King Henry does jack crap. Queen Margaret is gangster, and Joan of Arc is a riot grrrl. Clearly, they should be our entire focus."

"*This* is what the play should be," says Piper. "We focus on our favorite characters, pick key scenes, cut them to their essence. The remix sparks discussions Americans aren't supposed to have anymore."

When Axl reemerges, he's pushing a hunk of scenery on wheels. It's a section of a plum-colored drawing room from *The Mousetrap,* an Agatha Christie murder mystery the community theater put on decades ago. He duct-tapes a giant sheet of paper to the wall, hands Gigi a marker.

It doesn't take long to come up with characters and scenes everybody agrees are essential. Gigi writes them on the big sheet:

1. Wars of the Roses: The beginning of the civil war, when everyone chooses either a white rose to help York overthrow the crown or a red rose to help King Henry stay in power.
2. Joan of Arc's life as a teenage heroine: seeing religious visions, leading French soldiers into battle, being burned at the stake.
3. Queen Margaret: Taking over for her husband, King Henry; leading the army against York; capturing, taunting, and murdering York.
4. King Henry: Going into hiding, ruminating on the evils of war.

They also decide to show King Henry being crowned as an infant, as Skeletor suggested. A scene that doesn't exist in the play but sets up the story.

It's more than enough to fill an hour.

By the end of rehearsal, the Thespians are in high spirits. They've had two successful meetings without Ms. Lee. They're trading quotes from the film *The Princess Bride* (*"Inconceivable!" "Anybody want a peanut?"*) when a thud shakes the whole theater, and a shrieking horn makes everyone cover their ears.

Axl says, "Nobody move." Leaps onstage, bolts into the wings.

Xia catches Gigi's eye.

For a few seconds, everybody seems paralyzed.

A woman shoves open the lobby's velvet curtains.

Long, scraggly blond hair. Bleeding forehead. Sweatshirt, sweatpants, flip-flops. About the same age as our parents. Walking in a wobbly way, like she's either in shock, drunk, or both.

She looks around the big black room. At the catwalks, the darkened tech booth. Over the softly lit stage.

She says, "Will y'all look at *this* shit."

Piper snaps into business mode, approaches her. "Are you okay? Can I help you? Are you—do you need—"

A small boy wearing only a diaper pushes through the curtains, waddles into the theater behind the woman.

Axl is right behind him. He must've left through the side exit, come back in through the front. He's breathing heavily from running. His face is unreadable.

"What can I do for you?" Axl asks.

The woman turns to face him. "Y'all ain't supposed to be *here*, huh? I'm about to buy a truckload of weed with my cash reward."

Axl's vibe is dead calm. "Nah, don't fuck with the party. You know it takes them forever to pay. Lemme hook you up. I got the best shit, anyway. . . ."

This catches Gigi off guard. Axl can hook this person up . . . with *weed*?

"Car's okay, just took a wrong turn." Axl keeps talking, his voice low, soothing. "Fucked up your fender, broke a lot of glass. I'm gonna call a guy, get you fixed up. Lemme show you the sink. There's a washcloth in there. Kid want a treat? I got candy."

The Thespians are exchanging tense looks. Emma is trembling so hard she's gripping both arms of her chair to try to be still.

The woman scoops up the child with one arm, looks over her shoulder at the Thespians. "My boyfriend says I've got a photographic memory. One, two, three—"

She seems to be counting the Thespians. Puppy Dog slumps in her seat.

"Yup," says the woman, swaying on her feet. She looks at Axl. "Gonna need cabbage to fix my car, son."

"I got you. Let's—talk out here."

Axl leads the woman carrying the child back into the lobby. The velvet curtains fall closed.

Emma starts to sob. "I can't. I *can't.*"

Hal rushes to her, helps her up. "Let's go. Backstage exit."

Yolanda buttons her coat.

"My uncle," says Butt, throwing his bag over his shoulder, "he's gonna wonder where I'm at."

Spatz stands. "Everybody needs to clear out. But *I'll* be back for the next rehearsal, as planned."

The rest of the Thespians gather their things quickly, a couple saying *see you tomorrow,* most saying nothing.

When everyone is gone, Gigi and Piper take seats together in the front row to wait for Axl. Gigi has the sensation that their bodies are relentlessly bright in the black theater, glowing, attracting moths, refusing to disappear into the night.

"He's dealing—weed, now, I guess," says Gigi. "I mean, probably other stuff."

Piper looks at her. "You didn't know?"

"Did you?"

Piper shakes her head. "I mean, Frank was known for . . . that."

Gigi nods. She supposes that dealing drugs isn't even on the list of the "three things" Axl is keeping from her. If he gives that woman cash to "fix her car," she'll come back to him for more. Gigi wonders how many other situations like that Axl is involved in. Protecting Gigi doesn't seem quite so . . . grandiose, or something, now. Maybe it barely registers on the list of things Axl is keeping track of.

Gigi digs in her purse, passes Piper a Red Vine.

They sit together in silence, *Henry VI* notes posted onstage in front of them, candy dangling from their mouths.

They're wiped out. Tired in that way that's particular to making theater, the kind of tired that means you're building a new world from your imagination and can't quit until the dream is real—and tired in that way that's particular to now, the kind of tired that means you'd appreciate a night with a total lack of surprises, an absolutely dull and predictable experience, once in a while.

13

LOOK NOT UPON ME, FOR THINE EYES ARE WOUNDING

The Auroras' farmhouse is a century-old rambler north of town. Rosebushes bloom out front, a tumble of red and yellow blossoms carefree as ketchup and mustard.

The Thespians finished out the week with two more successful rehearsals—minus Emma and Butt. Since they quit, the mood has been considerably more sober.

On Sunday, Gigi pulls the Malibu into the circular drive and is flooded with a need so strong it hurts.

It's painful to be so close to a life you once wished was yours.

She's about to throw the Malibu into reverse and jet when she sees Piper's mother, Melinda Aurora, waving from the porch. Mrs. Aurora is wearing jeans, white Keds tennis shoes, a burgundy mock turtleneck, and an apron with a bowl of cherries on it. Her neat auburn bob hangs at jaw length; the silver streak swooping from her widow's peak is more pronounced now than Gigi remembers.

Gigi braces herself. Opens the door of the Malibu, inhales the perfume of sunbaked soil, feels her throat tighten. It's the scent of afternoons turning to evenings as she sat on these porch steps, waiting for her mother to pick her up. Gigi would insist on staying outside until dark, and the crickets started.

Eventually, Mr. Aurora would carry Gigi inside, where Mrs. Aurora would tuck her into the bottom bunk in Piper's room, and Gigi would lie there, teaching herself how to become numb.

You start with your toes. In silence, one by one, you turn them off.

Turn off.

Off.

When you can't move your toes, you do your feet. Your ankles. You must work slowly, concentrating as you go up. Paralyze your calves. Disappear your knees.

By the time you get to your heart?

It's easy, like pouring concrete into a pond.

If you make it to your head?

You win.

You can stop feeling pain.

You can stop feeling everything.

Gigi described it to me once, this ritual she created to avoid a hurt so huge, she was sure it would devour her.

Mrs. Aurora embraces Gigi, and Gigi flushes with shame, embarrassed by how easy it is to access her childhood desire to pretend that Mrs. Aurora is her mother.

Together, they go inside the farmhouse, where Piper is helping her father set the dinner table.

John Aurora looks exactly the same. Wiry build, fluffy blond mustache, grass-green eyes. Like someone who climbs mountains in knee shorts, carrying an accordion. Only instead of an accordion, it's a hunting rifle. Mr. Aurora is always improving the farm in subtle ways he explains to Gigi in clear, specific detail. Gigi might not need to repair any screen doors today, but she's always liked knowing that Mr. Aurora thinks she could, if she had to.

"Long time no see, pumpkin," says Mr. Aurora.

Gigi feels herself blushing. It wouldn't be inaccurate to say she's always had an innocent crush on Piper's dad.

At dinner, the Auroras pass plates of hot green beans with butter, fluffy mashed potatoes, buttermilk-fried chicken, saucy baked beans. Gigi inhales it all unthinking, savoring every crumb. The first square homemade meal she's had in ages has, for now, melted her concerns about the Auroras into nothing.

Only Piper doesn't seem to be enjoying dinner. She's dangling a green bean from her fork, looking out the window toward the sunset.

Mr. Aurora watches Piper, and at some point, Gigi starts watching him watch her.

Mrs. Aurora dabs her lips with a linen napkin, replaces it in her lap. Opens her eyes wide. "Piper, would you like to rejoin us?"

Piper shakes her head.

"We have company tonight."

"It's Gigi, Mom."

"Well, even family deserves our full attention, especially when we haven't seen them in so long."

"I see Gigi every day."

Piper is being rude to her mother.

Gigi has never witnessed this.

Mr. Aurora's expression is unchanging. Piper is very pointedly not looking at him.

Mrs. Aurora turns to Gigi. "Now, Giselle. Tell us how your father is doing. How does he like his new job?"

Mr. Aurora chuckles. "Dick doesn't much like assistance. Had to twist his arm. But I was glad he came to see the benefit to his family."

Piper drops her fork. "You guys just can't leave people alone."

Gigi feels panic. Confusion.

First of all, the Auroras' house isn't supposed to have any tension. It's supposed to be serene and perfect.

Second—

"We don't meddle, unless it's family. Family takes care of its own." Mrs. Aurora smiles at Gigi with a possessiveness that Gigi used to love to soak up. Someone wanting to take ownership of her care was a very welcome thing.

But what are they saying?

Did the Auroras arrange her father's job at the Round Barn?

"Dick wouldn't accept the Party Protector designation, naturally. But not everyone has to join the party to benefit from it. And we need men like Dick out there, working the front lines. Making sure we rout out those doubters who wish to inhibit our freedom to—"

"Dad!" shouts Piper. "Stop it!"

"Piper," says Mrs. Aurora, calmly, "Please—"

"It's okay," Gigi interrupts, her heart pumping at breakneck speed, trying to outpace the disintegration of her fantasy family. She shouldn't have come back here. She doesn't want to spoil the only childhood memories in which she actually felt like a child. She pushes out her chair. "Thank you. For the job. I mean, for our jobs. I need to use the restroom."

Mrs. Aurora collects plates. "You know where it is."

As Gigi starts down the narrow hallway, she hears Piper talking. "I used to think you were so smart, Dad. Now you only repeat everything they tell you."

"Piper Jean, I agree with your mother. We have a guest."

"No, seriously. You just made Gigi thank you. For forcing her father to compromise his values, because you know they're fucking desperate."

We cringe.

Gigi and her father aren't desperate.

They're poor.

"Desperate" implies that you have nothing. And the Durants do have something. Trust. A sense of humor. Integrity. Each other.

Gigi closes herself in the bathroom and lingers, washing her hands with apricot-scented soap, drying them carefully with the soft towel. The soap and towel almost force her to feel better. Like she's worth more, somehow.

She won't allow herself to be upset.

The Auroras are trying to help.

When Gigi returns to the table, creamy china plates with rippled edges gleam at everyone's places. Mr. Aurora presides over an apple pie.

As Gigi takes her seat, she looks at Piper. It's normal that Piper would argue with her parents. She's a teenager. Why should this annoy Gigi?

It's fantastic, actually—isn't it? Didn't Gigi avoid Piper all summer because she assumed Piper didn't question her role in the Royal Family?

The pie conversation is light, and Gigi can't participate. Mr. Aurora is a Chicago Bears fan, and Piper inherited this obsession. Mrs. Aurora chimes in, and the family seems like they get along again.

Which is a relief, but confusing. How can the Auroras argue so bitterly, then go back to talking about quarterbacks?

Gigi used to ask me the same thing, about the political shouting matches I would have with my father. How we could go back to geeking out over olive oil or, like, forcing Gigi to watch our vacation slide shows, blurry photos of fountains and plates of spaghetti, while we laughed our heads off, reminiscing.

When your love is forever, you have to take care of it.

You can't let these arguments destroy you.

After pie, Gigi clears plates as if no time has passed since her last dinner at the farmhouse. She used to relish the feeling of pitching in. Stacking dishes beside the sink, rinsing them carefully before sliding them neatly into their slots in the dishwasher. And she loved that the rest of the Auroras stayed seated at the table talking while Gigi cleaned up. Gigi could pretend she was part of the family instead of a guest.

She decides to allow herself this one last indulgence for the night.

To pretend, for a few more minutes, that the Auroras are just people, like everyone else.

Gigi is enjoying the warm, silky suds, thinking that it's comforting, actually, to be working at the Round Barn again—she *appreciates* the Auroras' help—when Mrs. Aurora clamps a warm hand on Gigi's shoulder.

"You're a good fairy, straightening up in here," says Mrs. Aurora.

"Thanks for dinner," says Gigi.

The swoop of silver in Mrs. Aurora's hair is so bold and elegant. Gigi decides on the spot that she won't dye her hair when she gets old, like her mother does. She'll age gracefully, like Mrs. Aurora.

"You know, Giselle, one thing you girls must learn is that ideas are seductive. A man with a dazzling smile who sings you a love song. But ideas are not real. And like that traveling Romeo, ideas lose their luster. They'll leave you stranded on the side of the road, pregnant and ruined."

Gigi stops scrubbing a fork. The faucet keeps running.

"Piper will grow out of her rebellious phase. She has us. I want you to know that you have us, too. But"—Mrs. Aurora turns off the faucet—"you mustn't keep pushing your mother away. She only wants what's best for you. Marty has worked very hard to earn his place in the party. And he'll be rewarded for it. Cutting out your parents leaves you vulnerable. John and I hate to see you in that position. We hate to see anything happen to you. Be a good girl for me and show some respect to your parents. Okay? You only get one mom. I've got the rest of these dishes."

Piper pokes her head into the kitchen from the backyard, oblivious to the conversation that just happened. "Wanna take a walk, Gigi? We have a new barn cat."

Wordlessly, Gigi follows Piper outside.

Piper and Gigi walk in silence down the dirt path that leads to the pear grove. Piper's hands are deep in the pockets of her overalls. The trees' rusty-orange leaves flash with the sun's last light.

Gigi's rib cage hurts. It's taking every cell in her body to hold in the tears.

She keeps replaying Mrs. Aurora's words in her head. Does Mrs. Aurora think that Didi Eckhorn abandoned her daughter because her daughter wasn't obedient enough? Not respectful enough? Has Mrs. Aurora always felt this way about Gigi? That the distance between Gigi and her mother is Gigi's fault?

When they get to the barn, Piper and Gigi automatically climb the ladder to the hayloft—their childhood hangout. Gigi's legs take the familiar rungs effortlessly. The salty scent of hay and animals used to feel like a trusty blanket. Now she feels herself slowly shutting down. Toes. Ankles. Calves. Knees. Thighs.

A huge cotton-colored cat leaps from out of nowhere onto a rafter.

Gigi ducks.

She's not numb at all.

"That's her," says Piper, nodding at the cat. "She doesn't trust people. That's why she's good at her job. She survives by her own intuition. Mom named her Roses. I'm like, *Really, Mom?* You're gonna *name* a barn cat? She wants nothing to do with you. Except she'll take the food."

Gigi doesn't reply. She plays with a dry piece of hay, snapping it in several places.

"Thanks for coming over tonight," Piper continues. "I'm guessing you heard the rumor that we abducted Ms. Lee, and now we're, like, feeding her pig slop, and you needed to, like, double-check if it was true? But it's still nice for me to have you here."

Gigi looks up. "Come on, Piper. I know that isn't true."

For the first time, Gigi notices that Piper is losing the roundness in her cheeks. Her face looks sculpted, not cute. The sprinkle of freckles on her nose looks pretty, just a taste of something, not like a storybook princess. Piper is practically an adult. And she's beautiful.

"I'm sorry, Piper. People are awful. And I mean—I've been awful lately too."

Piper fiddles with a piece of straw. "I used to think the rumors were because they hated us, because of Bud and Christie. I thought they cared about the things the party was doing. Starting wars and calling it self-defense. Turning Americans into Anti-Americans. And the reeducation camps, just like every other awful government in the history of the world. I thought people cared that my family was involved. But one day I realized. That isn't why they avoid me."

"Of course not," says Gigi. "They wish they *were* you. They want to be on the inside, not the outside. They're scared of you, Piper."

Piper leans over her crossed legs. "Nobody likes me for me, and nobody hates me for me, except the Thespians. Which I wouldn't have joined if it wasn't for you. Trying to be artistic, like you. Which I'll never be, but."

"Come on."

"Without you, I wouldn't have found Axl."

Piper meets Gigi's eyes, and Gigi steels herself; she doesn't want to hear about this.

"Thank you, Gigi. For letting me be a part of all of your friends. I mean—Axl was my first."

Gigi must change the subject. But she doesn't want Piper to think she's being a bitch again. Blowing her off—

"Piper, I'm so happy for you," Gigi says, way faster than normal, like she's spitting out something she can't swallow. "Listen, I have to ask you something. About your parents."

"Yes," says Piper. "They really do believe the Hills are saving America. They believe in the New American Way. They think it's loving. They believe that the party is generous. Mom binges on Success Stories. She says we need to be hopeful for people who haven't found the New Way yet. She talks about discouraging people from Anti-American Thought all the time . . . like that's a real thing. To her, it's the same as praying for sinners. I'm sorry you had to listen to that shit tonight. They're brainwashed."

That wasn't what Gigi was going to ask Piper, but it's interesting. It reminds Gigi of what I used to say about Dad.

"Do you believe in any of that stuff?" Gigi asks. "I mean, have you ever?"

Piper shrugs. "I mean, they're my parents. Of course, at first, I did. Like I . . . wanted to. But . . ." She looks down, as if she's trying to find something in the hay. When she spots the barn cat hunting in the corner, near the pitchfork, she seems to relax. "I don't think it matters if the SYXTEM works for some people. The party took away everything. Education. Music. And they act like these wars are so important, when they obviously made them up. We have no idea how many people we're killing in other countries, because they took over the news and don't report it. If the party was fundamentally good, Bud wouldn't be trying so hard to shut down every other fucking idea that wasn't his. It's like—"

Piper leans forward and drops her voice to a whisper. "Christie? I saw her this summer. She's nuts. I'm sorry, but she is. And Bud *only* talks about himself. All the time. He lists things he's done, and tells you why he did them, again and again. Like you can be talking about, like, the Bears, and he'll be like, 'Thorny had the right idea, but I had the methodology,' and the room has to stop and listen to him recount his, you know, business birth story, or whatever, all over. My father is so patient—he asks more and more questions. At some point, I realized, Oh. Bud Hill is just a human being who's a jerk. And Christie is a catastrophe. I'm sorry. She totally didn't used to be. And I know we're blood relatives. But still. It's like, they're people. The thing is? It doesn't matter who Bud and Christie are anymore. Millions of people have bought into their bullshit. That part isn't a lie. *Millions.* It doesn't matter if the SYXTEM works, or if it's fair. If Bud walked off the job tomorrow, plenty of people are ready to take his place."

"Millions *haven't* bought into it, though, too," says Gigi. "People like us. And the Defiance is also, you know. Working on stuff."

She isn't sure what she's allowed to say about Orin's internet project—better to err on the side of nothing.

Piper presses her lips together, like she's contemplating something. "Can I ask you a question?"

"Of course."

"What do you see in Orin Ellis?"

Gigi blinks. She feels her neck muscles tense. She wishes she'd finished her numbing exercise—fucking barn cat—

"Well, unlike most people in this town, Orin is a genuinely interesting person."

"Is he? He seems—I mean, no offense, Gigi. But he seems . . ."

"What? He's not perfect?" Gigi snaps. "Like Axl?"

That came out . . . harsh.

She's happy for Piper and Axl.

She really is.

"Sorry," says Gigi. "I—you know. I don't know." She keeps an eye on the cat, which is prowling the perimeter of the lower level of the barn, sniffing for something.

"No problem," says Piper. "I just hope that if anything with Orin ever feels strange to you, or—"

Wow. Gigi could physically, like, actually stand up right now and throw a bale of hay at Piper's head. Piper is completely condescending to her. Just like she was condescending about Gigi's father, earlier tonight. Calling them *desperate*.

Piper is still talking, hemming and hawing and dancing around what is obviously her opinion—that Orin can't be trusted.

Is this where Axl picked it up, his newest injection of anti-Orin sentiment?

From Piper?

"Gigi? Shoot. Gigi? I'm sorry. I know you really like him."

"I do like him, Piper. I've always liked Orin. People don't have to be completely comprehensible to everyone all the time to be trustworthy. Or just, like, decent people. Your family, for instance, are murderers. So be careful what you say to me about Orin. Or anything else."

Okay.

That is *not* what she meant to say.

Or how she meant to say it.

In fact, a few minutes ago, Gigi had been going to ask Piper if the Auroras really loved her, or only pitied her. Mrs. Aurora's disapproval had sent a hot shock of pain straight through her heart.

Gigi says, "Sorry. Sorry, I'm sorry, Piper—"

"Stop! Apologizing to me," says Piper, one hand over her eyes, the other in front of her, holding Gigi off. "If you want to say something, say it. If you don't, then have some self-control and don't! Grow up, Gigi! Just . . . !"

Gigi's head throbs, and she really could vomit.

Piper is right. Gigi needs to grow up.

And Mrs. Aurora is right. Gigi is vulnerable. She'd fall for—what did Mrs. Aurora say? Ideas that will get her pregnant, or something?

I mean yeah. Of course she would, because she's desperate.

Like Piper said . . .

But is that *all* Gigi is?

Desperate?

Gigi closes her eyes. She imagines Ms. Lee, stroking her long hair, backstage, after *A Streetcar Named Desire*. Comforting Gigi when her mother didn't come to the show.

She remembers the elated feeling she'd had only twenty minutes before that, when she'd been onstage, in her final scene. The feeling that everything she needed to express was expressible, in the most poetic language. The feeling of being whole.

Her mother had killed that feeling when she hadn't shown up that night.

Just like she'd killed that feeling every time she hadn't shown at the Auroras' to pick her up, when she was a little girl.

But the feeling of wholeness is Gigi's to re-create.

Again and again, night after night. Whatever the sky gods send to torture her, however badly they rip her apart, Gigi can take the stage again and grow back.

She can heal herself.

She has to.

No one can do it for her.

Gigi looks around the weather-beaten barn. "Piper, I don't want to talk about boys with you. Or politics. I'm just glad we're doing the play together."

Piper looks at her lap. "The play is the most important thing to me too, you know."

"I know."

"Okay."

"Okay."

The cat darts out the barn doors, chasing something. Outside, the wind is ferocious, punting tumbleweeds across the prairie. Maple trees shake violently, shedding their leaves. Songbirds curl in dry nests, beaks tucked under wings, as the big sky stares its vacant stare and the restless stars explode in the big dark night.

How I long to join them. To leave this land of confusion and rest in eternity, where I belong.

14.

FOR LIVE I WILL NOT, IF MY FATHER DIE

I used to love Easter.

Daffodils. Marshmallow chicks. Baskets. Hymns about a dude who loved sinners so much that he literally rose from the dead.

The Easter of 1991 was twisted. Church bells chiming on streets plastered with posters of Bud Hill's airbrushed face. Hungry-looking Americans lying on a sun-drenched sidewalk below a SYXTEM billboard that said, *Your Best Life Is Yours for the Taking!* While Party Protectors patrolled the streets, guns visible in their holsters, wearing American flag outfits. What were they hunting? Who knows! Not sure when the American flag started scaring the shit out of me, but it had definitely happened.

I was walking down Neil Street, emptying my wallet, handing out Dad's hard-earned cash, missing the old days. Dyeing eggs with Grandma Bowl, oblivious to Bud Hill's infomercials running in the background.

Still. It was Easter. I was a religiously promiscuous cultural Catholic, and it was Jesus Christ's resurrection day. A resurrection day is bigger than a birthday. It's an extra birthday Jesus got for being awesome.

And maybe also because his dad was God.

Point being: today was about *Jesus*.

Not Bud Hill, or life before or after him.

And I dug Jesus.

I'd always felt we had a lot in common.

To quote Billy Joel—yes, Axl Fischer, I'm quoting Billy Joel, and you can't stop me—Jesus and I would both *"rather laugh with the sinners than cry with the saints."*

For Jesus and me, solidarity with the sinners was always a point of pride.

For instance. Back in the day, me and the Fischer brothers were obsessed with the original punk rock icons, the Sex Pistols.

In particular, we worshipped the bass player, Sid Vicious.

Sid Vicious was a motherfucking *sinner*. Drugs. Assaults. Maybe did, maybe didn't murder his own girlfriend in a death pact in the Chelsea Hotel. The very existence of Sid Vicious feels like a giant fuck-you to sainthood. He's the kind of sinner you *know* it'd be fun to laugh with.

Of course, hanging out with Sid Vicious would also be a great way to get stabbed in the face.

Still.

The Fischers and I watched *Sid and Nancy* dozens of times.

But that Easter, I wondered. Did I need to change my definition of sinner? Was Sid Vicious a sinner compared to Bud Hill?

I didn't want to laugh with Bud Hill. I didn't want to do anything with him. Yes, I laughed at jokes *about* him, but the things he did weren't funny at all.

There are sinners.

And then there's evil.

Not the same.

I wondered what Jesus thought about this.

Must I learn to cry with the saints?

I stopped at the pay phone outside what used to be the local television station. The building was boarded up, but Dad and I had always liked its flat, modern exterior. I was full of wacky nervousness, the kind that can make you trip over something impossible, like a wall, as I dropped my quarter in the box and dialed the phone number I'd coerced Orin into giving me.

"Yes?" said a woman's voice.

A voice that sounded nothing like Smith's.

"Yes," I said. *"Yes, uh—hi."* All I had to do was repeat the lines I'd rehearsed. *"My name is Maximus Bowl. I'm calling about my father. But first—who am I talking to? Not Smith, right? Not the Vice Principal of CHS . . . ?"*

The voice was silent.

I watched a row of starlings line up on top of the Bud Hill billboard. Wondered which one would be the first to take a dump on his face.

The voice said, *"Okay, hon. Go."*

"Oh, so—you? You definitely aren't Smith. But you know who I, why I'm . . . ?"

"You're calling about Commissioner Bowl. I'm listening."

My heart felt like it got punched in the head.

This was Orin's party superior.

She knew why I was calling.

Finally, someone who could help!

"So! Uh. Thank you! I'm—much obliged. Much—well, okay, let's see here." What did I rehearse? I remembered nothing. *"There are, is, some sort of . . . list? If I'm not wrong? Not sure, how to—the best way—"*

I was shitting bricks.

No wonder Ms. Lee never gave me juicy parts in the plays.

This role got away from me, like, instantly.

"If your father is on one of my lists," said the voice, *"or if he is not is confidential information that I am required to keep confidential. I can tell ya that all contact with the individual you want your details to funnel down to goes through me. I determine when and how to pass those messages along. I'm givin' you two minutes, hon. Defend your Commissioner."*

Defend my Commissioner?

Holy fuck!

I remembered what I'd been planning to say.

"Okay—look. My dad loves you guys. The party. The Hills. I wish he didn't love you so much. You definitely don't want to lose him."

The voice was silent.

"Listen, Mrs.—Miss? You guys are all about information, right? Confidential shit—excuse me—stuff? I got you if you got me. That's really my entire, the reason for my call. My whole thing. Leave Bernie alone, and I can help the party."

"With what?"

"Whatever the fuck you want! Fuck! Pardon my French. I mean—I have all the information on this planet, in this whole one-donkey town, starting, like, now, if you have—a promise. That my father won't be . . . you know. You know."

"Gotcha, hon. I was told you'd be calling, and that I would need to make my own decision with regard to what to do with you. So I did give it some thought. You go to the high school, correct?"

"I absolutely do."

"Tell me about Fiona Lee."

Ex-*squeeze* me?

I removed the receiver from my ear, made a face at it.

I was talking to some party big-shot, right?

Why the fuck would she care about a high school theater teacher?

I tucked the receiver under my chin, palmed my pants looking for a clove. I couldn't hide my astonishment. *"Why?"*

"Oh, it's personal, hon," said the voice. *"Life's a personal business, all the time. But it's full of happy coincidences. Like you calling me, today."*

This person could not possibly be Orin's party superior.

She must've been an assistant or something.

And she was a local.

Whoever my dad had pissed off, they'd delegated his punishment to some peons in the 'Paign.

Not a problem.

I could handle locals.

I was one.

I lit my clove, started riffing.

"Ms. Lee? Gah. Ya know, I don't know. People think Ms. Lee is this, like, goddess. She's not all that. Overrated, basically, in all categories. What else you wanna know? There's a stash of stolen porno mags in the CHS gym closet, with the medicine balls—"

The voice cleared its throat. *"So what can I get Fiona Lee brought in for?"*

She wanted to have Ms. Lee—questioned?

My butt cheeks clenched. I tried to find a relaxed position, leaning against the side of the phone box. Forced myself to sound casual.

". . . Dude. Nothing. She just, you know. Goes around being how she is. Pretending to be important. Not even that hot . . ."

Not true. So hot. I was vomiting words.

"Your dad's in trouble, kiddo. Big trouble. They're real mad at

him. Lists are my job. I do all the lists. Keepin' 'em updated. The one he's on? You don't wanna be on it. But if you tell me a little something about Fiona Lee, I'll work with ya. I'm not gonna hurt her. I just need her to feel the pinch. Which she does deserve. If you knew the details, you'd know. It's gonna be a sort of practical joke."

I felt the saliva accumulating in my mouth. My eardrum itched.

Maybe I was only talking to a local getting off on her taste of power.

There's a problem with power, though.

And it's massive.

Even if you *are* only a peon in the 'Paign.

A nobody.

A speck of dust in the infinite mindfuck of time—

In the party, or just in life—

You have it.

Power.

We all do.

Anyone can screw up somebody's life.

It's not even that difficult.

The question was: Could I use my power to help Dad?

I felt like, yes.

If I played my cards right?

I could negotiate what the SYXTEM refers to as a "win-win deal."

The air was getting denser. The sky was bulking out. It felt like it might overflow and fall down.

"You want to scare Fiona Lee," I said. *"Catch and release?"*

"Like fishing."

Strange, wasn't it? That people made a hobby of scaring fish?

"And in exchange, you'll protect Commissioner Bowl. He'll, like.

You'll tell them he's been warned, or whatever. You'll get him off the list. Immediately. And whatever he did will be gone."

"Yup," said the voice. *"I'm the list person. I'm in charge of the lists."*

I took a breath.

That night, at Easter dinner with my parents, I felt like a hero. Not the second coming of Christ, precisely—but I can't act like the expression didn't cross my mind.

The entire next day was a clusterfuck. At CHS, I looked for Ms. Lee between classes, couldn't find her. VP Smith called me in for dealing acid-laced Laffy Taffys to some freshmen who were now roaming the hallways seeing snakes. When I reassured her that the freshmen were hornswoggled—they were just regular Laffy Taffys for which I overcharged—she made me clean the boys' bathroom with a toothbrush.

When the last bell rang, I was bolting out of marketing class when Knoxville slapped me with a punitive essay, a five-paragraph apology for answering every question on our last exam "your mom."

Upon its completion (*"In conclusion, I'm sorry I got obsessed with your mom, but I still think that she is very special"*) I sprinted to the CHS theater.

Gigi was onstage as King Henry, working one-on-one with Ms. Lee before the real rehearsal started.

"Woe above woe! Grief more than common grief! O that my death would stay these ruthful deeds! . . ."

I was sweating buckets as I squeezed through the third row to get to Ms. Lee.

Ms. Lee side-eyed me.

When Gigi finished her speech, Ms. Lee said, *"How was that for you?"*

"Good," said Gigi. *"King Henry feels everything that's happening around him. He can't control it, but he's stuck in this role, watching the tragedy. He won't participate and make it worse. But he isn't looking away, either."*

"He isn't looking away. Right."

"Let me embrace thee, sour adversity, For wise men say it is the wisest course," I proclaimed, a single finger raised above my head. *"And on that note—Fiona, may I speak to you a moment?"*

Ms. Lee gave me her demented smile. *"Are you auditioning for a Cap'n Crunch commercial?"*

"I need to speak with you about an important matter."

Ms. Lee stood, rolled down her suit jacket sleeves. *"Gigi, we have an hour until rehearsal starts. Why don't you go get something to eat."*

"Maxy, do you have antifreeze?" called Gigi. *"The Malibu is overheating again."*

"One minute, my love," I called back.

Ms. Lee says, *"We'll talk tonight, Max."*

"No—please. It's important."

"I want Arby's," said Gigi. *"Maxy, can you drive? We can stop by the 7-Eleven for the antifreeze. Axl is working, so I can use his discount."*

I looked up at her. *"My heart, I'm entangled here, temporarily. Catch."* I tossed her the keys to the Range Rover. It was a bad throw. The keys slid stage left; she scooped them up clankily.

I lowered my voice. *"Axl debugged all the restrooms last night when he combed the theater. Meet me in the ladies' room."*

"What do you want me to order?" Gigi called.

"A bunch of shit," I yelled back. *"And a large lemonade. And*

a Jamocha almond fudge shake for Fiona—shit." She didn't have the cash for all this. I wriggled through the row, digging in my pocket, hop-walked up the aisle as I fumbled with my wallet, pulled out twenty bucks, handed it to Gigi.

Gigi jangled my keys in a goodbye wave, disappeared.

I looked around.

Ms. Lee had left the theater.

Fuck.

The bathroom was lit by a single crusty bulb mounted beside a mirror that was permanently fogged. The words *Your ass or mine?* were written on the mirror in black Sharpie.

Ms. Lee was leaning against a stall.

"Thank the goddesses, you're here!" I exclaimed.

"What do you need, Max?"

"To tell you something." Hearing the urgency in my own voice agitated me even more.

She said, *"Spit it out."*

"I'm spitting it out right now! Jeez."

The quiet was punctuated by the dripping of a busted faucet.

I said, *"They know everything."*

She sighed. *"What are you talking about."*

"Someone in the party. Fiona, they cornered me. Well, I cornered them. Because they have something. On someone. Someone I—know. But then, they cornered me. And I told them about Henry VI. *And—about our oasis up there, in the scenery loft. Where we stash props and costumes. And the date of the show. And gave them specifics. About how we, you know. Pull these things off."*

Ms. Lee was silent.

"I—they—see, I can't tell you why. What they have on—not me.

I have to protect someone. And I did! So that part—yeah. Worked out great. Don't worry, though. What I must tell you is not to worry. They just want to fuck with you. Maybe you boinked the wrong dude— or dudette, no assumptions—maybe you stole the wrong baby— slashed the wrong tires—whatever. Look. They promised me it's catch and release. It's going to be okay."

Ms. Lee's nostrils were flaring. She seemed too unnerved to speak.

I held out my hands. "*Fiona, my position presents a major opportunity for us. In the future, when shit cools down. I gave the party something real. Henceforth, they'll trust me unequivocally!*"

Fiona looked above her head like she was hoping the jaws of life might appear, the *deus ex machina,* to airlift her out of this situation. "*You didn't, Max.*"

"*And yes. We're going to lose this particular production. But it's Henry VI, so, I mean, there's that. The thing is, it's all working out! I've infiltrated the party. After this blows over? Underground theater in the 'Paign will be more bitchin' than ever!*"

Fiona flicked her wrists like she was shaking off whatever she was feeling, so she could think clearly. "*They're using you.*"

"*They* think *they are. I know this. But the Maximus be a man of many masks. To trick the trickster, 'tis not so simple as . . .*"

Fiona walked past me; she appeared to be leaving.

"*Hey!*"

Ms. Lee turned around, squeezed my shoulder. "*Whatever you're thinking, baby, you're wrong.*"

Her voice was very un-Fiona-like. Very . . . tender.

This unnerved me. I didn't continue to try to persuade her. Instead, I followed her out of the bathroom like a shamed dog. Down the dark hallway, out into the parking lot, and she went her way, and I went mine, which was, you know.

Nowhere.

I just loitered on the chipped concrete stoop outside the door to the auto shop classroom, because Gigi had my vehicle.

And I knew I'd done the right thing. I'd saved Dad's life! I mean—

I had to do something.

Gigi's sleep is deep and heavy. Her blankets rise and fall with every breath.

I keep insisting. *I had to do something.* Like if I say it enough, Gigi will understand. Why I did it—why I betrayed her, and my people; why Ms. Lee is gone.

I had to do something, Gigi.

I had to do something.

You know?

15.

WE CAME BUT TO TELL YOU THAT WE ARE HERE

Yolanda is standing upstage center on top of a wooden ladder, wearing a hoodie and athletic shorts, holding the plastic Virgin Mary garden statue Spatz found at the dime store high above her head. She's playing Joan la Pucelle, also known as Joan of Arc.

The statue is banana yellow, celestial blue, strawberry red. The Virgin's mouth and eyes are downturned, like she's content to be concerned about everything, forever.

Below Yolanda stands Reggie, his arms hanging an unnatural distance from the sides of his body, as if they're levitating. Reggie is playing York, who is scheming to take the crown from King Henry. In this scene, he's battling Joan, who's leading the French army.

"See how the ugly witch doth bend her brows," Reggie / York says flatly, without looking up from his script. *"As if with Circe she would change my shape."*

It sounds like he's reading a bus schedule.

Yolanda / Joan of Arc, on the other hand, is vibing like she's possessed by the entire history of Catholicism.

"Changed to a worser shape thou canst not be," she hisses.

Gigi says, "Cut. York, Joan would like to murder you right now with her bare hands."

Reggie smiles politely, in the Midwestern manner.

"How do you feel about this?" Gigi asks.

"Prob'ly . . . not great?" says Reggie, like it's a question.

Yolanda closes her eyes.

"What's worse than not great?" Gigi asks.

Reggie twists his lips, like a kid struggling with a spelling test. ". . . Below average?"

Yolanda sighs.

Thespians are scattered around the house. Three are listening to Walkmans. Two are reading.

Spatz is sitting beside Axl in the front row, doodling in her sketchbook.

Gigi needs to work with Reggie one-on-one, like Ms. Lee did when an actor was struggling. She needs to teach him how to access some emotion. *Any* emotion.

But she doesn't want to lose momentum.

She claps, calls out to the group. "Shall we break, talk sets?"

Axl stands, stretches. "Me and Spatz have a concept."

"Which is?" says Gigi.

Spatz says, "Silent film."

Yolanda takes a seat on a ladder rung. "What do you mean?"

"Yolanda, you can act your ass off using, like, your earlobes, exclusively," says Axl. "Me and Spatz were thinking—"

"A dance," says Spatz. "Joan of Arc does a dance that shows she's the chosen one, an unstoppable force. The French army follows her. Reggie can just stand there, for the most part."

"I liked Piper's idea to project a film," says Axl. "So I found a silent film of Joan of Arc that's *gorgeous*. Hand colored in pastels, like an antique postcard. Directed by Georges Méliès. He made it in, like, 1900."

"Where do you get this stuff?" asks Leticia, who is sitting sideways in the second row, arms and knees draped across the armrests.

Axl says, "Places."

"Shakespeare with no language feels like a crime," says Gigi. "Yolanda, what are your thoughts?"

"I love the lines," says Yolanda. "But I haven't danced for an audience in years. I do miss it. It'd be incredibly challenging, Joan of Arc as ballet. I don't know if it's been done. That intrigues me."

Thespians are perking up. Closing books. Leaning forward.

"Could be fresh," says Zorro. "Depending on the music."

"And I wouldn't have to memorize any lines?" confirms Reggie, his voice hopeful.

Puppy Dog cocks her head. "You *volunteered* to play York."

"Yeah," says Reggie.

"Why?" asks Puppy Dog.

Reggie shoves his hands deep into the pockets of his khakis, smiles wide. "Because he's full of rage."

Leticia rewraps her blue-and-violet headscarf. "Straight white dudes are across-the-board twisted."

Hear, hear.

"Let's try it," says Gigi. "If it doesn't work, it doesn't work."

"Have you picked music yet?" asks Skeletor.

Axl and Spatz look at each other, shake their heads.

Zorro says, "I got a tune. . . ."

Axl tosses him the keys to the tech booth.

"If the tune doesn't suck, I'll choreograph the dance," says Leticia. "Assuming you're good with that, Gigi?"

Gigi says, "Go for it."

Leticia looks at Yolanda. "Yo?"

Yolanda says, "Fine with me."

"Be right back." Axl jumps onto the stage, disappears in the wings.

The sound of drums pounding in a warlike rhythm fills the theater. It's the Creatures, "Mad-Eyed Screamer."

"That'll work," says Gigi. "Leticia?"

"Agreed." Leticia faces the house. "Anybody want a piece of this dance scene?"

As the Thespians take the stage, Gigi realizes that she might love directing as much as she loves acting. You get to envision the whole story, instead of just one character. Plan how everything flows.

And directing like this, with everyone collaborating, means the Thespians are creating the show they want to perform in.

Not that this way of working is better than Ms. Lee's way, of sticking with the script and telling everyone what to do.

It's just different.

It's Gigi's style.

Behind the dancers, Axl reappears, holding a large hunk of plywood. He dodges them, hops offstage, stalks to Gigi, who has taken a seat in the front row.

"Beb. Check this out."

He flips the plywood around.

It's a tombstone.

MAXIMUS BOWL

1972-1991
DIONYSUS OF THE MIDWEST
REST IN PEACE

The nerve!

What, I'm not dead enough for you? Who knew Big Strong Tragic Man would be so desperate to say goodbye forever to Li'l Ol' . . .

Dionysus of the Midwest.

Dionysus. God of wine, sex, and song.

Axl gave me a nickname.

Gigi is running her hand over the plywood gravestone. It's quadruple the size of an actual grave. You could read it from the last row in the house.

My new nickname.

That Axl gave me.

Does this mean . . . he's forgiving me?

"This is exquisite," says Gigi, inspecting the Gothic lettering. "How are you not a painter or something?"

"I am a painter or something," says Axl.

"Should we be weird and keep the grave downstage, in its own light, during rehearsals?" asks Gigi.

"Purple light, like Purple Rain," says Axl. "We should."

Gigi braces herself, sees me crumpling in the street, in Rolling Acres. Hears the fatal shot echo through the prairie, all night long. Sees the scene she invented for herself to try to understand what happened, sees it on replay, again and again.

Axl leans my grave against the stage, sits beside Gigi.

Axl could tell her that I informed on the Thespians.

It's one of the "three things" he's keeping from her, I assume.

But I died before I could tell him why I did it.

Now that we know that I was the party's target, I'm praying he'll figure it out.

Meanwhile, he won't tell her.

He'd rather die himself than break her heart.

Gigi rests her head on Axl's shoulder while the music plays, and onstage, the Thespians dance.

A couple of weeks of rehearsal go by without incident. Nobody else stops by Axl's theater unexpectedly. Nobody else quits. There's the usual hum of Bud Hill's voice on the television, on the radio. Party Protectors in the streets, parroting him, in their raucous parades. Things feel almost normal.

Except for Gigi's nightmares. Soldiers' faces morphing from children to grown-ups to animals and back again. Chasing her as she pushes through stalks in a cornfield, looking for the stolen zine. Looking for Stu Perloff and Ms. Lee.

Gigi is still reeling from a particularly nauseating dream when she gets to school Monday morning. Horndogs full of unhinged energy swarm the CHS hallways.

Axl lands in front of her, out of breath.

"Come to my theater after school."

"Can't," says Gigi. "Your girlfriend and I are meeting to polish the script. After, it's dinner shift at the Round Barn."

If Gigi doesn't work some shifts at the restaurant, she'll run out of cash. While their director slings cow flesh, the Thespians will rehearse without her.

Axl says, "Cancel Piper."

His eyes are alive with a distinctive force, an energy Gigi can't quite label.

"What's going on?" she asks.

Axl shakes his head. His eyes linger on hers just long enough to get her confirmation, a small head nod, that she'll meet him.

Then he leaps away, a prima ballerina who is also a swarthy gorilla, disappears back into the crowd.

After school, Gigi meets Piper in the parking lot.

"Can we hang out tomorrow instead?"

"Why?"

"Axl needs me."

Piper looks confused.

Gigi feels an unwelcome pang of superiority.

What a miserable feeling.

She's genuinely happy for them.

"It's totally okay," says Piper in a cheery voice that does a lousy job of masking her mild case of the feeling-left-outs.

"Tomorrow." Gigi takes Piper's hand and squeezes, the way Piper sometimes does with hers. It doesn't feel remotely comfortable. Didi Eckhorn has never squeezed Gigi's hand, not once in her life.

Gigi isn't her mother, though. And regardless of what Mrs. Aurora thinks, Gigi has to grow up by herself.

In Axl's theater, the *Henry VI* sets the Thespians built on the weekends are lit by the floods: Joan of Arc's pyramid of painted plywood triangles and crepe paper flames, with hidden fans to animate them, when she's burned at the stake. The Wars of the Roses backdrop Spatz designed, a garden sprouting from cracks in the sky in an apocalyptic version of Washington, DC, the Lincoln Memorial covered in posters of the SYXTEM icon, the fist clutching the hundred-dollar bill. Capitalist detritus on the battlefield where Queen Margaret smears the blood of York's slain son across his face—car phones, briefcases, wristwatches, charge cards. Looking around, Gigi feels the same way she does every time the sets start coming together.

Alive.

Axl's head pokes out from the wings. "Come."

"You're going full caveman on me."

"Please," he adds before he disappears again.

Gigi puts a hand on my plywood gravestone in its home downstage left, in the purple spotlight, surrounded by offerings the Thespians left this weekend, Arby's wrappers and gummy bears and cloves.

Midwestern Dionysus. That's you, Maxy.

She gives me a kiss, follows Axl.

Backstage, only the red emergency lights are on. Gigi doesn't see Axl; he must've gone down to his bedroom.

A plywood rainbow from a performance of *The Wizard of Oz* is placed strategically in front of the door to the basement, which is open.

Gigi passes through it, locks the two dead bolts and the chain behind her, as per Axl's rule.

The stairs are lit by a single dangling bulb. Gigi descends carefully, keeping a hand on the uneven concrete wall to steady herself.

It's such a cave down here that Gigi is never prepared for how good it smells. Like ancient wood polish and freshly peeled oranges.

Bright light shines from a film projector. Axl's hulking silhouette stands out against the white sheet he's hanging on the wall to act as a screen. It's across from his bed, a headboard made of milk crates and a mattress on the floor, green sleeping bag unzipped, neatly tucked under.

Axl goes behind the crates, futzes with the projector.

Gigi peels off her Navy jacket and her sweater, tosses them on the mattress with her backpack. "Boiling hot down here."

"Sit." Axl catches himself, adds, "Please."

She sits on the mattress.

The whirring *tick-tick-tick* of the film beginning.

We're just diving right in, apparently.

Gigi feels the heat of Axl's body as he sits beside her, wraps his arms around a pillow.

She notices the pillow, looks at Axl's face. The Greek nose, the set jaw. His silver eyes almost innocent. She flashes to a memory of him when he was a boy, riding his bicycle around Rolling Acres.

He feels her looking at him, nods at the screen.

Together they watch . . . aw. Axl.

What is *up* with you, man?

All emotional about me lately and shit?

It's my favorite film, *Entr'acte*. A short live-action stop-motion from the 1920s. All manner of experiments in surrealism, including a corpse riding a roller coaster, hurtling toward oblivion, set to a soundtrack by the wacky French composer Erik Satie. When the ride ends, turns out the corpse was alive. It's everyone else who carked it.

A couple of years ago, Axl stumbled on the footage, told me it made him think of me. I enjoyed it so much, I forced everyone around me to watch it, dozens of times.

When the film ends, the reel keeps spinning; the bright light makes the sheet blinding white.

Tears stream down Gigi's face. She wipes her nose on the front of her thin undershirt.

She's seen *Entr'acte* before, of course.

Just never without me.

"Why did we watch this?" she asks.

Axl's eyes are totally still, like certain eerie nights.

"Before Max died, he told me he was moving to Japan."

Gigi's eyes pop open. *"What?"*

The ceiling vibrates. An avalanche of footsteps, pounding.

"Axl Fischer!" shouts a man. "You're wanted for Anti-American Thought. Do not attempt to evade arrest!"

It's a raid.

Axl yanks Gigi to her feet. In silence, they stumble across his mattress toward the brightly lit sheet.

The locked door at the top of the stairs rattles.

Gigi looks over her shoulder at her backpack, lying on the mattress. Pulls away from Axl, grabs it.

Axl pushes aside the sheet, opens a door.

Gigi rushes through.

He bolts it behind them.

They sprint down a dank brick hallway. Around a corner.

Above them, hacking; a hammer or an axe.

Axl crouches. A penlight is attached to his belt loop with a chain. He flips it on. Pulls keys from a pocket in his cargo pants, unlocks a hatch in the floor.

Gigi feels her pulse throbbing in her skull.

Axl opens the hatch. The stench of something overripe nearly knocks Gigi over. Axl aims the penlight at a rusty-looking ladder attached to the wall, nods in a way that means *You first.*

Gigi lowers a foot onto the first rung, its surface thin but solid.

She rushes down the ladder. Iron railings are cold. Rust flakes in her hands.

Above her, Axl's body blocks the light as he locks the hatch from beneath.

Gigi takes the last step, dangles her toe to find the floor, a couple of feet down.

She jumps.

Lands on concrete, looks around.

An orange bulb in a cage attached to a wall illuminates a small domed space, like a fallout shelter. There's a battered wooden table with piles of papers and a wallet. Tons of vinyl in milk crates. Two ashtrays overflowing with butts. Gigi's own clothes, a blue sweater and a yellow scarf she's been missing for, like, a year, draped over the back of a chair.

And—wait.

Is that *RiotRite*?

Is that Stu's zine?

Before she can ask Axl what's going on, he's opening a small refrigerator, removing bottles of water at warp speed. Detaching shelves. Crouching inside the fridge, using a cordless drill to unscrew a panel in the back of the appliance.

Axl backs out of the fridge, whispers, "Go."

Evidently, those *MacGyver* reruns the Fischer brothers and I used to watch together after school made an impression.

Gigi climbs inside the cramped white fridge.

It smells stale, like a hotel ice machine.

Gigi sticks a leg out through the open back. One of her Chucks lands with a squishing noise. The ground is flat but slimy.

Her palm finds a damp wall. When she feels steady, she pulls her body through the appliance, into a tunnel.

She covers her face with her undershirt to filter an even fouler stench, cow-shit-meets-curdled-milk.

It's freezing. She left her Navy jacket in the theater, and her sweater. All she's got for warmth besides this undershirt is her backpack.

Axl's boots land in the muck beside Gigi.

He hands her the cordless drill.

For a bizarre second, she thinks it's a gun.

Axl climbs back inside the refrigerator, replaces shelves, restocks water, somehow pulls the appliance's door shut.

Lands in the tunnel again, digs in his pocket, passes Gigi a handful of screws. Sticks the penlight between his teeth, lifts a large steel panel that's leaning against the tunnel wall. Holds it over the opening. Looks at Gigi.

Gigi pops up between Axl's arms. For a few minutes, there's just the humming of the drill as Gigi attaches the panel to the wall, her body shuddering with fear and cold.

When the panel is secure, she hands Axl the drill, which he leaves on the floor.

They clasp hands again, run down the mucky corridor to an intersection of tunnels, where Axl guides them to turn left.

For ten minutes, they run in the blackness, attached at the hands. Gigi feels vertigo, like she's falling into a ravine.

They approach a green lamp that offers hazy, unconvincing light, stop.

Gigi is panting but warmer.

Axl unlocks another heavy door.

On the other side, the tunnel continues, but it's an archway, built of brick.

Gigi's nose adjusts to a new variety of the funky, cheesy smell. Axl shines his penlight over three bicycles, each leaning on a kickstand, three backpacks hanging from their handles.

Three.

Two for them.

One for . . . me.

"What the hell," Gigi whispers. "How long have you been planning this?"

"You can talk normal," says Axl as he chains the door behind him. "No way they make it this far. We've gotten way the fuck convoluted. And if they get to the fallout shelter, I left Stu's zine there, your clothes, mine, a wallet with a bunch of fake IDs in it, a fat wad of cash, and some quality hip-hop on vinyl. The soldiers will feel accomplished, divide up the best shit to sell or keep, turn in the rest for brownie points. They'll wrap up as fast as possible so they can get back home to watch Johnny Carson and jerk off."

Gigi blinks.

"Do I start with who jerks off to Johnny Carson, or I can't believe you stole my shit?"

"I asked you several times to not keep contraband in your car."

"My clothes?"

"Your clothes make it realistic. Like they found the real spot where I deal with people, and can quit looking. Lie to their party superiors, say that when they got there, I wasn't home."

"You took my clothes. *Ew.*"

"That's what you have to say to me?"

"Sorry. I'm trying to pretend we're not—"

"I know," says Axl. "Look—I'm sorry, Gigi. I mean, right. I'm a fucker. I put the Thespians in danger. Doing the play in my theater was a bad call."

"No self-flagellation right now. I don't have the energy to make you feel better. Where are we?"

Axl opens his arms wide, turns in a circle. "The intestines of Champaign-Urbana."

"They smell like cheese."

"We're near the Kraft factory. Remember when Frank worked there?"

"He barely worked there is what I remember."

"Yup. But he did dick around and find this tunnel."

Gigi remembers Orin telling her that he used to sneak into the University of Illinois through the steam tunnels, to work in the supercomputing lab.

"Are there tunnels running under the whole town?"

"Dunno. Frank assumed they'd built this place especially for him. A nice quiet place to shoot up."

"Delightful. Maybe we can get married here."

"You could fit a lot of guests," says Axl. "They'd just have to sit in, like, a long, narrow line."

"Why am I joking? I'm going to barf in a minute. I'm shivering, and I can barely see."

"Joking about how bad shit is is, like, thirty percent of your charm." Axl grabs two backpacks, unzips them. "Headlamp?"

Gigi puts one on; Axl does the same.

Axl unbuttons his flannel.

The tunnel is covered in sludge. They're standing in shallow water.

Axl gives Gigi his shirt.

Gigi takes off her backpack, slips into Axl's flannel, comforted that it smells exactly like him, even though he's standing right here.

"Pop-Tart?" asks Axl, offering her a box.

They polish off an entire box of brown sugar Pop-Tarts in silence.

I'm starting to feel an exquisite sense of relief.

For the moment, my friends are safe.

And apparently, I'm safe too. Axl told Gigi about Japan, and that was that.

For all my talk about needing to tell Gigi everything, I find myself immensely relieved that she still doesn't know that I informed on the Thespians.

She never heard me confess.

Axl didn't have the heart to tell her.

The End.

The truth is overrated.

Not the lesson I expected to learn in the Purgatorio, ya know? I expected I was here to become My Best Dead Self—all halos and profound observations. When I did, the bouncers would let me into Club Paradiso, where I'd smash my face into a big bowl of nacho cheese—or Club Inferno, where I'd boil in hot nacho cheese, eternally.

Instead, I'm like, phew!

Dodged that bullet.

I mean—not literally, of course.

Axl claps his hands to dust off Pop-Tart crumbs. "The thing is, Max was an informer."

Now—

Really, man?

"Max told the party that the Thespians were gonna do *Henry VI.*"

Gigi squints. *"What?"*

Here on my knee I beg mortality, Rather than life preserved with infamy.

"Listen, Gigi. When you said the party was after Max the night he died, things started making sense. Soldier wanted Max; he got him. And then he left. If he'd wanted me, he'd have kept looking. How many houses are in Rolling Acres? Fifty? And what are we surrounded by? Flat fields of corn, for miles in every direction. If he'd wanted me, he would've tried to find me. And he might've, because I wasn't prepared. I was just so self-absorbed, I didn't imagine they'd want Max. But they did. Marty wasn't lying; Max was who they were after."

"But why Max? And why would Max inform on the Thespians?"

"The night he died, Max told me he was moving to Japan. I didn't have time to process it before the soldier started shooting. But there's only one reason Mr. Bowl would move his family. He didn't think they were safe. Mr. Bowl, you know—he's a solid guy, Gigi. It wouldn't surprise me if he saw through the party's bullshit, even if it took, you know. Time. I'm pretty sure Max informed on us because he was trying to protect his dad. No idea what went down, but it's the best theory I can come up with. Max's family was the only thing more important to him than us."

Gigi closes her eyes. "Max . . ."

"The party let the rumors fly, about an accident. They kept the truth tight. But I finally found a soldier who could confirm it. Told me the dude assigned to kill Max was ordered to keep it quiet; they relocated him to some other state. Max's dad knows, though. And—well. Every other Commissioner could basically guess. The party killed Max to send a message to his father. And any Commissioner who's thinking about asking questions."

Axl gets on a bike. Gigi does the same.

Axl looks over his shoulder. "We should go."

Gigi says, "Wait. I need—one thing. How do you know that Max informed on the Thespians?"

Axl looks down. "Yeah. Kind of a long story. I'll tell you when we get to our next stop."

16.

THESE EYES, LIKE LAMPS WHOSE WASTING OIL IS SPENT, WAX DIM, AS DRAWING TO THEIR EXIGENT

After I confessed to Ms. Lee in the ladies' room, she held the *Henry VI* rehearsal as scheduled but ended it early.

The next morning, I was in homeroom, racked with guilt, when VP Smith made the announcement over the sound system:

"Fiona Lee is deceased. Students in her classes should report to the gymnasium for drill team for the remainder of the semester."

I screamed.

After class, I found Gigi on the floor of the hallway. She was sobbing so hard, I was afraid her body wouldn't be able to withstand it.

I was afraid she'd dry up.

I was afraid she'd drown.

* * *

By nightfall, the Thespians had gathered at Axl's theater. There was no discussion; it's just what happened.

The official report was out: Ms. Lee had committed suicide.

When I walked in, two dozen Thespians were sitting in a circle onstage, arms wrapped around each other like the maenads of Dionysus, weeping and moaning.

Gigi and Spatz were sitting together in the audience, eyes like vacant lots.

I crossed the house, jumped onstage, hopscotched around the mourners.

Frank Fischer had died less than a month ago.

I was worried about where Axl was right now.

What he might do.

I found Axl in his basement cave, a lump wrapped in a sleeping bag.

"Dude," I said. *"Talk to me."*

Axl said nothing.

I dropped my backpack, stripped off the thick L.L.Bean sweater I'd donned for the chilly spring day. *"Hot as the ninth circle of Hell down here. . . ."*

Axl said, *"Shut up."*

With Axl, sadness is anger.

Didn't shock me.

Just a fact.

"Axl, I'm here, man. I am here. This is the most fucked-up thing that could've happened right now, and I'm—" I caught my breath.

Started to shiver.

Ms. Lee was dead.

And it felt like it might be—

My fault.

I inhaled, and inhaled again, and gasped for air, and groaned, like an elephant seal, and swayed, like I might fall down.

When Axl stood, the sleeping bag slipped down around his ankles like a snakeskin. He stepped out of it, stood in front of me.

"You big, dumb baby."

That felt . . . personal.

"What?"

"What did you do, Max?"

Alarmed, I held up my hands. *"I— What?"*

"What did you do."

"Nothing!"

Axl grabbed my T-shirt, like the bully in the '80s movie.

"The fuck *did you do, Bowl."*

"Let go of me!"

Axl kept holding my T-shirt.

"Axl!"

He threw me backward several feet.

"Jesus!" I yelled. *"What the fuck?!"*

Axl was staring me down like he was the bull and I was the matador.

"You did *something. You* said *something. You tried to* be *something. And now she's gone."*

"I did not!" I said—knowing, though.

Knowing that he was right.

I did do something.

And say something.

And somehow, Axl knew it.

I turned sideways to hide my face, started to cry.

"Max Bowl, you are a privileged bag of dicks. Get out of my theater. I never want to see you again."

I was crying already. *"Wait. What?"*

Then I saw Axl, his back to me now.

He was heaving. Convulsing, but making no sounds.

I went to him. *"We're both in pain! You have to talk to me!"*

"You know, man," said Axl, and his eyes were wet, I saw them, *"you act like everything is fucking funny, because you don't have to take life seriously, because you are safe. Because you're a rich kid whose father got hosed by Bud Hill's pyramid scheme, and you're out of their reach. Yet for some unfathomable reason, you informed on Fiona Lee. And you can't even admit it to your best friend."*

"My best friend? Who's that supposed to be?"

"I used to think it was me."

He did?

I wanted to tell Axl what Dad told me—that the party wasn't hosing him anymore—but before I could, Axl said, *"You wouldn't have the balls to cross me, though. That much will let me fall asleep tonight without worrying you're going to trade my friendship for whatever they offered you for Ms. Lee."*

I don't know why being accused of the truth was the thing that set me off.

"Why is every analogy with you about the size of your balls? As long as we're comparing, believe it or not, mine are fucking ginormous. I'm working for the Defiance," I said, referring to the narc-ing I never got around to doing for Orin. *"Yes, it's true; I am. Whereas you are working for one person in this world. Yourself."*

Axl's resonant laugh echoed in the basement of the theater. *"You rich kids are all the same. You take responsibility for nothing. You take a dump and blame someone else for the stink."*

I couldn't tell what was happening. I couldn't tell where we were going in this argument. Where we were coming from, what we were talking about, or where we were at. It felt like we were in a tornado of feelings; some of them were just jumping in to get some stage time, you know, announcing themselves, and I couldn't tell, anymore, what was about what.

"I'm sorry that my family is rich," I said, *"and yours is—was—poor. That it always comes back to money for you. There are advantages to not being poor, though. It's sad you didn't have a few of them. I used to feel sorry for you. That you had nobody to show you and your brother how to give and take actual love. Frank needed love, so he married the white lady. Heroin stole his soul. Was Frank a wuss, like me? Did he trade information for cash, the rumor nobody will tell you? Survey says—maybe!"*

I was about to say something else about what a shithead Frank was—Frank, who had been dead less than a month—when I felt the crack of bone against bone.

My jaw was breaking.

And I saw Axl's fist receding, landing in his other hand, his teeth gritted like if he opened his mouth, something evil would leap out.

In that moment, I understood that Axl was one of them.

Every bully I'd ever tried to outrun.

Every kid who wanted to be my friend for a while, until he didn't.

Everyone who had ever shit on my heart.

"Gosh!" I exclaimed, my hand doused in the blood gushing from my busted lip, which sang with pain. *"What a man! That's just some—"* It physically hurt to speak, but I kept going. *"Some classic masculinity, right there! Message sent; message received! No need to talk when you're a man, right?"*

I curtseyed.

Axl didn't look up from his fist.

I went back upstairs, exited through backstage, through the

side door, to the gravel drive. I wouldn't have minded showing the Thespians what he did to me, to build sympathy—

But what if I cracked and told them what I'd done to them?

That night, I crashed hard.

"To prevent me from hurting myself or anyone else," I repeated, for the fifth time, to my father, who was sitting beside me on my velvet duvet, in my room, with the door closed, so Mom, who was downstairs practicing piano, wouldn't overhear.

Dad's face reflected a mix of confusion and annoyance. *"Maximus, I'm going to need more information before I agree to lock you, a grown man, in your bedroom!"*

"Dad! I have to stop ruining people's lives!"

My heart felt like it was pumping poison. I needed to go back in time and undo everything I'd ever done. I needed to go back in time and never be born.

Dad sighed loudly. *"Teenage problems often feel insurmountable. Whoever it is, some girl—or—boy—if you'd like to talk about it, why, I'm your father. And—"*

"It's not me, Dad!" I yelled, louder than I expected to.

And I felt something inside me crumble, a scaffolding that had been holding me together.

I had to be real with someone.

I had to tell someone everything.

And the person sitting next to me was my father.

My father, who, despite it all, I trusted.

"Dad, you're on some party shit list. Okay? When I found out, I tried to talk to them—"

"—What?"

"And they told me you were a problem, or whatever, gonna be

fucked. And I said, look, I can help you. Just, get him off that list. And they said—I mean, I said—and then I just—"

I kid you not: Dad's face went white. He was the ghost of a marshmallow.

I couldn't even finish the sentence.

I got played.

Just like Ms. Lee said.

I should've gone straight to Dad.

What. Is. Wrong. With. Me?

"Okay, Maximus," said Dad, nodding in a rhythmic, unconscious sort of way. *"All right. I've been—your mother and I have been, we've been—well, we've been planning something. A . . . something. For the family, and it's looking very much like it's going to work out. I was going to wait to tell you until the night before. But."*

Planning "a something" for the family. This is what Dad says before we go to Europe.

I wished this was a moment like that. I could sit there all excited about what ancient ruins I was about to get inspired by.

Dad said, *"The Bowls are moving to Japan."*

My head snapped up. I saw a hundred masks, screaming with horror and laughter.

"Yes," I said.

"Your mother isn't enthusiastic, but I—"

"Yes, Dad. Yes. And we have to bring someone."

"Ah—"

"Dad, I fucked up. I have to make it right."

Dad looked at me like he was listening, and I told him who we were bringing. He gave me a single, solid nod.

I stood. *"When are we leaving?"*

"Friday."

It was Tuesday.

Fuck.

Dad told me what I should do next, where I should go, and I said I would, but I didn't. I grabbed the keys to the Range Rover.

Axl wasn't at his theater. I stood outside, looking up at the crescent moon, hoping for divine inspiration about where he might be. Glimpsed taillights pulling out from behind a pile of car parts in the junkyard up the road.

Axl's Toyota.

I jumped back into my vehicle, stepped on the gas.

With no streetlights, it wasn't difficult to keep Axl's Toyota in view. He was driving south. I was going to tell him about Dad, plead my case, beg his forgiveness, and offer him a ticket out of this madness and despair, the Failed American Experiment, and the 'Paign.

Axl sped past the turn you'd take to get to Weedman's Diner, the turns you'd take for the Round Barn, 7-Eleven, the gas station, food.

Now we were in the cornfields south of town, and there were only two places Axl could've been going.

He could've been going to the cemetery to have sex with someone.

But he was alone.

And it's not the kind of place where you wanna have sex with yourself.

He was going to an outlying planet of a neighborhood, a half mile by a quarter mile, plopped in a galaxy of corn.

Axl was going to Rolling Acres.

Either to see Gigi—which felt unlikely; this time of night, if she needed to see him, she'd go to his theater—

Or to a stash I know about, a pool house on the cul-de-sac on Berniece Drive.

I do hate Axl, and I know that Axl hates me.

It's true of all brothers.

Sooner or later, you're gonna have to brawl.

But we love each other too.

I couldn't see it, or touch it, but I knew it was there.

Our love.

I was counting on that.

I was standing in a cornfield, peering through the floor-to-ceiling window into the pool house. I felt like one of those goofy-looking child murderers from Stephen King's *Children of the Corn*. I had a strong urge to press my nose against the glass, gripping a scythe, and scare the piss out of Axl.

Wrong moment for that.

I went to the door, knocked our secret knock.

The rhythm of this knock was the song "Axel F," from the 1984 film *Beverly Hills Cop*.

Axl opened the door midknock.

We looked at each other.

"You look like—"

"Shit," I said.

My lip was busted, crusted with blood, malformed.

Axl covered his face with both hands, rubbed it hard, like he'd like to rub it off. *"I punched you."*

"It's okay."

"It definitely isn't."

"No, it isn't."

"I'm sorry, Max. I, uh—fuck me. I don't know how to—"

"Later. I need to tell you something urgent. Right now."

Our eye contact was complicated. It worked out an agreement. For this moment, Axl and I would put what happened aside. Just for long enough to get us away from it.

Get us to another place, another time, when we could deal with it for real.

Axl put his fist on his forehead. Closed his eyes. *"Talk to me."*

"My parents and I—we're taking a trip."

"Eiffel Tower? East Berlin?"

"It's—not a regular trip."

"A regular trip for most of us is, like, going all the way to Urbana. So."

Axl walked away from me to the Ping-Pong table, picked up his soldering iron. He needs to keep his hands busy when he's overwhelmed, so his brain doesn't short out. He was repairing some old recording equipment, something too broken for Frank to sell for drug money before he died.

"Have you ever thought about Japan?" I asked.

"That's a haul."

"Yeah. But, I don't know. Have you ever thought about what it would be like. To like. Live there?"

"No. You?"

"Um—sort of."

"Cool. You're moving to Japan."

I peered out the window. From the inside, you couldn't see shit. It was making me nervous.

Axl stopped soldering. *"Hold up, Bowl. You're moving to* Japan?*"*

"If I said yes," I whispered, *"would you come?"*

An explosion made my ears sing. The window was shattered. Glass skidded across the Ping-Pong table.

Axl yelled, "Fuck!"

Dropped his soldering iron.

Ran for the door.

For a split second I was looking straight ahead, into the blackness, down the barrel we'd been living in fear of, for so long.

I didn't wonder where I'd gone wrong.

Your mask dictates your fate.

Always.

It's never the other way around.

Gigi is cradling her head in her hands, like if she doesn't, it might explode.

Axl just told her everything.

We've both thought a lot about what happened. Not the kind of thinking where you interpret and reinterpret things to justify what you've done.

The kind where you try to see yourself clearly.

To see who you actually are.

"This is a nightmare," says Gigi. "And I still don't understand how you knew that Max informed on the Thespians."

"Ms. Lee told me after rehearsal," says Axl, "the night she left."

Gigi looks up.

"This is—the part you kind of. Yeah. Um—" Axl coughs. "Gigi, you're gonna be—not too happy. With me."

Gigi's voice is wary. "There's fucking *more*?"

"On our last night of *Henry VI* rehearsal, Max warned Ms. Lee that he'd told some party superior about the show. He wanted to play double agent, apparently. Told Ms. Lee he could work for her, from inside the party."

Gigi closes her eyes. "No, Max. . . ."

"After Ms. Lee called off rehearsal, she pulled me aside. Told me she needed to hide. Remember last fall, *Streetcar*?"

"When I told my mother about the underground show? Yes, Axl. I remember."

"It scared the fuck out of Ms. Lee. She didn't let on, because she didn't want you to feel worse than you already did. But apparently, the warnings VP Smith gave Ms. Lee after *The Brig* were nothing compared to what the soldiers said when they raided her house. They told Ms. Lee they'd let her go if she—paid them. So . . . she did. Regularly. They told her if she wasn't careful—if she was ever caught by anyone else, if she was reported again, they'd have to—ah. Yeah, she didn't make that part real clear. So when you told Ms. Lee you fucked up, after *Streetcar*, she was waiting for the other shoe to fall. Getting more and more stressed. And when *Max* told Ms. Lee he fucked up? She called it. Asked me for help."

"And you helped her."

"I told Ms. Lee I had a connection who could drive her wherever she needed to go. Get her through the checkpoints, out of town. And she said thank you. And then she said . . . *'I have nowhere to go.'* That's when Piper came out of the dressing room. We didn't realize she'd been in there, listening. . . ."

Gigi's hand rises to her chest instinctively.

I clutch my pearls.

"Yeah," says Axl. "Ms. Lee is on the farm."

For a long time, Axl and Gigi are silent. Squatting across from each other, a few inches away from the slimy walls.

Axl and Piper have been lying to Gigi for half a year. It's so big, so unfathomable, that Gigi feels like she missed something fundamental. Or was born without it. Something critical about . . . how to live.

"Why?" she finally asks quietly. "Why didn't you tell me where Ms. Lee was hiding?"

"Because you would've told Max."

"I wouldn't have!"

"Of *course* you would've. Max was your best friend. And also, you know. He was mine."

"Why didn't you tell me after Max died?"

"Because she still isn't safe. It's a tenuous situation, and it could turn anytime. I told you I'd tell you when Ms. Lee was free. And I meant it."

"You thought I'd tell my mother. You thought I'd tell Didi Eckhorn."

"Or Orin."

Gigi exhales. She wants to bang her head against a wall. But she doesn't want anything but the bottoms of her shoes to touch this tunnel.

"Why the farmhouse? That feels like the most dangerous place in town!"

"Me and Ms. Lee thought so too, at first. But Piper convinced us. It's the only place the party is too scared to raid. No matter how good their information, nobody in town would ever act on it. The Auroras are untouchable. The Royal Family. Piper knew we could use their status. At least, we could use it for now."

Thinking about Piper, Gigi's heart stops.

"Axl, the Thespians! They're gonna go to the theater tonight for rehearsal!"

"Hopefully, the soldiers will be gone by the time they get there. We can't help them, Gigi. We just have to outlive tonight."

* * *

After an ungodly amount of time has passed, Axl stands. Climbs an iron ladder that has apparently been beside them this whole time. Disappears above Gigi in a passage.

Gigi is too exhausted to ask where he's going.

Axl rustles with something that thumps and clangs. Calls down, "We're in."

"In what?" Gigi mumbles.

"Someplace fun."

Gigi stands. Her thighs are stiff. She grabs the railing, climbs the skinny rungs, remembers a playground structure that used to blister her hands.

She wishes tonight was some melodramatic wild-man fantasy Axl cooked up, like when they were sophomores and he went to live in the woods outside town for a week. He told her he needed to learn to survive alone. When she responded that nobody survives alone, he said, *"Not without practice."* He came back filthy and happy. She found him at his house in Rolling Acres, flopped on his davenport, eating Cool Ranch Doritos and listening to Run DMC.

When Gigi reaches the top of the ladder, her head pops into a room. Her headlamp pans red carpeting, red walls. Crystal balls. Studded belts. Hats with holsters for beers, straws protruding. Glasses with naked women on them. A rack of buttons with sayings: "Party Animal." "Where's the Beef?" "I'm so broke I can't even pay attention." "You're ugly and your mother dresses you funny."

Axl is looking around like he's reached the summit of Mount Everest.

"Are you *shitting* me?" says Gigi. "Did I just wait six hours inside a leaking intestine to get into Market Place Mall?"

"Spencer Gifts," says Axl.

Gigi crawls out of the hole in the floor, stands beside him. "You secretly love your life."

Axl stalks to a rack of neckties, each one decorated with a different hairy butt. As he knots his tie, he says, "My connect works the night shift. We're good here as long as we need."

"There is no *we*," says Gigi.

"True. You can leave in the morning with my connect. How do I look?"

Gigi considers Axl's appearance. His tie hangs over his black long-sleeved T-shirt. His hair is bonkers, and he smells like sweat. She straightens his tie. "You look—"

She's hit with a full-body chill. The flannel Axl lent her isn't cutting it. "I need another layer."

Axl pulls a folded square of what looks like aluminum foil out of his backpack. "Heat blanket."

Gigi is shivering wildly—how did this just hit? Shaking her head no, she walks the aisles of Spencer Gifts until she finds a hooded sweatshirt with a pair of sagging naked boobs on the front. She grabs an XXL. Takes off her backpack, drops it on the ground. Pulls on the sweatshirt. The boobs reach her knees. She puts the hood up.

"What now?" she asks.

"Every morning before the mall opens, my connect checks the store for a message from me. Tomorrow morning, you'll be the message."

"But I have to work tonight! My dad is expecting me at the Round Barn."

Axl touches Gigi's elbow. "Giselle. You're not going to the Round Barn tonight."

Axl and Gigi are lying together on their backs on the red carpet, headlamps glowing, casting them in a yellow cloud of light.

Gigi thinks, *What happened, Max?*

I've given up trying to explain myself to Gigi.

Ideally, Gigi would explain myself to me.

She digs her hand into the open bag of chocolate pretzels that's resting on Axl's chest, pops a few into her mouth. Says, "These are displeasingly stale and revolting."

Axl lays his hand on Gigi's forearm.

She looks.

Their faces are inches apart.

"I'm very sorry we didn't tell you, Giselle. About Ms. Lee. I know it hurts. Maybe I was wrong on this one."

Gigi sighs. "Maybe not. I mean . . . what could I have done about it?"

Axl leans over Gigi and turns off his headlamp so it isn't shining in her face.

Gigi feels a charge, turns off her own.

She's going to let it happen.

Axl can kiss her.

Tonight is unreal. A lost night. It will be like it never happened.

"Swear to me you won't tell Orin where I'm hiding," says Axl. "Or that you were there when they raided my theater. Promise me, Gigi. Orin knows nothing about tonight. Ever. Nothing."

Gigi feels the embarrassment wash over her, quickly followed by annoyance. "Can you please stop telling me what to do?"

"I'm asking. Please, Gigi. It's important to me."

"Fine!" She sits up. "Whatever."

"And promise me you'll go to school tomorrow."

"What?"

"If they made it as far as the fallout shelter, the soldiers who raided the theater will want to close the file on last night fast, so nobody discovers what they stole. They're gonna leave you alone, Gigi, but *only* if you don't draw attention to yourself. You cannot skip school."

Going to school tomorrow is an absurd idea.

"What about you?" she asks.

"It's over for me. I can never go back."

The words land heavily.

"And—don't tell Piper about tonight," says Axl more quietly.

Gigi wants to ask why not, but she doesn't. Instead, she says, "fine" again, lies back down, putting a bit of distance between herself and Axl, so she doesn't get any more unoriginal heterosexual ideas.

17.

SWIFT-WINGED WITH DESIRE TO GET A GRAVE, AS WITTING I NO OTHER COMFORT HAVE

Gigi follows Axl's "connect," the soldier with the royal blue uniform, through the predawn mall. Last night's dinner of gummy wieners and canned cheese left her stomach especially iffy. Plus edible underwear tastes like stale Fruit Roll-Ups, which is a thing she didn't need to know. Between that and the smelly cocktail of ammonia and lemon-scented floor wax, she's pretty sure she's gonna blow chunks.

She cannot fathom what she was thinking last night, wanting Axl to kiss her. It was mall fever. The stress of danger. Both.

Still, she wasn't eager to leave him this morning. After he replaced the floor in Spencer Gifts, he went down to hide in the tunnel of stank, where he'll do who knows what all day. Breathe rat poop.

The soldier lets Gigi out through a door near JCPenney. She walks between two dumpsters to the bus stop. It's a private transportation company with no set schedule, but the stops are the same as in the old days, when she was a kid and she and Piper would ride the city bus to the mall to buy gum and nail polish.

The sky is pale and looks sleepy. After an hour or so, the bus approaches, a lumbering roll, and Gigi gets on. Two other riders look as sick as she feels. Nearby, there are a couple factories; maybe they're coming from there.

The bus picks up speed, flies through the prairie into town.

I tell her *I'm sorry*, again and again, as if quantity can counteract futility.

Gigi leans her head on the seat, closes her eyes.

The Malibu is parked in the junkyard near Axl's theater. Gigi gets off the bus at a stop a mile away, walks.

When she sees the beast in the distance, she's so relieved she almost cries. Unlike her father, her car hasn't been worrying about her. It's the simplest significant relationship in her life.

As Gigi unlocks the Malibu, she thinks about the zine. That Axl is the one who stole it from her is a relief, and also aggravating.

For the millionth time, she wonders what happened to Stu Perloff.

And she needs to find out what happened to the Thespians.

Cigarette smoke collects under the skylight above Dick Durant, who's leaning over his coffee at the dining room table.

"I'm so sorry," says Gigi, rushing to him.

Dick puts out his butt in a tin ashtray shaped like a spade. "Heading to bed."

"You haven't slept."

Dick looks at Gigi more carefully than usual. The grooves

in his face read especially deep. "I'm gonna choose not to worry about you, Giselle. This teenage shit will kill me, otherwise. Promise me you'll say goodbye before you and Fischer leave town together. Otherwise, I'm gonna assume you're all right."

"Last night—"

Dick holds up a hand to interrupt her. "Tell me nothing."

Tell me nothing is the new *I love you.*

Magic words meant to protect them both.

The light on Gigi's answering machine is blinking furiously.

Gigi presses play.

"Gigi?" It's Piper, nearly out of breath. "So the theater was un-locked and everything is a mess, the um, sets? And everything—it was raided—nobody can go there tonight. I ran and I'm at the pay phone near, um, the copy shop? I paged Axl—I'm starting the calling tree, but also just calling everyone until I run out of quarters. Can you call people? Fuck! I gotta get off this phone, Axl is gonna call, don't go to the theater tonight—"

Gigi dials the Auroras' number; Piper picks up on the first ring.

"Meet me after school," says Gigi.

"Gigi! Thank god! Did you get my message last night? Have you talked to Axl?"

She should let Piper know that Axl is okay.

"Meet me after school," Gigi repeats.

"I will," says Piper. "Have you talked to him?"

Gigi says, "See you then."

She knows she should tell Piper that Axl is fine.

And Piper should've told Gigi that Ms. Lee is alive.

A lot of people should do a lot of things, right?

Gigi hangs up.

Later that morning, Gigi is sitting in homeroom, tapping her fountain pen on the desk, feeling dried out and useless, like an empty husk of corn.

Yes, a corn metaphor will always be the first one to pop into our heads.

Being from Illinois doesn't make you corny.

It just makes you corn-y.

I'm still here, by the way. I, Maximus. Perched on my sagging branch, unsinging. A cheerless monkey.

Gigi hasn't kicked me out of her consciousness. I suspect I'd feel the door hit me where the Lord split me if that happened. So I'm trying to enjoy myself until she does. For instance, when she picked out those metallic gold leggings this morning, I offered some gently passive-aggressive best-friend advice: *You're wearing those today? That's a choice you're making. . . .*

She didn't respond, of course.

If she hasn't heard me by now, I'm guessing she won't.

But she knows the truth. Not the truth I thought I was going to tell. Something bigger. Something with no clear beginning and no obvious end.

Sometimes, the truth is atrocious.

Sometimes, you solve a mystery, and it's like, uh . . .

Can I unknow this?

Regain my innocence?

Restore my virginity?

Unopen that door?

Gold legs crossed, Gigi waggles her foot fast, like it's a fire she's trying to put out.

Max sabotaged the Thespians.

The party killed Max to punish his father.

Piper joked about hiding Ms. Lee on the farm, but Ms. Lee is actually there, hiding.

Nobody except me trusts Orin.

Gigi will try to see Orin later, before she goes back to the mall. Find out what he knows about the raid without mentioning it.

She used to think that sex would make her grow up. She doesn't think that anymore. But maybe she'll make out with Orin again, anyway. Get it out of her system before she sees Axl tonight.

After school, Gigi and Piper are parked in the Malibu, near Hessel Park. They're looking out the window at the fire truck on the playground where they ate custard cones when they were little girls.

Where is Ms. Lee, exactly? Gigi wonders. The log cabin where the Auroras store firewood? The grain silo, out past the soybeans? The spidery basement of the Auroras' house?

Maybe she's in the big barn. Maybe she was listening to Piper and Gigi's conversation that night. Maybe Piper felt superior, knowing this, the way Gigi sometimes does when she knows something Piper doesn't.

"I paged Axl again at lunch," says Piper. "He didn't call. I stayed at the pay phone for, like, twenty minutes."

"He doesn't always call," says Gigi. "Try not to worry about it."

It's a shitty thing to say. Piper knows that Gigi knows what happened to Axl and his theater. If she didn't, she'd be twice as nervous as Piper.

Gigi pulls out the *Henry VI* script. "Let's work on the Queen Margaret scene."

Piper looks at Gigi like she just suggested they streak across the playground. "We're still doing the show?"

The theater is gone. The sets are destroyed. Axl is in hiding.

Art doesn't matter now.

Yet a stubborn voice inside Gigi is insistent.

Art is the *only* thing that matters.

If she abandons the play, she abandons hope.

When hope is gone, the party wins.

"Gigi, can we be real?" asks Piper.

"I'm real," says Gigi.

"Then will you please tell me what happened to Axl?"

Gigi sighs. "He's okay."

"I gathered that much. But where is he? What happened?"

Gigi looks at Piper pointedly. "Sometimes you can't tell someone everything you know. You know?"

Piper holds Gigi's cold stare for a few seconds. If Piper suspects why Gigi is angry—that she knows that Piper is hiding Ms. Lee on the farm—she doesn't let on. Instead, she looks out the window.

"Do you think it was that lady who informed on us?" asks Piper. "The one who crashed her car?"

Gigi doesn't think it was her. If Axl said he'd hook her up, he did. It could've been payback for the house party. What Frank said, about not making them look like fools. Then again—

"Who knows?"

For a few minutes they sit in silence, watching children crawl over the fire truck. It seems impossible that children could still exist.

"When should we have rehearsal?" asks Piper.

"Tomorrow night," says Gigi.

"Not tonight?"

"I have plans tonight."

Piper is probably debating whether to ask Gigi if her plans involve Axl.

But she doesn't.

"Where?" asks Piper.

Gigi hasn't thought about it. For a moment, she forgets the tension between them.

"Do you think anybody will even *come*?" asks Gigi.

"I mean, some will," says Piper. "Probably not Reggie."

"Some people, though?"

"Yeah. Some."

Gigi says, "Let's do it at my house."

"There's space in your sunroom," says Piper. "I'll make calls tonight. Tomorrow, *Henry VI* rehearsal moves to Rolling Acres."

Gigi parks the Malibu near the Espresso Café and jogs across the street, her legs still sore from last night's bicycle ride.

Orin is leaning against the building.

When he sees her, his face brightens. He clasps his hands behind his back. "Shall we grab a table?"

Shakes her head. "To go. Walk and talk."

Gigi leads the way to a quiet Urbana neighborhood with brick streets and huge elm trees whose massive branches interlock, like they're joining forces to block the glare of the sky.

Gigi used to believe the sky watched over her. When she was sad, its clouds made shapes to amuse her. When she was scared, its constellations schemed to protect her, centaurs and scorpions writing her fate like a monologue, waiting to be spoken aloud.

Gigi knows now that her childhood didn't end when she lost her virginity.

It ended long before.

When she realized the sky was bloodless.

That there was nobody up there writing her future for her.

For ten minutes or so, Gigi and Orin walk together in perfect silence. She'll respect Axl's request not to mention the raid, but it's frustrating, having to dance around the truth.

Gigi stops beside a gnarled tree trunk.

"Why am I the only person in town who trusts you?"

Orin nods once, like the question is normal. "I need to tell you something. But it has to stay—"

"Secret?" asks Gigi, almost sarcastic. "All these secrets make me feel like an eight-year-old."

"I know. You remember how I told you that the work I'm doing to lay the foundation for revolution isn't sexy? It won't make me a star—won't make anyone admire my talent. . . ."

"I do."

"Gigi, I informed on Stu Perloff."

Gigi's lips part, but she doesn't speak.

"I told them he was working on a subversive coding project, malware to disrupt the party's control of the internet."

"Is he?"

"Yes."

Game over, O-dog.

Your dubiosity just lost you the girl.

"Why?" asks Gigi. "Why would you—"

"Wait. First, I asked my sources, the soldiers who work with me, to tell Stu that this was happening. So Stu would have time to hide."

I sigh my icy death breath.

O, Orin.

You and I are just two sides of the same crappy album.

Gigi scrunches her eyes shut.

"I was *there,* Orin. At the Round Barn, when the soldiers came. I was reading the illegal book *you gave me.* And *RiotRite* was shoved in my skirt! I barely got out of there—"

"I know. That was—horrifying. I didn't know—they didn't tell me they were going to the Round Barn."

"You should've guessed!"

"I—maybe." Orin shakes his head. "I just needed the party to believe I was willing to inform on my peers. And, Gigi? Look at me. Please."

Gigi forces herself to take in his complicated expression. The long eyelashes and strong lips she's gotten to know so well. The shadows in his eyes.

"I needed every known actor for the Defiance to hate me. But I should've been selfless enough to not drag you into it. Affiliating with me is bad for you. People won't trust you. They won't tell you things you need to know. I've been meaning to find a way for us to talk about this."

"Wait. Are *you* breaking up with *me*? I mean—I'm not saying we were dating—"

"It felt like we were. Or, at least, we were starting to. If I had more self-control, I wouldn't have put us in this situation in the first place."

They sit on a metal bench in Carle Park, near piles of leaves in shades of amber and violet. The setting sun coats the park in liquid gold.

"You're right," says Gigi. "We have to end this."

"My greatest hope is that it will be temporary."

"Nothing is temporary," says Gigi.

"Everything is temporary," says Orin.

Orin has been letting Gigi in, to be with him, in his darkness—the place she's always wanted to go.

And he's looking at her in a longing way, like her eyes contain a faraway land he's been trying to reach too.

His explanation for why he informed on Stu fits who Orin is, the person Gigi has come to know.

She believes him, that he did it so the party would trust him, so he can dismantle it.

No one else will.

"I'd like to stay friends," says Gigi.

"That word." Orin smiles at her sadly. "I hate the idea of moving the other direction, with you. It's the opposite of what I want . . . but of course we'll stay friends, Gigi. Could I just—possibly—kiss you goodbye?"

They kiss, and it's, like, way better than it ought to be.

They pull away from each other.

This is over.

They both know.

In the darkness outside JCPenney, Gigi signals the security camera like Axl showed her. A few minutes later, his connect lets her inside.

Gigi and I agreed that Market Place Mall is haunted. The dead eyes of the mannequins; the poltergeisty pay phones; the mirrored shoe displays that turn a pair of penniless penny loafers into infinite penniless penny loafers; all those limp clothes.

After hours it's even eerier. Dry fountains, concrete planters holding plastic trees. The echoes from Gigi's footsteps. You can feel the lives that have passed through this place, the hometown dramas, come and gone.

Gigi is going to miss Orin's peculiar beauty. The way he challenged her. She'd assumed that eventually the boyfriend thing would click, and sex would be fun too.

Maybe someday, it will be. With someone else . . .

She's been trying not to worry about Axl, brooding all day in the smack tunnel. But now that she's inside the mall, she's desperate to give him something to eat. She made him a Bugs Bunny, the fat veggie-and-cheese sandwich on whole wheat that he used to order at the cozy café in downtown Urbana that closed after the vandals moved in. Axl is the only vegetarian in the Midwest, as far as Gigi knows. There are just a few things he can order easily anywhere, and the Bugs Bunny had been one of them.

The soldier pulls up the metal gate to Spencer Gifts.

When Axl steps out from the Adult Games aisle, Gigi feels something she has never felt before, upon seeing him.

Elation.

Axl is standing before her, in the flesh.

They came for him, but they didn't find him, and he's here.

With Gigi.

Alive.

The metal gate rattles loudly as the soldier pulls it down, locking Gigi and Axl inside the store.

She reaches into her backpack, pulls out his sandwich.

"Holy mother of Satan," Axl says, unwrapping the waxed paper. "You made this for me?"

"I couldn't find Colby cheese, so I used Velveeta. I know it's grosser. Sorry. I bought lettuce at the IGA. And cucumber. So it's crunchy. There's red onions, tomatoes . . ."

Axl is thumbing through the assemblage of multicolored slices of bread, cheese, and veggies like he's flipping pages in a book. "No mayo?"

"Come on. Would I put mayonnaise on your sandwich and ruin it?"

"You really do love me."

"I do."

Axl fishes out a tomato slice and eats it. Then he takes a giant bite of the Bugs Bunny.

Gigi crosses her arms and watches him chew. It really shouldn't be so compelling, watching Axl eat.

She looks away. "What did you do all day, underground?"

"I worked out," he says, mouth full.

She smirks. "Haven't lost your sense of humor, at least."

Axl swallows, wipes his lips on the shoulder of his black T-shirt. "Why do you think you have any idea what I do when you're not around?"

"Because I know you."

Axl sets his sandwich on the checkout counter. Peels off his shirt.

"Ew! What? Put that back on!"

"I've been working out for years. You don't know everything."

Gigi lets herself look.

It wouldn't have mattered if Axl were a chiseled muscleman or had a belly like a bowl full of jelly. It's just that he's standing here, alive, half dressed.

A feeling washes over Gigi, the same feeling she had last night.

Gigi and Axl have never been just friends.

They aren't *just* anything.

Axl takes a step toward her.

"Thank you for the sandwich. That was very sweet."

Gigi twists her earrings. What was she supposed to do? *Not bring him a sandwich?*

Axl is looking at her in a curious way.

This time, Gigi isn't imagining the sexual tension.

She's encouraging it.

About time you bozos boinked! I hoot. *Let's get it on!*

Nothing can happen, thinks Gigi. *I'm single again, but Axl isn't. I refuse to do that to Piper.*

"We need to talk about something," she says.

Axl nods, like he's bracing himself. "Okay."

They need to talk about this—the tension between them.

But there's something else they need to talk about.

Something more important than that.

The thing that has the power to hold them together as the world around them falls apart.

"Axl, we need to do the play."

Axl holds up both hands. "Oh, we're *doing* the play."

"Right?"

"No question. As soon as possible."

"As in?"

"Like, this week."

"We're not ready."

"We can get ready."

"Why so fast?"

"We cannot let them take this from us, Gigi. We have to strike back immediately, with force."

Strike back with force.

And isn't this exactly what nonviolent action looks like?

Isn't this a show of strength and power?

"The longer we wait, the riskier it will be," says Axl. "We do the show, we get the fuck out."

"*Get the fuck out*? What does that mean?"

Axl shakes his head. "Just—we do it; we move on."

Gigi doesn't disagree that they need to act fast. The moment feels precarious. They need to put up the show before the next terrible thing happens. Something she doesn't care to imagine.

For the first time, she wonders something.

"Does Ms. Lee know about the *Henry VI* remix?"

"She's proud of you, Gigi. And everybody. I mean—apparently. Piper is the only one who talks to her."

Piper talks to Ms. Lee.

Of course.

"Even if we got our shit together, where would we perform?" asks Gigi.

"Dunno."

"What about our sets?"

"Dunno."

"We could break into the school and make new ones," says Gigi, thinking aloud. "But with Knoxville in charge, it'd be complicated. The Thespians are coming to my house tomorrow night, for rehearsal—well, whoever doesn't bag—"

Axl interrupts. "You already scheduled rehearsal?"

"I'm way ahead of you, beb."

Axl smiles in that peculiar way again. "Always."

Gigi feels another powerful pull between them.

She looks at the grimy red carpet. Reminds herself that her momentary lust for Axl—*Axl,* of all people!—is mall fever. A thing she would've been shocked, before last night, to think it was possible for her to have.

"But we can't perform in Rolling Acres," says Gigi. "My house is too small. There's no parking."

"There's tons of parking at the mall, but we can't do it here."

"Because it's, like, your new home. . . ."

"Could be worse. There's, like, novelty playing cards and shit."

Gigi stops breathing.

"Axl." She grabs his forearms. "Axl. Axl."

Her eyes are wide. She's seeing something clearly.

"Epidaurus."

Epidaurus. Ancient Greek amphitheater, built in the fourth century BC, finished in the second century BC—a round venue, with the greatest natural acoustics of any theater in the history of the world . . .

O, shit.

O, *shit.*

Axl raises his chin. "Theater in the round."

"Theater in the *Round Barn.*"

"*Hell* yes. What's today, Tuesday? We'll do it Sunday. During all-you-can-eat fried chicken. Built-in audience."

"Whoa—really? That doesn't even give us a week. . . ."

"The Thespians will be down. They live for this dramatic type of shit. But don't tell them where I am now, or about the raid. The more they know, the more danger we're all in. I'll sneak into the barn to work tech."

"No, you will certainly not!"

"Gigi, I'm working this show. I have to leave here anyway. I can't live in the mall. I can get to the Round Barn undetected, not a problem. And afterward, you know. We'll see—what happens next. Make a plan."

"Mm-hmm. So what's the plan?"

"I mean—that's what I'm saying."

"Axl Fischer, you told me there were three things you were keeping from me. One, I assume, is the fact that Max informed on us. Two, I'm guessing, is the fact that Ms. Lee is hiding on the Auroras' farm. Which leaves the third thing. What's the plan?"

Axl tilts his head like he wasn't expecting that.

"Okay," he says. "So, there are, like, one or two more things."

"Or *two*? Axl!"

"Happening. In motion. And I need you to trust me."

"No, I need *you* to trust *me*!"

"I do trust you, Gigi. But I can't tell you about the plan yet. It's not safe."

"You are never not needlessly condescending."

"I'm not trying to condescend to you. I'm saying I can't let anything happen to—"

"You don't have that ability."

Axl takes a deep breath. "I'll tell you the rest soon. I'm not *trying* to be a dick. But I love you. I love—" He looks away, like he didn't mean to say that.

Gigi tries very hard not to register Axl's bare torso.

"—Everybody," he says. "The Thespians . . . look. I'm doing the best I can. Please. Let me handle this the way I need to handle it."

"I know that Orin informed on Stu Perloff."

Axl looks at her, several questions in his eyes.

"He did it to maintain his credibility inside the party, so he could keep working, to sabotage them. He made sure Stu got the information first. To warn him."

Axl is still looking at Gigi, like he's trying to decide how to say what he wants to say.

"Axl, you don't have to trust Orin. You shouldn't, maybe. But I do. And we broke up. Because I need people to trust *me*. It's for the best. And you don't have to tell me he's lying to me, or whatever. You can think what you want to think. But I know."

18

NOW THOU ART COME
UNTO A FEAST OF DEATH

The Midwestern United States is the most overlooked geography on the planet.

I see you smirking.

You think it's flat.

You think flat is boring.

You know what isn't boring?

The sky.

You know how much sky you can see when there is zero altitude gain in every direction?

All of it.

The sky is a searing chrome blue with jagged silver brush-strokes, remnants of the storm clouds that the wind swiftly shredded and left behind. Wednesday after school, Giselle is speeding from CHS south through the country, the only car in sight, while hundreds of starlings soar above her over acres of fields dotted with rusty farm equipment and stranded structures, a solitary silo here, a buckled barn there, the sculpture garden surrounding Rolling Acres. It's so heart-achingly open in every direction that you can, yes, to borrow the expression, *see forever*—but not only literally. There's simply no excuse not to see past your own delusions of grandeur to the horizon.

Not that we do.

Typically, people don't.

But here there's no excuse.

The Midwest is nothing you want it to be and whatever you want it to be, simultaneously; it's an ever-shifting stage set a thousand years wide, ready to serve as the portentous backdrop for your personal shitshow, however you want to play it.

Tonight is the Thespians' first *Henry VI* rehearsal in Rolling Acres. To prepare for their arrival, Gigi makes a pot of coffee, curls up on the love seat in the sunroom, and rereads the Jean-Paul Sartre play *The Flies*. It's not that she doubts her decision to go on with the show. But she wouldn't mind reassurance from the theater gods that she's doing it for a good reason.

Of course art won't save her from Death; Orin is right about that.

But nobody's safe from Death.

The question is, What do you stand for while you're alive?

"Some men are born committed to action: they do not have a choice, they have been thrown on a path, at the end of that path, an act awaits them, their act. . . ."

Gigi thinks, *What's important about the Thespians performing the* Henry VI *remix isn't the play itself. Not precisely. How "relevant" it is, or how expertly we pull it off.*

It's the fact that we're doing it at all.

Like the townspeople in The Flies, *our power is our freedom to act. We can use our freedom to release ourselves from the curse.*

Gigi didn't create the dark truth of the world she was born into, but she knows how she wants to respond to it.

Maybe the play will make the audience feel it.

Free.

Reggie bagged.

So did Yolanda.

Piper, Spatz, Xia, and the other Thespians who haven't quit yet gather in the Durants' sunroom, taking seats in a highly charged silence on the wicker love seats and rotting wood floor.

Gigi stands by the screened-in windows, twisting her earrings. She's the planet's shittiest liar, but Axl has been gone for two days. She can't hold rehearsal without telling everybody something.

"Thanks for driving all the way out here," she says. "I know it's a haul. But, as you know, the theater was raided. We lost our sets, our props . . ."

She doesn't need to continue.

Everything is gone.

Spatz raises her hand.

Gigi's eyes pop open. "Don't raise your hand!"

"Is Axl okay?" Spatz asks. "That's all we want to know."

"He is," Gigi assures her.

Gigi looks at Piper, whose expression is blank.

Puppy Dog and Leticia are sitting together on the rickety love seat.

"She totally knows where he is," whispers Puppy Dog.

"Of *course* she does," whispers Leticia.

Gigi clears her throat loudly, to shut them up. "The show must go on!" she announces, although she'd explicitly decided not to say that, the most obvious, cheesiest, basic, clichéd thing.

But apparently, sometimes, the obvious thing is the one people need to hear.

There's a smattering of applause.

"When?" asks Zorro.

"This Sunday," says Gigi, "at a new venue."

"This Sunday?" asks Hal.

"Where?" asks Spatz.

Gigi looks out the sunroom windows at the silent cornfield. In the violet sky, low, black clouds press down on the land like a curse. She imagines that the clouds are made of flies.

She looks back at the Thespians in their monochrome uniforms of black T-shirts, black hats, a rainbow of shades of Chucks.

Gigi says, "Epidaurus."

As Axl predicted, the Thespians are amped about the Round Barn as a venue, and up for rehearsing their asses off to be ready for a Sunday show.

Xia volunteers to take over Joan of Arc for Yolanda; Piper takes Reggie's role, York—an easy switch, since the Thespians took away his lines.

Tonight they tackle the Wars of the Roses, the only scene they hadn't yet remixed. It's one of the play's most straightforward moments. Characters pick roses to choose sides: red for King Henry, white for the house of York. Next stop, civil war. The audience gets the vibe of the confrontation even if they don't understand all the dialogue.

But the Thespians need to distill it, adapt it in the same music-video style as the other scenes, and make it work in their new, round venue.

Zorro / Plantagenet and Leticia / Somerset face off in front of the screened windows. Thespians representing the House of York and the House of Lancaster surround them.

"Somebody want to shout out a word that captures the mood of this scene?" says Gigi.

"Escalation," says Leticia.

"Escalation," Gigi repeats. "The audience needs to feel the escalation, immediately. There's this Butthole Surfers song I keep thinking of that seems to fit here. If you guys like it, maybe we play it while everyone picks roses."

"What if they keep picking and picking, hoarding them?" Puppy Dog is flopped on the wicker love seat, head in Skeletor's lap, black Doc Martens dangling over the armrest. She's playing Queen Margaret, who isn't in this scene. "Like they're contestants cleaning the shelves on *Supermarket Sweep.*"

"Nice," says Skeletor, who is packing his corncob pipe with tobacco, above Puppy Dog's head. "The bloodthirsty aristocracy decimates all life in the garden."

Spatz is kneeling on her leather jacket on the splintery floor. "Love that. Rose garden shopping orgy."

The black boom box from the Malibu is at Gigi's feet. When she presses play, guitars screech with feedback. The Butthole Surfers scream, *"U.S.S.A.! U.S.S.R.! U.S.A.! U.S.S.R.!"*

Hal, who's leaning in the doorway to the dining room, covers his ears.

"Why doesn't someone hide in the Round Barn hayloft, dump a buttload of tissue-paper roses on the audience for the ending," says Leticia.

"And the roses are black. Scene," says Spatz. "Beautifully grotesque."

"Thumbs up," says Gigi.

Piper is sitting on the coffee table, taking notes. "How many paper flowers do we need?"

Gigi shrugs. "A hundred?"

Skeletor says, "A shower of black flowers. I approve."

"He approves!" says Leticia, feigning excitement. "We have the approval of this bald ass!"

Ha. Leticia will *always* love me more than him.

Everybody starts laughing, chiming in with technicolor insults.

Gigi automatically looks at Piper, to share the joke.

Piper ignores her. "Make a hundred paper roses in three days," she says dryly. "Because I'm magic, apparently. I'll see what I can do."

THURSDAY
Queen Margaret's Revenge

Puppy Dog / Queen Margaret places a paper crown on Piper / York's head. Skeletor, who took over Emma's role as Lord Clifford, Hal / Prince Edward, and Leticia, who took over Butt's role as the Earl of Northumberland, flank her, all evil grins. They're wearing red roses—King Henry's color.

Queen Margaret gives one of her famous withering speeches to York, insulting his living son and one of his dead sons, both:

QUEEN MARGARET:
And where's that valiant crook-back prodigy,
Dicky your boy, that with his grumbling voice
Was wont to cheer his dad in mutinies?
Or, with the rest, where is your darling Rutland?
Look, York: I stained this napkin with the blood
That valiant Clifford, with his rapier's point,
Made issue from the bosom of the boy;
And if thine eyes can water for his death,
I give thee this to dry thy cheeks withal.

Queen Margaret pantomimes smearing the napkin soaked with York's dead son's blood across his face, to wipe his tears.

"Cut," says Gigi.

"Goddamn," says Zorro, who is sitting on a plastic side table, playing with his Zippo. "That bitch is cold."

"I love her so much," says Spatz from the wicker armchair, shaking her head.

It's hitting Gigi for the first time how gruesome this scene is. The queen wipes a father's dead son's blood on his face. This is sicker than some of the low-budge horror films she's watched with Axl.

She thinks of me and my dad. The idea that the party murdered me to punish him is almost too demented to comprehend.

I also preferred the old story. The party was aiming for the king of cool, shot the king of fools instead. I was punished by a fair and just universe, killed for informing on my friends. I'd met no gods, but I'd met karma, and she was a saucy bitch, as advertised. It all felt right and made sense.

This shit? Killing the son to punish the father?

It's Shakespearean.

Ms. Lee wasn't right about some things.

She was right about everything.

Including the play she chose.

Piper is scribbling in her notebook. "And how are we going to do this," she says. It's a question that her tone of voice turned into an accusatory statement.

Gigi looks up. "What do you mean?"

"The cloth, the blood, cleaning York's face for the next scene, all of it."

Spatz raises her eyebrow at Gigi.

"I mean—we do it," says Gigi. "It's what we do. I don't know."

"It's what I do, actually," says Piper. "While you throw out ideas at random. So tell me what you want."

Skeletor and Puppy Dog make a sassy face at each other.

"Ketchup and a napkin?" says Gigi.

Piper sighs heavily. "Which means I now need to add ketchup and a napkin to my prop list, which is helpful to know. . . ."

Gigi has to find a way to talk to Piper about Axl. Everyone is catching the bad vibe between the director and the stage manager.

It won't be long until the tension between them starts to hurt the show.

FRIDAY

Friday afternoon, Gigi is sitting cross-legged in Orin's La-Z-Boy, holding a steaming mug of coffee.

Orin is standing near the window, his hands behind his back. "You're performing at the Round Barn. Wow. When?"

"Sunday."

"That's soon."

"It was a last-minute decision. We've been scrambling to get the show together."

"Is it together? The show?"

"Well . . ." Gigi smiles.

"Together enough," offers Orin, smiling back.

"All we need is an audience," says Gigi. "Not just the usual people, whoever the Thespians know. I want you to show me how to use the internet."

Orin inhales. "Gigi . . ."

"Obviously, we can't make flyers. Is there a way to use the internet to tell the kind of people who would want to see our show that it's happening? Who'd appreciate it, or just, I don't know. Are enough people using it, that word would get out?"

"Well, locally, more people are using it than the party is aware of. And those who are online could tell others, theoretically. But—"

"Great."

"Wait." Orin rubs his eyes, like he's trying to massage something away. "This is killing me. Public performance is so dangerous. I don't see the point."

"I know you don't. But you and I agreed that a revolution takes everyone, using their talents. This is my thing, Orin. I'm asking for your help."

"I don't want to help you, Gigi. At the same time . . ."

When he stretches his arms above his head, his faded Joy Division T-shirt grazes his body. Gigi can't help but remember what it felt like to slide her hands under the fabric. Orin may not be right for her, but it's not like he's suddenly not hot.

Orin drops his arms. "I mean, fuck, Gigi. If you're doing this, you need protection."

"Axl has people."

"It's not enough. Soldiers work multiple angles. You need redundancy. I can put the word out in some private groups online, about your play. But only if you let me help."

Gigi can hardly say no to more protection.

"How would you do that?" she asks.

"A few soldiers call me regularly, gathering information they use to make themselves look better to their party superiors. They owe me. Will your theater teacher be there?"

The question catches Gigi off guard.

"Ms. Lee? Absolutely not."

"Are you sure?"

"Yes."

"Excellent."

"Why?"

"Just confirming."

Gigi can't tell Orin how she knows that Ms. Lee won't be at the show. That in fact Ms. Lee is hiding on the Auroras' farm, as Orin suggested she was weeks ago.

And Orin didn't ask why *Henry VI* needs to happen so soon. Which means he *did* hear that Axl's theater was raided, and that Axl is off the map.

There's so much they can't say to each other.

So much they pretend not to know.

"I feel two percent better about the play, knowing I can help keep you safe."

"Me too."

When Orin traces Gigi's cheek with the back of his hand, Gigi closes her eyes—and misses Axl.

Which triggers a wave of guilt and confusion she has no desire to process.

"I have to go to rehearsal."

"See you Sunday night."

"You're coming to the play?" Gigi asks.

"Of course," says Orin, sounding puzzled that she'd be surprised. "I wouldn't miss it."

The Fatal Colours

Xia / King Henry kneels behind a wicker chair in the sunroom's makeshift battlefield, strewn with throw pillows and ashtrays, substitutes for props the Thespians need to rustle up before Sunday. Xia / King Henry just watched Piper / a son realize that he has killed his father in battle, and Spatz / a father realize that he has killed his son in battle. The son and father don't see each other—or King Henry, who is hiding.

There's a violent thunderstorm tonight in Rolling Acres, the kind that feels like it won't stop until it finds you and soaks you to the bone, which adds to the mood.

KING HENRY:

> Woe above woe! grief more than common grief!
> O that my death would stay these ruthful deeds!
> O pity, pity, gentle heaven, pity!
> The red rose and the white are on his face,
> The fatal colours of our striving houses:
> The one his purple blood right well resembles;
> The other his pale cheeks, methinks, presenteth:
> Wither one rose, and let the other flourish;
> If you contend, a thousand lives must wither.

SON:

> How will my mother for a father's death
> Take on with me and ne'er be satisfied!

FATHER:

> How will my wife for slaughter of my son
> Shed seas of tears and ne'er be satisfied!

KING HENRY:

> How will the country for these woeful chances
> Misthink the king and not be satisfied!

SON:

> Was ever son so rued a father's death?

FATHER:

> Was ever father so bemoan'd his son?

When Gigi played King Henry in Ms. Lee's production, the concept of a father mourning his son had been abstract.

It's not anymore.

This time, the nausea hits her hard.

"Cut," she says as she runs to her bathroom, kneels on the pale yellow tile before the throne.

She wants Axl. Beside her, holding her hair—

Not her hair—

Just holding her.

Piper appears in the bathroom doorway.

"What can I do?" she asks without emotion.

Gigi throws up.

That night, Gigi and Axl are kneeling across from one another in the Adult Games aisle at Spencer Gifts. Axl has gathered the lava lamps, for light. It looks like they're doing a satanic ritual. A teenage hobby from the 1980s that seems almost innocent now.

"I'm lying to everyone, pretending like I don't know where you are."

"They can't know, Gigi. It's not safe."

"Rumors abound," says Gigi. "VP Smith tried to get me to tell her that you're jetting. Leaving Champaign."

Axl leans back. "When?"

"This morning, when she called me in for questioning for the second time this week. You'd think Smith would know all about the raid. But *she* thinks *I* know about it. I feel like I'm cracking."

Axl drops a fist on Gigi's shoulder. "Don't crack."

"I need to tell Piper that I've seen you. I can't keep lying to her. Even by omission."

Axl scratches his earlobe, thinking. "I'll find a way to talk to her. I've just been trying to figure out what to say. How to say it so she doesn't hate me."

"What do you mean?"

Axl looks down, like he's searching for some words he left on the floor. "Piper and I hooked up, like, three times. She's someone I like a lot."

"You're breaking up with her."

"I'm not sure we were officially dating."

Gigi feels an unwelcome pang of hope, somewhere in her throat.

Spencer Gifts could really make you nuts.

"She'll be crushed," says Gigi.

"It's going to be okay."

"What's going to be okay?"

"Everything."

Gigi sniffs. "I love that you're saying that to me. Like we aren't from the same place where nothing is okay, ever."

Axl wraps his arms around Gigi, squeezes her like he's always done, as long as they've known each other.

Only this time, she wants to stay wrapped up in them. Her mind is telling her she's not thinking straight; she's surrounded by household items decorated with soft-core porn.

But her body is insistent. All Gigi wants is for Axl to never let go.

"I know how much you hate clichés," says Axl. "But we're alive, and we have each other. You told me once that we can't let them keep us apart. And we won't. That's all that matters to me, Giselle. That's all."

Confession:

I'm starting to feel incredibly left out.

Everybody's just rolling along, adapting to these ever-shifting circumstances like they've had ten thousand years of therapy.

Meanwhile, I lie here, literally rotting. Stranded at the bus stop, waiting for my ride to Heaven or Hell, but the bus ain't comin', and I can't do anything about it.

I mean, I've gathered intel. Drawn conclusions. Figured out Axl's mysterious third secret—but so what? If Gigi wasn't such a horndog, fantasizing about doing the wild thing with Axl, she'd know too.

Nobody gives a flying fart what I know, and frankly, neither do I.

And in the deepest of all ironies, I'm stuck watching *Henry VI*! Again and again!

Night after night!

I wish there were a concession stand in the Purgatorio. Popcorn, candy corn, and other corn syrup products, so I could stuff my undead feelings about all this.

I'm praying 24-7 to the goddesses—Aphrodite, Cinderella, Diana Ross, Judy Garland, Meryl Streep—that after the Thespians take their bows, an angel wearing a feather-trimmed negligee from Victoria's Secret will abduct me in her chariot and carry my tired ass home.

Home, where I can hang my masks for eternity.

Home, to rest my weary soul.

SATURDAY
Dress Rehearsal

Gigi is going to the kitchen to microwave a pizza before dress rehearsal when she sees, through the narrow window beside her front door, Piper, sitting on her stoop.

She's half an hour early.

When Gigi opens the door, Piper's eyes are puffy, and her hair is wet and stringy, like she just took a shower. She comes inside carrying a duffel bag of props.

Gigi says, "Hey . . ."

Piper walks past Gigi, drops the bag. Tosses her coat on the wooden bench in the entryway, kicks off her Chucks.

"Axl broke up with me. He's in love with someone else, apparently." Piper spits the words like arrows.

Gigi is confused. "He— What?"

"You cannot step out of the spotlight for five seconds. Are you happy now?"

"I mean—" Gigi shakes her head.

"When were you going to tell me? God!"

"You think—*me*? No! Axl and I aren't," Gigi stammers. "We've never . . . I mean, *I'm* not . . ."

But . . . isn't she?

Gigi looks up at the popcorn ceiling, white paint flaking around the damp spots. Feels her head getting lighter.

It was a fantasy. Induced by stress and red carpet and posters of people in bathing suits draped over sports cars.

She isn't trying to break them up.

She isn't!

Gigi feels the room getting hotter.

"No, Giselle," says Piper. "You're never happy. You're just fucking *sad*. Sometimes I don't even feel sorry for you. You're the most self-absorbed person I know."

Gigi's face crumples like a tissue.

Piper stares at her coldly as Gigi starts to cry.

Gigi is choking on the pain of the truth. Sunk by the absolute fact that Piper is right.

Gigi is sad.

So, so very sad.

"Nothing happened between us," says Gigi through the tears. "I've never told Axl how I feel. I didn't even know how I felt until, like, I don't know . . ."

Piper says, "*Please.* Give it up!"

Gigi keeps crying. Holding her belly loosely with her limp hands. Crying the way she never allowed herself to cry when she was a little girl.

Piper is frowning now; I suspect that the depth of her anger has been reached.

She and Axl only hooked up, like, three times.

And the whole time, Piper knew who he was really in love with.

I mean, she isn't blind.

I'm not in Piper's head right now; I'm just body-language-reading. It's like lipreading, but you get to make more shit up.

Piper looks at her watch. "You get to be miserable for ten more minutes, then clean up for rehearsal. I'll be in your bedroom. You got snot on your shirt."

Gigi is pretty sure Piper said she was staying for rehearsal, but she must've heard her wrong.

Gigi goes down the hallway to the bathroom. She needs to hide in there and finish crying. Now that she's started, ten minutes isn't gonna cut it, but if it's all she has, she's taking every second.

When the Thespians arrive, Gigi is still in the bathroom.

Sitting on the toilet, lid closed. Safe in the room where she used to take baths, yellow tiles the washed-out color of something scrubbed half to death.

Before theater, Gigi was afraid of people. They seemed to have so much power over her. They said and did things so quickly. With such clarity. Everyone seemed to know what they were doing.

Hiding in the bathroom, Gigi knows what she's doing.

She's giving up.

Piper nailed it. Gigi can't step out of the spotlight for five seconds.

Orin is right too. Artists only care about attention. They don't change anything.

Nobody needs to see Shakespeare tomorrow night.

People should stay home, where it's safe. Watch a sitcom, eat a burger. Go to sleep and enjoy their silent dreams. Live their lives inside their heads, where they can't hurt anyone or get hurt.

There's pounding on the door. "Everyone is waiting for you, Giselle. Congrats on getting the attention you so desperately . . ." Piper pauses, like she's got to control something or redirect it. "It's dress rehearsal. Okay? It's time."

"I'm not doing the show," says Gigi quietly.

"Oh, get *over* yourself." Piper pauses again; changes her tone. "Just—come do your job."

Her job.

That's all it is.

Piper is telling Gigi to do it, and it seems like she'll be pissed if she doesn't.

Fine.

For now, that's reason enough.

* * *

It's the most bizarre dress rehearsal the Thespians have ever experienced.

Which, as far as most of them are concerned, makes it the best one.

They've never rehearsed in the venue where they'll be performing. Random customers in the audience will have no idea what's happening. And nobody knows what lights and sound will be like, because the tech guy is in hiding. They haven't discussed costumes, so nobody knew what to wear. Calling what's happening Saturday night in Rolling Acres "dress rehearsal" is like calling an apple a clam.

It takes all of Gigi's energy to work through potential scenarios with the troupe. For the next several hours, she forgets herself entirely.

It's an incredible relief.

Theater has always allowed Gigi to forget her own story for a while. Set aside her fears and live with purpose.

She needs it now.

Even if it's selfish and changes nothing.

She needs theater to survive.

The mood is optimistic as the Thespians funnel out the Durants' front door. Overcompensating, perhaps, for the fear they must feel about tomorrow. Gigi high-fives everybody, reassuring them for the millionth time that they'll get free fried chicken at the Round Barn after the show.

Piper is the last to leave, dragging her duffel bag outside. Gigi hadn't noticed how heavy it was before.

"Can I help you get that to your car?" Gigi asks, reaching for a dangling strap.

"No," snaps Piper.

Gigi's eye catches on something sticking out of the bag.

The edge of a sweater sleeve, hot pink with black zebra stripes.

Gigi's sweater.

"Get home safe," says Gigi.

Piper ignores her.

Gigi closes the door, flips on the porch light.

Well, you know.

Even Piper gets to lose her chill sometimes.

Gigi hopes she took a pair of earrings while she was at it.

WOMEN ARE SOFT, MILD, PITIFUL AND FLEXIBLE; THOU STERN, OBDURATE, FLINTY, ROUGH, REMORSELESS

She can't park the Malibu at the mall, so after dress rehearsal, Gigi takes the bus. It's nearly midnight, but Gigi needs to go over the finalized *Henry VI* script with Axl so he can run tech tomorrow.

The bus rolls north, in the dark, past billboards of Bud and Christie Hill, faces the color of canaries, hair all gloss.

The billboards are all that's lit up out here.

All the light you can see.

Gigi feels as confident as she can imagine feeling about performing *Henry VI* in her Midwestern Epidaurus. She always feels like she's acting when she's working at the Round Barn anyway.

She remembers when Ms. Lee told the Thespians about the Living Theater, in New York City. Oldest experimental theater group in the United States. If they still exist, we don't know about it. But back in the day, they were putting up the new shit, the hot shit. Brecht. Gertrude Stein.

And, in 1963, the anti-authoritarian manifesto *The Brig*. The Thespians' first underground production with Ms. Lee.

Doing Shakespeare at the Round Barn is the type of thing the Living Theater would've done. Dive-bombing a public space. Surprising the audience.

People talk like things that matter happen only in New York, or California.

But we're doing it here, Maxy.

We're guerrillas in Illinois.

Gigi is speaking to me.

Why?

Because . . . she loves me.

I did the best I could, and she knows it.

And finally, so do I.

Maybe that's why I've been stuck in Purgatorio.

Until you forgive yourself, there's no way out.

I know she's only imagining me, but I respond anyway.

You're doing it, Gigi, I tell her. *You're an official riot grrrl.*

Gigi watches the fields, all mud from last night's storm. As the bus swerves into the mall parking lot, she sees the low, dark buildings, imagines Axl inside. Doing push-ups. Eating Cheez Whiz. Wanting to protect Gigi from anything bad that could happen to her in this life.

She's so frustrated with him, for so many reasons.

But she does love him.

What kind of love, she doesn't know.

* * *

Axl is kneeling on the floor of Spencer Gifts, flipping through the final version of the *Henry VI* script. Noting changes, marking cues for sound and light.

Gigi is sitting cross-legged across from him, watching him closely. His serious brow. His huge hands. Wondering if she'd ever recover if she lost Axl. Whether there'd be anything she'd regret saying, or not saying, if Axl was gone.

"I'm going in to the Round Barn early tomorrow, to set up," he says. "Stereo system is decent, and the lights in the dining room are all on dimmers. If I accomplish half of what I think I can, rewiring, it'll feel like a real theater. I'll hide a video camera so I can watch in real time, get the cues right, and record the show. Just gotta work around your dad."

"Dad won't want to know what's happening."

"Believe me, I know."

Gigi takes in the thin red carpet, the emergency lights, the dirty-jokey knickknacks that comprise Spencer Gifts. The sensation of the recirculating air drying her eyes. Observes how normal it's starting to seem that this is their office.

"Axl, I need you to tell me the third thing you're keeping from me."

He exhales in a puff. "I know. So . . . look. You know I've never wanted to leave Champaign."

Gigi blinks.

What?

"But Ms. Lee can't stay," he says. "If the soldiers find her, it's over. Or Piper's parents. I mean, fuck. Piper can't live with them anymore. Piper and Ms. Lee have both gotta go. And I'm still tight with Ito. . . ."

Ito, the bassist from Frank's old band, Pater Cida.

"They asked me to come with them," says Axl.

Gigi's stomach falls into a bottomless pit.

"Where?"

"Chicago."

That Defiance art commune, in Chicago, Gigi recalls a Thespian mentioning, sometime back.

"And you said . . . yes."

"No fucking way. I said *no.* For weeks. Finally, Piper said, fine. Asked me what my plan was. My *plan,* Gigi. Like I've ever had the luxury of creating a fucking road map. I'm like, my plan? My plan is to NOT DIE. Piper let me rant a bit before she shut that down. *'You don't have the right to be a nihilist. You survived. Ms. Lee survived. I'm here, and so is Gigi.'* I said, exactly. And I go nowhere without Giselle. We argued about it after my party. I said, we both go, or you go, without me."

Axl locks eyes with Gigi like he needs to drive this home.

"But I do not trust Orin. I do not. I will never. So I couldn't tell you. Because I will not fuck things up for Ms. Lee. I don't even like Chicago. But I get why—I mean, it's, of all the options, especially now . . ." Axl's nostrils flare. "If I'm going, I need you to come. I mean—I want you to."

"When are you leaving?"

A pause.

She said *you,* not we.

"Tomorrow night after the show."

Gigi laughs quietly, a breathy laugh, the way you laugh when you're astonished about something that shouldn't surprise you at all. "The plan was to kidnap me."

"Not— Come on."

"No. No, you weren't going to kidnap me. . . . You thought it through. You arranged this with my father."

Axl looks down. "I didn't tell Dick *when*. I just asked for a connect with his friend Mosquito. I needed an Oldsmobile Cutlass Supreme, like the soldiers drive. He knew why. I have a driver, obviously. I put it out there. I asked your dad, if I ever leave town with Gigi, will you kill me. As I mentioned, my plan is to not die, so. Anyway, he said, *'I expected we'd have a conversation like this someday. Take care of her.'*"

"How utterly medieval of you. You and Dad worked it all out. You were gonna go *Seven Brides for Seven Brothers* on me. The men agree, the woman protests, but ultimately she loves her new life."

Axl sniffs. "Ouch."

"You are such an absolute dumb boy."

"Yeah. I'm a boy. Often dumb. But that isn't the entire issue. We're all trying, you know? I mean—Chicago? Giselle, I have *zero* desire. You know this. As in, *zero*."

Gigi presses her lips together, closes her eyes.

Axl's plan is flat-out ridiculous. It wouldn't have worked, throwing Gigi into a SYXTEM Olds after the show. She would've been furious. She would've refused to go.

But that's not how it played out.

"I find this hard to swallow," says Gigi.

Axl holds out a hand weakly. "Look, I'm very sorry," he says, his voice uneven. "I did not at all intend to be a jockstrap about this."

"All men are jockstraps, on some level."

"False."

"I've seen your pornography collection. It's not exactly a feminist film library."

"Oh Jesus Christ. You sound like Max."

"Max was right sometimes."

"Yes." Axl's eyes are weary. He's lost weight this week, despite Gigi's sandwiches. "He absolutely was. But if you *do* decide to come. If you do decide to—trust me. I just, I might—*gently* ask. If you would not tell Orin that we're leaving. And . . . please, Gigi. Humor me, and don't tell him about the play."

Gigi presses her lips together.

Orin is providing an extra layer of protection for *Henry VI*. The soldiers who owe him will help prevent the Round Barn from being raided.

He's also providing the audience.

Axl doesn't know these things.

Now Gigi can't tell him. If she does, he might try to call off the show.

Gigi will tell Axl as much truth as she can.

Just like he did.

"Orin is coming to the show."

"Oh."

"Yeah."

"Okay."

"But I won't tell him the rest."

"As in?"

"I won't tell him I'm leaving with you, after."

MY CROWN IS IN MY HEART, NOT ON MY HEAD

Sunday morning in Rolling Acres, Gigi takes a long, hot shower. Washes her shag of rapidly growing hair with coconut shampoo. Switches around her earrings, replacing the loops with studs, the studs with loops.

Dick Durant is still sleeping from his Saturday-night shift.

She promised she'd tell him goodbye. And she will, tonight at the Round Barn, before the Thespians' one and only performance of *Henry VI*.

Gigi limits her makeup to a quality red lipstick she splurged on once, from Carson Pirie-Scott, a shade that reminds her of apples. Apples for fall. She's also wearing a white turtleneck sweater and a silky white skirt from the 1970s that she bought with me at a garage sale in the Castles at Worcestershire.

She slips on her ruby Chucks to take a walk.

Her first stop is the house she still thinks of as the Fischers'. The pale blue siding, the backyard sycamore tree. The new owners put a plastic gymnasium in the front yard for their toddlers, two kids who will grow up under the New American Way. To them, the party won't feel like a darkness our eyes have slowly adjusted to. It'll just be how life is.

She steps around piles of dog shit, spies the culprits, a handful of mutts foraging in an overturned garbage can they've rolled into the drainage ditch.

The sky is the color of mud. It's not the least bit warm out, but it's not freezing yet. It's the type of dreary autumn morning when you're forced to let go of last summer forever.

And Gigi is ready to do this, even if it means letting go of the wish that it didn't really happen.

She needs to let her best friend rest in peace.

And I need to let her let go of me.

I bit the bullet at the end of her very own street, Berniece Drive.

Now Gigi must make a pilgrimage to the place she's spent so much energy imagining. It's been waiting for her, steps from home.

When she reaches the cul-de-sac, the scene appears before her, overlaid on the landscape like a hologram.

Night falls.

The wind blows her skirt around her bare ankles.

She sees me, huffing and puffing her way.

Hears me thinking, *You know what, Dad? Your coworkers are some real ass-pods. I can't fucking wait to get to Japan.*

Watches Axl, the back of his flannel shirt, as he climbs a fence.

She faces me. When the shot rings out—the second and final shot of the night—I stumble into her arms.

She holds me as I heave, and the pain shoots through my body, electrifying me, shutting down my nervous system. She strokes my cheeks as my thoughts turn to smoke and the hot blood begins its long leak out.

She places her palm over the wound in the back of my head. Feels the sticky shards of my skull. My tangled hair matted with my blood. I smell of iron, and Ralph Lauren cologne, and smoke, and doughnuts.

My body is heavy and warm.

With Gigi, I was laughter. Dirty jokes and boundless glee.

I used to wonder if Axl was right, that my friendship with Gigi was shallow.

It wasn't.

We shared the most mysterious connection.

We were baffled, together.

Gigi kneels, lowering me to the asphalt. Tears stream down her face as she curls up beside me.

I'm sorry, Max. That you had to die alone.

I wasn't alone, Gigi, I tell her. *Since the day we met, I've had you.*

Gigi weaves between tall cocktail tables to check in for her waitress shift and greet her father at the Round Barn bar, feeling like tonight is the opening of a play in an actual theater.

Painfully and blissfully aware that every instant only happens once.

"Evening," Dick calls wearily, from behind the bar, as he looks his daughter up and down.

She's not wearing her uniform. In addition to her all-white outfit, she's carrying a backpack of essentials.

"Hey, Dad. Someone is gonna stop by tonight."

Dick looks around. A cocktail waitress beside the jukebox is rolling silverware.

"Coulda waited for me to let him in, rather than screwing with my locks."

Axl is already here. Gigi tries to think of how to say what she needs to say, but her father gets there first.

"Must be tonight that you're blowing this pop stand. Lemme say goodbye now."

Some bartenders can read minds; Gigi is sure of it.

They embrace.

"I love you, Dad."

Dick pulls away. "I've decided I'm not gonna worry about you."

"You told me that already."

"Yeah, well. If I say it often enough, maybe it'll turn true."

Gigi is in the kitchen contemplating the steam drawer of dinner rolls, trying to convince herself that her guts can handle half of one before the show, when Piper grabs her elbow.

"The restaurant is packed. Xia seated as many people as she can; some are standing by the walls."

Piper, born stage manager, total professional.

Piper, who is leaving town after the show.

With Gigi.

And Gigi's pink-and-black-striped sweater.

Piper is shaking Gigi's arm. "Wake up, G. Puppy Dog is a no-show. Xia volunteered to play Joan of Arc *and* Queen Margaret, in addition to Bedford. Apparently, she memorized everybody's lines, so."

"Xia memorized everything?"

Piper nods.

Gigi couldn't love the freshman more.

"But that means we need you to take over as King Henry," says Piper. "Do you want a hard copy, or do you remember the lines?"

Gigi looks at Piper's adult face. Long, narrow, blush the color of apricots, little bumps where her makeup covers the pimples, eyes that complex shade of cinnamon, like a tea.

Piper is trying to shove a script into Gigi's hands. "Take it. Just in case."

"Thanks for packing my bag."

Piper flinches. "We have no time for this now. It's places."

"Two seconds," says Gigi, looking at the script she's now holding. Looking around the kitchen, where the new cooks pretend not to hear what's going on.

For the next hour, Gigi needs to focus.

Theater gets her through everything.

And it's going to get her through her last night in Champaign.

She also needs to ingratiate herself with the cocktail waitress. If Epidaurus is as packed as Piper says it is, and Gigi is playing King Henry?

She's gonna need help on the floor.

Guess what, folks.

The internet works.

The Round Barn dining room has never been so packed with bodies. Kids from CHS, Urbana, the Thespians' siblings and friends, art-punk kids in their early twenties leaning against the curved wall like some wandering hard-core orchestra. There are also random customers who don't know what's about to happen, here for the all-you-can-eat fried-chicken buffet.

Luckily, when teenagers commandeer a bunch of tables at a restaurant, they order the bare minimum required by that restaurant so as not to be kicked out. The cocktail waitress will have to shake a leg to keep up with the refills, but it's doable; for a quarter of the customers, "dinner service" will be coffee and pop.

Knoxville and Derry are here too. Gigi almost feels guilty.

She'd promised them anonymity on fried-chicken Sundays, and they're getting exactly none. Every new group of students who tumble in together stops at their booth to say hi. Knoxville looks like she's trying to shrink into her yellow mock turtleneck. Derry takes the opposite approach, overcompensating. Talking too loudly, and at great length, with every student, like he's chaperoning a school function.

Gigi spends a few minutes hiding in the server station in the center of the barn, enjoying its strange acoustics. Listening to fragments of various conversations, soaking up the audience's energy.

People came tonight because they need to experience something. Something to slice open their numbness, to make them feel.

Shock. Wonder. Terror. Excitement. Horniness.

Anything.

Tonight, it's the Thespians' job to make the audience feel alive.

And Axl is somewhere in this building right now, risking his life for his first sound cue.

Axl, who is leaving town with Gigi tonight.

Gigi pokes her head out of the server station, looks toward the hostess stand; Xia feels her looking, turns around. They both nod.

Curtain up, horndogs!

Welcome to the theatron.

Thespians, may you break your faces.

Everybody else, please.

Enjoy the show.

Xia picks up the receiver of the phone at the hostess stand, presses the intercom button. The restaurant lights dim except the one above Xia, which brightens.

BEDFORD:

> Hung be the heavens with black, yield day to night!
> Comets, importing change of times and states,
> Brandish your crystal tresses in the sky,
> And with them scourge the bad revolting stars
> That have consented unto Henry's death:
> King Henry the Fifth, too famous to live long.
> England ne'er lost a king of so much worth.

Apparently, Axl's rewiring was successful. Xia's lines—Bedford mourning the death of Henry V, King Henry's father—are heard through multiple speakers in the amphitheater.

The dining room quiets.

Normal customers look confused.

A light goes up on a stool in the dining room. Skeletor / Gloucester is seated on it, swathed in his green crushed-velvet cape, a doll representing baby King Henry in his arms.

GLOUCESTER:

> I'll to the Tower with all the haste I can
> To view th' artillery and munition,
> And then I will proclaim young Henry king.

Axl hits the sound cue. The dining room fills with the fast drums and upbeat chord progression of the MC5 song "The American Ruse."

> *"They told you in school about freedom*
> *But when you try to be free, they never let ya."*

The cocktail waitress is frozen in her tracks beside a booth crammed with CHS students.

Gigi puts on one of the royal blue masks that Spatz made to represent the military.

Soldiers (Gigi, Zorro, Leticia, and Hal, all wearing royal blue masks) swarm the baby King Henry, dancing violently, thrashing and head-banging.

Gloucester tosses the infant king into the mosh pit.

Leticia's choreography energizes the audience. You can feel the heat pulsing through the crowd.

Axl turns down the volume. The soldiers keep dancing, and Spatz / Exeter reads from a script, to get everyone amped about warring with France:

EXETER:

We mourn in black; why mourn we not in blood?

Henry is dead and never shall revive.

Upon a wooden coffin we attend,

And Death's dishonorable victory

We with our stately presence glorify,

Like captives bound to a triumphant car.

What? Shall we curse the planets of mishap

That plotted thus our glory's overthrow?

Or shall we think the subtle-witted French

Conjurers and sorcerers, that, afraid of him,

By magic verses have contrived his end?

Violet light flashes in the hayloft. Changing venues from Axl's theater to the restaurant meant scrapping the silent *Joan of Arc* film—nowhere to project it. So in the Rolling Acres rehearsals, the Thespians decided to have Joan appear upstairs, to add variety to the staging. And with Yolanda out, they cut the dance. To-night, Joan of Arc has lines.

Xia appears upstairs in the light, a swath of celestial white fabric draped over her shoulder, a silver sword on a belt around her waist.

Joan of Arc is trying to convince the French king to let her lead the battle with the English. She challenges him to prove her might as a warlord.

JOAN OF ARC:
Dauphin, I am by birth a shepherd's daughter,
My wit untrained in any kind of art.
Heaven and Our Lady gracious hath it pleased
To shine on my contemptible estate.
Lo, whilst I waited on my tender lambs,
And to sun's parching heat displayed my cheeks,
God's Mother deignèd to appear to me,
And in a vision full of majesty
Willed me to leave my base vocation
And free my country from calamity.
Her aid she promised and assured success.
In complete glory she revealed herself;
And whereas I was black and swart before,
With those clear rays which she infused on me
That beauty am I blest with, which you may see.
Ask me what question thou canst possible,
And I will answer unpremeditated.
My courage try by combat, if thou dar'st,
And thou shalt find that I exceed my sex.
Resolve on this: thou shalt be fortunate
If thou receive me for thy warlike mate.

The audience is silent, even the fried-chicken people.

Xia has their full attention.

Gigi smiles.

Another violet light appears over Zorro / King Charles, standing with his chest thrust out at the bottom of the stairs to the hayloft, brandishing a sword.

Brandishing.

I've always wanted to say that.

KING CHARLES:

Then come, a' God's name! I fear no woman.

JOAN OF ARC:

And while I live, I'll ne'er fly from a man.

Zorro / King Charles draws his weapon, hops up the bottom three steps. Xia whips out hers, and they engage in a sword fight on the stairs.

It's true, what Axl said.

Thespians *live* for this shit.

Gigi checks on the audience. *Everybody is paying attention. They're awake and curious. They're willing to experience a certain amount of danger to see what happens next. Even I want to know what's going to happen next!*

Me too, Gigi.

Me too.

Strange as it may sound, the rest of the show is totally normal. Just another low-budge abridged Shakespeare adaptation with a punk rock soundtrack.

But besides the fact that our performance is short and illegal, it's standard stuff. Piper plays a more-than-adequate York; the black tissue-paper roses look beautiful when Gigi tosses them from the hayloft during the Wars of the Roses scene, and they land gracefully in several people's mashed potatoes. Xia, playing Joan of Arc and Queen Margaret, proves herself to be both a versatile actress and a massive overachiever—traits that are almost always intertwined.

About a dozen audience members have left, including Knoxville, director of the CHS Thespians. Maybe she's going to tell VP Smith what's happening. Maybe she rushed home, inspired to punch up the *Top Gun* script.

Derry stayed. Apparently, his teacherly curiosity overrode his Party Protector vigilante mandate tonight.

Dick Durant is in the dining room now, standing near the kitchen doors, scanning the crowd, probably looking for potential trouble. He must've spotted Axl's protection, the soldier in plain clothes who is lingering near the hostess credenza. Dick's face is drawn, but he isn't likely to interfere. With Gigi leaving tonight, he wouldn't want to end things on a sour note.

Orin's soldiers are also in plain clothes, but just as obvious, if you're looking—three of them are communicating with walkie-talkies in whispers that are rather loud and rude.

Gigi is kneeling by Derry's booth, giving King Henry's monologue from Part III, Act II, Scene V, when he laments the cost of civil war:

KING HENRY:
O piteous spectacle! O bloody times!
Whiles lions war and battle for their dens,
Poor harmless lambs abide their enmity.

Weep, wretched man, I'll aid thee tear for tear;
And let our hearts and eyes, like civil war,
Be blind with tears, and break o'ercharged with grief.

Tears roll down Gigi's cheeks.

The lights go down.

For about ten seconds, Epidaurus is silent.

O'ercharged with grief.

The show is over.

They did it.

It's done.

The lights come up with a reprise of the MC5 song from the opening of the show. The audience applauds.

The Last Thespians Standing—Gigi, Piper, Spatz, Xia, Leticia, Skeletor, Zorro, and Hal—gather near the server station in the center of the dining room, clasp hands.

Together, they bow.

Gigi's eyes lock onto a mostly empty tabletop in one of the booths. She lets go of her fellow Thespians' hands, flashes the customers seated in the booth a polite Midwestern smile as she climbs on top of their table.

Gigi and Axl know what's happening now.

But they didn't tell anybody else.

Dim lights flutter above Gigi, like sunlight through moving clouds.

"Some barns were built round," Gigi announces, "so no ghosts could take residence in their corners. Tonight, the dead swirl around us. Can you feel them?"

Axl turns on the sound cue: a tornado. Beams cracking, trees being ripped from their roots.

"Together, the living and the dead will triumph over those

who would stop us from feeling. Who would dehumanize us, to create their machines of war." Ms. Lee said that, about the machines of war. We never forgot. "The Thespians would like to dedicate this performance to the loved ones we've lost, and to the love we'll use to heal ourselves again."

The lights come back up softly.

The deads love you too, Gigi.

I do.

Gigi is glowing. Vibing with that particular postshow high of exhausted, elated, and complete.

But the mood in the barn has shifted. The play was a play. Gigi's speech was an explicit political critique. Some of the audience seem a little freaked out.

Axl's soldier cups his hands around his mouth. "Clear out! Everybody!"

People hustle toward the barn doors. Thespians hug, saying rushed goodbyes. Everybody seems to have forgotten about the fried chicken.

Standing on the table, watching them leave, Gigi can almost feel Ms. Lee cheering her on.

The idea makes her deeply happy.

A handful of customers linger. Perhaps they're not quite ready to let go of what happened in our makeshift theatron, tonight. The possibilities the Thespians revealed. The way it made them feel.

Piper and Xia go to the booth where Gigi is still standing on the table.

Gigi smiles down at Xia. "You were outstanding."

"I'm, like, on fire right now," says Xia, her face flushed. "When should we do the next one?"

Piper and Gigi exchange a look that's charged with something.

It's not that all is forgiven between them. It's that whatever is wrong in their friendship, they need each other.

To leave town together.

Their lives intertwined, like a braid.

Tonight, they'll disappear on Xia, leaving her, a freshman, to run the CHS underground theater department, alone.

Gigi has no doubt that Xia will keep it going.

No doubt at all.

One of Orin's walkie-talkie soldiers strolls over to Gigi, speaks without conviction. "Anti-American Thought divides this great nation in a time of war. All staged performances must be approved in advance by the Culture Commissioner. I'm issuing you a warning and a fine. American freedom is at stake."

"Brother, isn't that the truth." A stocky man in a blue plaid shirt is walking toward them, limping in an obtrusive way, like he's trying to take up space.

I don my opera glasses.

Who's this?

"You *love* Anti-American Thought, huh?" asks the man, peering at Gigi. "Real fuckin' proud of yourself right now."

Gigi is too startled to respond.

Piper and Xia exchange a look.

"Jimmy, take it down a notch," says Dick Durant, calmly approaching them. "That's my girl."

Gigi exhales. It's reassuring to have a father who's a professional asshole-wrangler.

"Well, go on, Dick," says the man. "Handle your girl. I'm waiting."

Axl's soldier joins Dick. "Sir, it's under control."

"Is it?" The man's arm shakes as he points at Gigi. "You seen this smart-ass, standing up here, mouthing off? You're not gonna do anything about her, I sure as shit am. I'm a Party Protector—"

"Get down, Gigi!" yells a woman's voice from the hayloft— a voice so familiar that Gigi feels she's dreaming it.

Is Ms. Lee giving her direction?

Lights flash, but this time it isn't Axl's doing—

Holy mother of Muses.

It's Fiona. Standing up there in her white suit jacket, black ponytail—

Ms. Lee is watching from the hayloft.

"Ms. Lee!" Gigi jumps off the table, runs to the stairs.

A uniformed soldier appears from the shadows in the hayloft.

"*No*, Gigi! Leave *now*! *Run!*" Ms. Lee's voice echoes through the barn as she tries to tear herself away from the soldier who has grabbed her.

"Fiona Lee, you're under arrest for Anti-American Thought," yells the soldier. "Do not attempt to evade arrest!"

Gigi stops halfway up the stairs, looking around for help.

Sees Axl slipping into the closet beside the hostess credenza.

The soldier yelps; he's bent over in pain.

Ms. Lee kneed him in the nuts.

When she runs, uniformed soldiers swarm her, drag her toward the back stairwell.

"Giselle!" yells Dick. "Get down here!"

Orin rushes up the stairs to Gigi, whispering urgently, "You said she wouldn't be here!"

Gigi feels the hot blood pulsing in her neck. "Did *you* do this?"

"No! I mean—" Orin puts his hands on his head. "You told me she wouldn't— I had no intention—"

Dick is arguing with Axl's soldier, who's holding his hands up, eyes wide, confused.

From the coat closet, Axl watches Gigi and Orin's argument escalate. He ran tech from the downstairs office with the video monitor. I'm guessing he heard the commotion, glanced at the screen, dropped everything. The way he's leaning forward, one hand on the doorframe, it looks like he's considering intervening.

Do I go over there, Maxy? thinks Axl. *Do I chase Ms. Lee? What do I do?*

I say, *You should—*

I stop.

I squeal like dude just ripped my bodice.

I HEARD AXL THINK THAT.

Stay where you are! I tell him.

Axl asks, *Why?* Like a confused child.

HE CAN HEAR ME!

The gates of Axl's consciousness have fallen open. His thoughts are clear and unobstructed. As if the barriers were only made of smoke—

You want them to send you to North Carolina? I ask.

No! thinks Axl. *I want to leave this place forever. With Gigi. Tonight.*

I say, *Then don't move.*

Dick Durant is livid. "Giselle, go home. *Now.* Everybody!"

Piper and Xia are crying. They rush toward the barn doors.

Gigi nods. The evening has turned. She pushes past Orin down the stairs, stalks toward the barn doors, her head swimming.

What did Orin do?

As she passes the coat closet, Gigi doesn't look in at Axl. But she almost looks—to show him that she'll meet him later, at the mall. Reassure him they can still leave tonight. It can be accomplished in a gesture as subtle as smoothing her hair.

The angry man intercepts Piper and Xia at the barn doors. "Did I give you girls permission to leave?"

Dick intervenes in a flash, Axl's soldier by his side.

"Jimmy, get out of my restaurant."

The man pulls a gun out of his pants.

Points it at Gigi's father.

People scream.

The man yells, "Nobody move!"

Don't do it, Axl, I tell him, but of course he can't not.

Axl steps out of the coat closet to stand between Gigi's father and the gunman.

Axl says, "Let's talk."

The man leans around Axl, waves his gun at Dick. "You're just totally cool with your girl disgracing America with her potty mouth. Who's the boss in your house, Dick? Wanna clarify that for me now?"

The few remaining customers, people who were too stunned to leave, or couldn't stop looking, are now sprinting upstairs to the hayloft.

"Nobody move!" repeats the angry man.

He shoots a rafter.

Screaming people drop on the stairs, and to the floor.

Piper and Xia are holding each other by the barn doors, crying.

Orin gives up arguing with his soldiers, who don't seem motivated to intervene. Pulls a gun out of the back of his pants, walks toward the angry man, pointing it.

"Hell yeah!" yells the man. "Let's get the party started!" His laugh is so empty that it doesn't even function as a laugh. It's the sound of something opening wide enough to swallow you whole.

"The guns!" cries Gigi, pressing her hands over her ears. "Put down the *guns!*"

A walkie-talkie soldier wanders to the gunman like he's got all night. "Lay down your weapon, Jimmy. That guy will drop his, too. The girl was helping us arrest that theater teacher. Bitch was on the run for months."

Gigi feels the heat rush to her head.

"That's not true," she practically spits. "I'm *with* her. *I'm with Ms. Lee."*

When she shoves Axl aside, he's so caught off guard that he moves.

"What's your name? Jimmy?" asks Gigi.

The angry man smirks. "Call me anything you want. I'm a Party Protector. Proud citizen of America. An America I can finally be proud of again."

"Well, Jimmy America, it's nice to meet you. I am also an American. Two Americans should always be able to have a conversation."

"Sweetheart, you're an Anti-American. Time's past for conversation with those."

"Really?" Gigi's eye is on his gun. Her throat is so swollen she's practically choking. "Am I really that threatening to you?"

"You've got it twisted, baby girl. I'm the one who's threatening you. You and your pussy faggot friends pull some disrespectful horseshit like this again? Insulting those who died for our freedom? None of you will live to regret it. Guarantee plenty of folks around here agree with me."

"But wait," says Gigi. "You're talking about, like, three different things right now. We all love freedom. My grandfathers fought in World War II—"

"I don't need a history lesson from a white trash bitch. America is no longer willing to let those who don't love this land poison the melting pot." Still pointing his gun at Gigi, the man looks at her father, who is ghostly pale, humiliated by the fact that he's standing here, unable to figure out how to wrangle the weapon from the man's hand or physically remove him from the premises.

Gigi is filled with rage. She thinks of the hundreds of times men have referred to her as a girl, or a bitch, or trash, while looking at her like she's a steak. Threatening her with insults and leering at her breasts.

Gigi has one life.

And she's free.

To feel how she truly feels.

And to say it.

Because this man is telling her she can't.

Because he's pointing a gun at her, a gun he believes is more powerful than her words.

A weapon he plans to use to take away her freedom and replace it with his own.

Gigi smiles at Axl, who is standing to her right, the arm he has instinctively extended in front of her like it's a seat belt shaking madly, his brain short-circuiting as he tries and fails and tries and fails to figure out how he can tackle this man without his gun going off and killing Gigi or another innocent person.

It's a moment that will torture him for the rest of his life.

Gigi smiles at her father, on her left, who is going through the same thought process as Axl, only with a deeper sense of shame.

"I'm going to do it again, sir," says Gigi. "And again, and again, and again. You'll have to kill me with that gun to get me to stop making theater. If I'm that much of a threat to you, that's your weakness. Not mine."

The man laughs, and casually shoots Gigi in the chest.

The bullet slides in like a dry pill. Gigi needs water. To wash the burn. A sinkhole is turning her inside out. The dryness is in her mouth now, and her eyes are so dry she can't see.

She needs water.

She tries for a breath.

Gigi falls into Axl's arms.

Orin shoots the man. He drops.

Everyone is screaming.

Axl is holding Gigi's body, trying to support her, shouting.

Dick Durant and Orin and Piper have closed in around Axl and Gigi. The few remaining customers sprint out of the restaurant, through the hayloft. Xia is still lying facedown on the floor, her hands clasped over her head. Orin's soldiers are shouting into their walkie-talkies, hunched over Jimmy, the man Orin killed.

Axl has lowered Gigi to the ground. She isn't moving. She isn't breathing. He's crying without knowing he's crying. Seeing without knowing what he sees.

Axl cries silently, *Max!*

I'm here, I tell him. *I'm here.*

A walkie-talkie soldier arrests Orin.

"She needs a medic!" cries Orin. "Do you not have an ambulance on-site?"

"You can't just kill a Party Protector," says the soldier.

She's still alive, right, Max? asks Axl, his head resting on Gigi's chest. *Tell me I'm too much of a dumbass to hear her heart beating.*

My friends lie together, bathed in blood on the dining room floor.

I'm not inside Gigi's head anymore.

She's gone.

Tears stream down Axl's soldier's face as he leans on the hostess credenza, trying to reach a private ambulance on the grimy phone.

Tell me, Maxy, Axl pleads, his face covered with snot and blood and tears. *Tell me I'm wrong. . . .*

I try to think what to tell him. I can't think anymore, of course; I can only share what I know. What I'm learning by lingering here, clinging to warm bodies, trying to understand everything I never did; everything I still don't.

I can't see her, Axl. I can't hear her.

But I know that Gigi is joining the dead.

Dick Durant is kneeling beside his daughter, rubbing her limp arm, tears streaming down his face. He shouts, "Do we have an ambulance?"

Axl's soldier is still on the phone. "I'm trying."

Oh God, Max. Oh, God! thinks Axl. *What am I going to do?*

A THOUSAND SOULS TO DEATH
AND DEADLY NIGHT

Last night, everyone was supposed to be speeding north on Interstate 57 under the blameless sky, crammed inside the less-than-stylish cover of Mosquito's revamped Oldsmobile Cutlass Supreme. Axl had already bribed the checkpoints. Maybe they would've made it.

If they had, today they'd be doing something Chicago-y.

Eating a deep-dish pizza.

Watching a Cubs game.

Or at the very least, hiding together in Ito's art commune, noodling on musical instruments, figuring out what happens next.

Instead, in the Cliffs of Capri, the Bowls' doorbell rings.

Gigi's death didn't eject me from the Purgatorio, but it tore a hole through the dimensions.

I know that when I'm done here, I can go.

Home.

To the all-you-can-eat fried-chicken buffet in the sky.

But there's one thing I need to do first.

Axl couldn't leave Gigi's car at the Round Barn. Last night, he took Gigi's backpack, got the keys to the Malibu, parked it in the Durants' driveway in Rolling Acres. Refused Dick's invitation to come inside. Sat in the driver's seat all night, covered in blood, wide awake, the wind of Death blowing through his body.

At daybreak, I told him, *Take my father downtown.*

So he drove the Malibu to my house.

Now he's standing on my front porch.

The Bowls' giant red front doors open.

Dad is standing in a morning sunbeam, clutching his Janis Joplin LP like a security blanket.

O, Dad.

You have no idea how much I've wanted to see you.

Having said that . . .

Ya look like homemade Hell.

Hair?

Bananas.

Eyes?

Bloodshot.

White button-down untucked, chest hair poppin'. Dress shoes gleaming on the marble floor.

I spy a blanket on that floor.

Did he sleep there?

Where's Mom?

Bernie nods to Axl. "Morning."

Axl nods back.

Axl and my father bonded, once.

But that's another story.

Bernie looks Axl up and down.

Axl looks like a crime scene.

Except, in the Dictator's America, killing a peaceful protestor is the type of crime that tends to go unpunished. The party prefers it when citizens take justice into their own hands.

My father doesn't ask what happened.

He knows what's happening now.

Dad follows Axl to the Malibu, takes shotgun.

When they near their destination, Dad says, "Park here."

Axl finds a spot near a group of Americans huddled around a garbage-can fire. A woman who looks like my dead grandma is selling drugs to a boy with sad eyes. Two men are pissing close enough to the fire that you can smell it. Around the edges of the parking lot prowl the dogs.

When Axl and my father step out of the Malibu, the crowd eyes them and the beast.

Axl thinks, *Please attack me. Just beat the shit out of me. Beat me until I can't see, or hear, or speak. Break all my ribs so I can't move, and leave my flesh to the dogs.*

With his genuine wish to be mauled by these vulnerable humans, his blood-soaked clothing, the perfume of a week without a proper shower shrouded in the stench of Death, and the junker car that says he has nothing left to lose, Axl is vibing hella menacing.

And then there's Dad.

Surly, burly, and unkempt, sporting a fucked-up energy, wearing a pair of incongruously expensive Italian loafers, it's obvious that my father could thump you.

The whole package is a challenge that none of the hungry, exhausted, depressed people have the remotest desire to meet. In fact, they share a collective hope against hope that Axl and my father will ignore them.

They do.

They're going to G. Harold's.

The old department store is about eight blocks southeast.

Axl grabs his backpack, follows Dad.

G. Harold's is a four-story building with an ornate exterior, opulent botanicals cast in concrete. Back when, its design was modeled on the elaborate turn-of-the-century shops of Paris, France.

Its owners were widely regarded as oddballs. Wealthy beyond anybody's ability to comprehend, with a mansion on the country club golf course. No children. As far as the local peeping Trinas and Terrys could tell—the ones who drove slowly past the Harolds' home, hoping for a glimpse of something grand and difficult—they also had no pets.

The Harolds were early adopters of the flee-to-Japan response to the New American Way, and they didn't bother to lock up shop when they left. For a few months, several dozen citizens called G. Harold's home, even without plumbing or lights.

When the party slated the building for demolition, my father intervened with a business proposal. He couldn't bear to see fine architecture go to waste, so he'd turn the place into condominiums. Sell them to the wealthy citizens who were sure to follow in his footsteps—Midwestern party members with money and taste. A penthouse was his vision, with sweeping views of the plains o' grain below.

He'd call it the Majestic Prairie.

When I came home that night and told Dad everything—that he was on the party's shit list—I learned about the basement apartment.

Dad built it in case we Bowls ever needed to disappear in plain sight.

When, precisely, he realized this—that one day we'd need to hide—I'll never know.

Dad leads Axl to the alley behind the department store, stops beside the basement entrance he equipped with a spankin' security system.

"I told Max to stay here until we left the country. He promised me he would, but—"

Dad chokes. The alcohol has been mostly metabolized. Tears flow anew.

O, Dad.

Axl waits for my father's crying spell to pass. He doesn't have the strength to manage anyone else's pain this morning.

Dad shakes his head like he's getting water out of his ears, tries to smile, which gives his face a sour look, like he just smelled my laundry.

"Memorize the codes," he says, looking at the door. "There's another lock at the entrance."

Axl repeats the codes, looks above his head, toward the catwalk in the clouds.

When Dad tried to give me the studio, I picked codes Axl would never forget. The first is Gigi's phone number. The second, Axl and Frank's old number, from the house in Rolling Acres.

I knew Axl wouldn't come to Japan.

When he said no, I was going to give him this place.

"I'm powered by a generator. That isn't to say they won't find me. You; me. I monitor—fairly well. But there's always a loophole.

I'm sorry about the windows. Even a basement should have windows. I'm going to create a glass ceiling, so light pours in from a hidden channel. Have you been to the Louvre museum? Below the glass pyramids?"

Axl can't decipher my father's ramblings.

It doesn't sound like important information.

Dad lifts the tail of a concrete lion who is missing his head.

Axl enters the first code into the keypad beneath.

With a click, the door unlocks.

"Go in quick now. And ah—"

Dad inhales, long and deep. The downtown morning smells graceful, like laundry detergent. Why? Some tree with branches above them is still breathing its sweet breath; still sharing its beauty, even now.

Axl impulsively puts a hand on my father's arm. "Thanks."

Dad nods, fending off tears again. He'd been going to say, "Be careful," I suspect, but it's implicit.

Besides. In the end, the deciding factor is never how careful you are.

They've both learned that.

Axl is standing in the secret apartment in G. Harold's, my father's first foray into architecture.

And like a good Bowl, when Dad forays, he forays the hell out.

It's a small space with terra-cotta floors covered in Turkish rugs and a tall ceiling with oak beams. Immediately, Axl can tell it's soundproofed; he can't even hear his own footsteps.

Axl goes to the small sink Dad had imported from Italy, washes his face.

What's special about Italian sinks?

Who knows.

I wish I knew more about what happened to my parents after I left. Like . . . where's Mom? How's . . . my mother?

Perhaps the gods aren't only comedians.

Perhaps they granted a mother's prayer for privacy, even from the quiet eyes of the dead.

Beside the sink, on the counter, is a VHS tape, unlabeled.

Axl picks it up.

Maxy, how did your dad get the Ms. Lee video? he asks.

How do you know that's what it is? I ask.

Because it's one of my tapes, says Axl. *I mark them.*

I swear! You cannot leave the living alone for five minutes without them going off script.

Where did Dad get the tape?

Why did he leave it here?

I don't know.

And I'll never know.

Axl is in the safe house.

My work in the Purgatorio is done.

Axl slides the tape into the VCR. He's seen it before. . . .

But I haven't.

I can't not stick around for this.

Axl plops on a white leather couch shaped like a kidney, grabs the remote.

Presses play.

On the screen, Stu Perloff is sitting on a stool, visible from the shoulders up.

"All is cold, cold. All is void, void, void. All is terrible, terrible—"

Mary, Joseph, and a box of demons.

Stu Perloff was with Ms. Lee.

Stu's bright eyes shine with warm intensity. *"The bodies of all living creatures have dropped to dust, and eternal matter has transformed them into stones and water and clouds; but their spirits have flowed together into one, and that great world-soul am I! . . . I understand all, all, all, and each life lives again in me."*

Chekhov, I say. The Seagull. *A hundred-year-old play—*

Axl finishes my thought. *That never gets old.*

Well . . . here we are. I don't know if anybody out there was listening to me—but what else is new? I'm one of those sidewalk preachers standing on an overturned milk crate, crowing into the crowd.

Save yourself! he yells, like he just saw Jesus on a Harley, speeding through the cornfields, back for the sequel—one more round of teaching humans how to love—and it's our last chance to get schooled.

Good old Jesus Christ our Savior. He really did it right, no? Dude has been dead for thousands of years, and people still talk about how *nice* he was. Plus the sandals, the Fabio hair, the whole hot-teacher thing—I gotta tell you, Ms. Lee, he's your main competition in that department.

But you know what I love most about Jesus?

His dad. I bet Jesus dug his pop as much as I dug mine, even if the way they showed unconditional love didn't always legit make a ton of sense—

Save yourself! says the soap-box preacher, and that's what the SYXTEM says too.

You know what I say?

Forget saving yourself.

Forget saving anyone.

Love your friends. Love your family. Love your enemies, too.

And when they're gone?

Love the dead.

On the screen, Ms. Lee is looking directly into the camera.

"Stand up," she says. "Talk back. You heard me. *Act.*"

Axl feels his chest aching, the tears burning.

Gigi? He calls silently, hoping to hear her voice the way he hears mine.

But there's nothing.

Only the silence where she used to be. The emptiness in his soft heart.

Ms. Lee is still talking. "And when they tell you you can't do it? You do it anyway. You do it *louder.* You never stop."

Cut to black.

END OF ACT I.

ACKNOWLEDGMENTS

Thank you doesn't begin to convey the gratitude I feel for the critical support I received from so many generous readers and friends as this series took form.

MATT PILCHER: *Rolling Acres, Ye Olde Donut Shoppe, driving old cars into ditches together, horror flicks, lifelong friendship born in the corn*

MATT WEEDMAN: *Loompanics, cult films, diagramming Market Place Mall, driving old cars in circles together, "Let It Be"*

JEREMY B. COHEN: *Long conversations about this project since it was a seedling, History of the Western Theater at Oberlin in the '90s (how many times?), your blessing ("bippity-boppity-boo")*

CORI CLARK-NELSON: *Early, infectious excitement about this project, gloriously sharp notes, all the reads!*

AMRITA RAMANAN: *Generously sharing your Shakespeare expertise*

KATE WISNIEWSKI: *Talking with me about Upstart Crow Collective's astonishing* Henry VI *adaptation,* Bring Down the House

ADRIANA X. JACOBS: *Reading fast when I needed it, the coveted "Holy fuck"*

JONATHAN REGIER: *Exchanging many versions of many writings over many years . . .*

LISA (PARKER) THORNTON: *That time when we were fourteen and wrote "Just Be" on our Chuck Taylors, spending the next several decades trying to figure out how to do that*

GINNY WIEHARDT: *Important feedback on the prelude to the earliest drafts*

RON HORNING: *The records, the letters, the poems! And a swift read at the right time*

LIZ WINSLOW: *That critical note a hundred years ago:* She has to take the zine!

GWEN JONES: *Link to FBI files, Budapest when things looked so bright, applying the right shade of lipstick and closing the door*

BLAKE RILEY: *Bicoastal bivalve conferences, rooftop fashion, centuries of fables, covers, and other mysteries . . .*

TODD FLETCHER: *Photo archives . . . memories . . .*

JENNIFER DAVIS: *Photo archives . . . memories . . .*

MICHAEL ELYANOW: *Title blue-sky-ing*

TSITSI ZANA: *Winter term adventure! Lending your time, wisdom, and perspective*

ALVARO BARQUERO: *TikTok research, great conversations about the writing process*

JEFFREY YANG: *Sneaking in a read, forever generously answering my questions*

MATT SHARPE: *The whale!*

SUSAN HAWK: *Warmth, humor, and endurance*

KELLY DELANEY: *Acquiring the project with your usual enthusiasm, vision, and indefatigable positive energy*

ERIN CLARKE: *Razor-sharp editorial genius! Next-level insights—this book owes everything to our partnership*

GIANNA LAKENAUTH: *Easing an impossible transition*

MARISA DINOVIS: *Editor #3, stepping in for Act Two*

RENÉE CAFIERO: *Copyediting the regionalisms*

MELANIE NOLAN AND THE REST OF THE TEAM AT KNOPF: *Your time, creativity, and care*

CENTENNIAL HIGH SCHOOL THESPIANS AND OBERLIN COLLEGE THEATER DEPARTMENT: *The play is a family*

HAYWOOD JABLOWMIE: *Keeping it light*

MELANIE VESEY: *Professional makeover*

TRACY VAN STRAATEN: *PR assistance*

DAVID ARENAS: *Photography party*

MISHEL BROWN: *Makeup party*

BARBARA BALBACH: *Little getaways*

MICHAEL LARIVIERE: *Lots of CU memories*

DAVID LARIVIERE: *Champaign research*

TIM MAPP: *Taking care of everyone and everything*

IGGY AND LASZLO MAPP: *Laughter and love*

RIOT ACT—READINGS

I did a lot of research before, during, and after writing this novel.
Mostly, I wanted to know how people survive repressive regimes.
How they live, love, and thrive.

You can read a million books about this stuff. I'd never try to
make an exhaustive or "best of" list. This is just a glimpse of the
nonfiction that impacted me as I imagined the world of this tale.

On Tyranny: Twenty Lessons from the Twentieth Century,
by Timothy Snyder

Nothing to Envy: Ordinary Lives in North Korea,
by Barbara Demick

Stalin: Paradoxes of Power, 1878–1928, by Stephen Kotkin

Stalin: Waiting for Hitler, 1929–1941, by Stephen Kotkin

We Have Been Harmonized: Life in China's Surveillance State,
by Kai Strittmatter

A Moonless, Starless Sky: Ordinary Women and Men Fighting Extremism in Africa, by Alexis Okeowo

The Acts of My Mother, by András Forgách

Red-Color News Soldier: A Chinese Photographer's Odyssey Through the Cultural Revolution, by Li Zhensheng

Living Silence in Burma: Surviving Under Military Rule, by Christina Fink

The Body Keeps the Score: Brain, Mind and Body in the Healing of Trauma, by Bessel van der Kolk

The System of Dante's Hell, by Amiri Baraka

Mala's Cat: A Memoir of Survival in World War II, by Mala Kacenberg

The Commissar Vanishes: The Falsification of Photographs and Art in Stalin's Russia, by David King

Disturbing the Peace, by Václav Havel

The Politics of Nonviolent Action, by Gene Sharp

The Meaning of Freedom and Other Difficult Dialogues, by Angela Y. Davis

From Dictatorship to Democracy: A Conceptual Framework for Liberation, by Gene Sharp

Internet for the People: The Fight for Our Digital Future, by Ben Tarnoff

Cyberpunk: Outlaws and Hackers on the Computer Frontier, by Katie Hafner and John Markoff

Weaving the Web: The Original Design and Ultimate Destiny of the World Wide Web, by Tim Berners-Lee

A Brief History of the Future: The Origins of the Internet, by John Naughton

Where Wizards Stay Up Late: The Origins of the Internet,
by Katie Hafner and Matthew Lyon

Practical Anarchism: A Guide for Daily Life, by Scott Branson

*Shakespeare in a Divided America: What His Plays Tell Us About
Our Past and Future,* by James Shapiro

Tyrant: Shakespeare on Politics, by Stephen Greenblatt

The Cambridge Companion to Greek and Roman Theatre,
edited by Marianne McDonald and J. Michael Walton

The Art of Ancient Greek Theater, by Mary Louise Hart

Japanese Nō Masks, by Friedrich Perzyński

Happenings and Other Acts, edited by Mariellen R. Sandford

*Burning Down the Haus: Punk Rock, Revolution, and the Fall of
the Berlin Wall,* by Tim Mohr

Words Will Break Cement: The Passion of Pussy Riot, by Masha
Gessen

*Performance Art in Eastern Europe Since 1960 (Rethinking Art's
Histories),* by Amy Bryzgel

RIOT ACT—MIXTAPE

SIDE A

THE RAINCOATS— *"Fairytale in the Supermarket"*

PRINCE— *"Let's Go Crazy"*

VIOLENT FEMMES— *"Add It Up"*

BUTTHOLE SURFERS— *"U.S.S.A."*

THE SLITS— *"Typical Girls"*

MORRISSEY— *"How Soon Is Now?"*

THE CLASH— *"Straight to Hell"*

THE DOORS— *"L.A. Woman"*

THE REPLACEMENTS— *"Kick Your Door Down"*

SALT-N-PEPA— *"Tramp"*

BEASTIE BOYS— *"Brass Monkey"*

DIGITAL UNDERGROUND— *"The Humpty Dance"*

MC LYTE— *"Lyte as a Rock"*

SIDE B

MC5— *"The American Ruse"*

PUBLIC ENEMY— *"Fight the Power"*

DAVID BOWIE— *"Oh! You Pretty Things"*

NEW YORK DOLLS— *"Personality Crisis"*

B-52S— *"Rock Lobster"*

THE CREATURES— *"Mad Eyed Screamer"*

X-RAY SPEX— *"Germfree Adolescents"*

PIXIES— *"Here Comes Your Man"*

SEX PISTOLS— *"Pretty Vacant"*

R.E.M.— *"Pop Song 89"*

BIG STAR— *"The Ballad of El Goodo"*

PINK FLOYD— *"Brain Damage"*

TOM PETTY AND THE HEARTBREAKERS— *"American Girl"*